ROSS MACDONALD

The Zebra-Striped Hearse

Ross Macdonald's real name was Kenneth Millar. Born near San Francisco in 1915 and raised in Vancouver, British Columbia, Millar returned to the U.S. as a young man and published his first novel in 1944. He served as the president of the Mystery Writers of America and was awarded their Grand Master Award, as well as the Mystery Writers of Great Britain's Silver Dagger Award. He died in 1983.

The Zebra-Striped Hearse

ROSS MACDONALD

The Zebra-Striped Hearse

Vintage Crime/Black Lizard

Vintage Books

A Division of Random House, Inc.

New York

FIRST VINTAGE CRIME/BLACK LIZARD EDITION,
MARCH 1998

A condensed version of this novel was first published in *Cosmopolitan*.

Library of Congress Cataloging-in-Publication Data
Macdonald, Ross, 1915–
The zebra-striped hearse / Ross Macdonald.
p. cm.
ISBN 978-0-375-70145-0
I. Title
PS3525.I486Z3   1998
813'.52—dc21   97-47424
CIP

Random House Web address: www.randomhouse.com

To Harris W. Seed

The people in this novel are fortunately all imaginary, and were invented without reference to any actual people living or dead.

—R. M.

The Zebra-Striped Hearse

chapter 1

SHE WAS WAITING at the office door when I got back from my morning coffee break. The women I usually ran into in the rather dingy upstairs corridor were the aspiring hopeless girls who depended on the modeling agency next door. This one was different.

She had the kind of style that didn't go on with her make-up, and she was about my age. As a man gets older, if he knows what is good for him, the women he likes are getting older, too. The trouble is that most of them are married.

"I'm Mrs. Blackwell," she said. "You must be Mr. Archer."

I acknowledged that I was.

"My husband has an appointment with you in half an hour or so." She consulted a wrist watch on which diamonds sparkled. "Thirty-five minutes, to be precise. I've been waiting for some time."

"I'm sorry, I didn't anticipate the pleasure. Colonel Blackwell is the only appointment I have scheduled this morning."

"Good. Then we can talk."

She wasn't using her charm on me, exactly. The charm was merely there. I unlocked the outer door and led her across the waiting rcom, through the door marked Private, into my inner office, where I placed a chair for her.

She sat upright with her black leather bag under her elbow, touching as little of the chair as possible. Her gaze went to the mug shots on the wall, the faces you see in bad dreams and too often on waking. They seemed to trouble her. Perhaps they brought home to her where she was and who I was and what I did for a living.

I was thinking I liked her face. Her dark eyes were intelligent, and capable of warmth. There was a touch of sadness on her mouth. It was a face that had known suffering, and seemed to be renewing the acquaintance.

I said in an exploratory way: "'Abandon hope all ye who enter here.'"

She colored slightly. "You're quick at catching moods. Or is that a stock line?"

"I've used it before."

"So has Dante." She paused, and her voice changed in tone and rhythm: "I suppose I've placed myself in a rather anomalous position, coming here. You mustn't imagine my husband and I are at odds. We're not, basically. But it's such a destructive thing he proposes to do."

"He wasn't very specific on the telephone. Is it divorce he has on his mind?"

"Heavens, no. There's no trouble of that sort in our marriage." Perhaps she was protesting a little too vehemently. "It's my husband's daughter I'm concerned—that we're both concerned about."

"Your stepdaughter?"

"Yes, though I dislike that word. I have tried to be something better than the proverbial stepmother. But I got to Harriet very late in the day. She was deprived of her own mother when she was only a child."

"Her mother died?"

"Pauline is still very much alive. But she divorced Mark years ago, when Harriet was eleven or twelve. Divorce can be terribly hard on a little girl, especially when she's approaching puberty. There hasn't been much I could do to make Harriet feel easier in the world. She's a grown woman, after all, and she's naturally suspicious of me."

"Why?"

"It's in the nature of things, when a man marries for the

second time. Harriet and her father have always been close. I used to be able to communicate with her better before I married him." She stirred uneasily, and shifted her attention from herself to me. "Do you have any children, Mr. Archer?"

"No."

"Have you ever been married?"

"I have, but I don't quite see the relevance. You didn't come here to discuss my private life. You haven't made it clear why you did come, and your husband will be turning up shortly."

She looked at her watch and rose, I think without intending to. The tension in her simply levitated her out of the chair.

I offered her a cigarette, which she refused, and lit one for myself. "Am I wrong in thinking you're a little afraid of him?"

"You're completely wrong," she said in a definite voice, but she seemed to have some difficulty in continuing. "The thing I'm afraid of is letting him down. Mark needs to be able to trust me. I don't want to do anything behind his back."

"But here you are."

"Here I am." She relapsed into the chair.

"Which brings us back to the question of why."

"I'll be frank with you, Mr. Archer. I don't like Mark's battle plan"—she made the phrase sound ironic—"and I've told him so. I've done some social work, and I have some conception of what it means to be a young woman in the contemporary world. I believe it's best to let nature take its course. Let Harriet marry the man, if her heart is set on him. But Mark can't see it my way at all. He's fiercely opposed to the marriage, and determined to do something drastic."

"And I'm the something drastic."

"You're one version of it. Guns and horsewhips have also been mentioned. Not," she added quickly, "that I take everything he says seriously."

"I always take gun talk seriously. What do you want me to do?"

Her gaze had returned to the pin-ups on the wall. Killers, embezzlers, bigamists, and con men looked at her with unabashed eyes. She shifted her bag to her lap.

"Well, I can hardly ask you to turn him down. It would do no good, anyway. He'd simply find another detective and set him loose on Harriet and—her friend. All I really hoped to do was prepare you for the situation. You'll get a very one-sided view of it from Mark."

"I've gotten a very vague one from you, so far."

"I'll try to do better," she said with a small tight smile. "About five weeks ago Harriet went to Mexico. Her announced intentions were to visit her mother—Pauline lives on Lake Chapala—and to do some painting. But the fact is that she's not on very good terms with her mother, and her talent as a painter will never set the world on fire. I think she went to Lake Chapala deliberately to find a man.

"Any man. If that sounds cynical, let me add that I might have done the same thing myself, under the circumstances."

"What circumstances?"

"I mean her father's second marriage, to me. It's been quite apparent that Harriet hasn't been happy living with us. Fortunately for her, for all of us, her little Mexican expedition was successful. She found a friend, and brought him back alive."

"Does this live one have a name?"

"His name is Burke Damis. He's a young painter. While he's no great social prize—my husband tends to overrate the social —he is quite personable. He has no money, which is another of Mark's objections to him, but he does have artistic talent—a great deal more talent than Harriet possesses, as she knows. And, after all, she'll have money enough for both of them. With his talent and—virility, and her money and devotion, I'd say they had the makings of a marriage."

"She'll have money?"

"Quite a lot of money, and quite soon. One of her aunts left her a substantial trust fund. Harriet comes into it when she's twenty-five."

"How old is she now?"

"Twenty-four. Old enough to know her own mind and live her own life and get out from under Mark's domination—" She paused, as if the strength of her feeling had carried her too far.

I prompted her: "Domination is a strong word."

"It slipped out. I don't mean to malign my husband behind his back. He's a good man, according to his lights, but like other men he's capable of emotional foolishness. This isn't the first affair of Harriet's he's tried to break up. He's always succeeded before. If he succeeds this time, we could end up with a very sad girl on our hands." Her face was alive with passionate identification.

"You really care about Harriet, Mrs. Blackwell."

"I care about all three of us. It isn't good for her to live in her father's shadow. It isn't good for me to sit and watch it— I'm not the sitting and watching type—and it will become less good if it goes on. Harriet is so vulnerable, really, and Mark is such a powerful personality."

As if to illustrate this remark, a large masculine voice was raised in the outer room. I recognized it from Blackwell's telephone call. He said through the translucent glass door: "Isobel, are you in there?"

She jumped as if lightning had struck her, not for the first time. Then she tried to make herself small.

"Is there a back way out?" she whispered.

"I'm afraid not. Shall I get rid of him?"

"No. It would only lead to further trouble."

Her husband was fumbling at the door, his featureless shadow moving on the glass. "I wondered what you were up to when I saw your car in the parking lot. Isobel?"

She didn't answer him. She moved to the window and looked out through the slatted blind over Sunset Boulevard. She was very slim and tense against the striated light. I suppose my protective instinct was aroused. I opened the door a foot or so and slid out into the waiting room and closed the door behind me.

It was my first meeting with Colonel Blackwell. His phone call the day before had been our only contact. I'd looked him up afterward and learned that he was a Regular Army officer who had retired soon after the war from an undistinguished career.

He was a fairly big man who had begun to lose his battle with age. His brown outdoorsman's face made his white hair seem premature. He held himself with ramrod dignity. But his body had started to dwindle. His Shetland jacket hung loose around the shoulders; the collar of his shirt was noticeably large for his corded neck.

His eyebrows were his most conspicuous feature, and they gave him the air of an early Roman emperor. Black in contrast with his hair, they merged in a single eyebrow which edged his forehead like an iron rim. Under it, his eyes were unexpectedly confused.

He tried to shout down his own confusion: "I want to know what's going on in there. My wife is in there, isn't she?"

I gave him a vacant stare. "Your wife? Do I know you?"

"I'm Colonel Blackwell. We spoke on the telephone yesterday."

"I see. Do you have any identification?"

"I don't need identification! I vouch for myself!"

He sounded as though a yelling demon, perhaps the tormented ghost of a master sergeant, had taken possession of him. His tanned face turned red, then lavender.

I said at the purple end of the yell: "Are you really Colonel Blackwell? The way you came bulling in here, I thought you were a crank. We get a lot of cranks."

A woman with very tall pink hair looked in from the corridor, knotting her imitation pearls in her fist. It was Miss Ditmar, who ran the modeling agency:

"Is it all right?"

"Everything's under control," I said. "We were just having a yelling contest. This gentleman won."

Colonel Blackwell couldn't bear to be talked about in this fashion. He turned his back on me and stood with his face to the wall, like a plebe being braced. Miss Ditmar waved her hand benevolently and departed under her hive of hair, trailing a smog of perfume.

The door to the inner office was open now. Mrs. Blackwell had recovered her composure, which was mainly what I'd had in mind.

"Was that a mirage?" she said.

"That was Miss Ditmar in the next office. She was alarmed by the noise. She's very nervous about me all the time."

"I really must apologize," Mrs. Blackwell said with a glance at her husband, "for both of us. I shouldn't have come here. It's put you very much in the middle."

"I've been in the middle before. I rather enjoy it."

"You're very nice."

Like a man being rotated by invisible torque, Blackwell turned and let us see his face. The anger had drained out of it and left it open. His eyes had a hurt expression, as though his young wife had rejected him by complimenting me. He tried to cover this with a wide painful smile.

"Shall we start over, in a lower key?"

"A lower key would suit me, Colonel."

"Fine."

It did something for him to be called by his rank. He made an abrupt horizontal gesture which implied that he was in charge of himself and the situation. He cast an appraising glance around my waiting room as if he was thinking of having it redecorated. With a similar glance at me, he said: "I'll join you shortly in your office. First I'll put Mrs. Blackwell in her car."

"It isn't necessary, Mark. I can find my way—"

"I insist."

He offered her his elbow. She trudged out holding onto it. Though he was the big one and the loud one, I had the impression that she was supporting him.

Through the venetian blind I watched them emerge from the street entrance onto the sidewalk. They walked very formally together, like people on their way to a funeral.

I liked Isobel Blackwell, but I was sort of hoping her husband wouldn't come back.

chapter 2

HE CAME BACK, though, wearing a purged expression which failed to tell me what had been purged, or who. I took the hand he offered me across my desk, but I went on disliking him.

He was sensitive to this—a surprising thing in a man of his temper and background—and made an oblique attempt to get around it: "You don't know the pressures I live under. The combined forces of the females in my life—" He paused, and decided not to finish the sentence.

"Mrs. Blackwell was telling me about some of the pressures."

"So she said. I suppose she meant no harm in coming here. But dammit, if a man's wife won't go through channels," he said obscurely, "who will?"

"I understand the two of you disagree about your prospective son-in-law."

"Burke Damis is not my prospective son-in-law. I have no intention of letting the marriage go through."

"Why not?"

He glared down at me, moving his tongue around under his lips as if he had foreign objects between his teeth. "My wife has the standard female illusion that all marriages are made in heaven. Apparently she's infected you with it."

"I asked a simple question, about this particular marriage. Won't you sit down, Colonel?"

He sat stiffly in the chair his wife had occupied. "The man's a fortune-hunter, or worse. I suspect he's one of those confidence men who make a career of marrying silly women."

"Do you have any evidence along those lines?"

"The evidence is on his face, in his manner, in the nature of his relationship with my daughter. He's the kind of man who would make her miserable, and that's putting it gently."

Concern for her had broken through into his voice and changed its self-conscious tone. He wasn't the stuffed shirt I had taken him for, or at least the stuffing had its human elements.

"What about their relationship?"

He hitched his chair forward. "It's completely unilateral. Harriet is offering him everything—her money, her love, her not inconsiderable attractions. Damis offers nothing. He *is* nothing—a man from nowhere, a man from Mars. He pretends to be a serious painter, but I know something about painting and I wouldn't hire him to paint the side of a barn. Nobody's ever heard of him, and I've made inquiries."

"How extensive?"

"I asked a fellow at the art museum. He's an authority on contemporary American painters. The name Burke Damis meant nothing to him."

"The woods are full of contemporary American painters, and there are always new ones coming up."

"Yes, and a lot of them are fakes and impostors. We're dealing with one here, with this Burke Damis. I believe the name's an alias, one he picked out of a hat."

"What makes you think so?"

"The point is, he's given me no reason to think otherwise. I tried to question him about his background. His answers were evasive. When I asked him where he came from, he said

Guadalajara, Mexico. He's obviously not Mexican and he admitted having been born in the States, but he wouldn't say
where. He wouldn't tell me who his father was or what he'd
done for a living or if he had any relatives extant. When I
pressed him on it, he claimed to be an orphan."

"Maybe he is. Poor boys can be sensitive, especially under
cross-examination."

"He's no boy, and I didn't cross-examine him, and he's got
the sensitivity of a wild pig."

"I seem to have struck out, Colonel."

He sat back in his chair, unsmiling, and ran his hand over
his head. He was careful not to dislodge the wave in his metic-
ulously brushed white hair.

"You make it very clear that you think I'm taking the wrong
approach to this problem. I assure you I am not. I don't know
how much my wife told you, or how much of what she told
you was true—objectively true. The fact remains that my
daughter, whom I love dearly, is a fool about men."

"Mrs. Blackwell did mention," I said carefully, "that a similar situation had come up before."

"Several times. Harriet has a great desire to get married. Unfortunately she combines it with a genius for picking the
wrong man. Don't misunderstand me, I'm not opposed to marriage. I want my daughter to get married—to the right man,
at the proper time. But this idea of rushing into it with a fellow she barely knows—"

"Exactly how long has she known Damis?"

"No more than a month. She picked up with him in Ajijic,
on Lake Chapala. I've visited Mexico myself, and I know
what kind of floaters you can get involved with if you're not
careful. It's no place for an unattached young woman. I realize
now I shouldn't have let her go down there."

"Could you have stopped her?"

A shadow stained his eyes. "The fact is I didn't try. She'd
had an unhappy winter, and I could see she needed a change.

I was under the impression she would stay with her mother, my former wife, who lives in Ajijic. I should have known better than to depend on Pauline. I naturally supposed she'd surround her with the appropriate social safeguards. Instead she simply turned her loose on the town."

"Forgive my bluntness, but you talk about your daughter as though she wasn't responsible. She isn't mentally retarded?"

"Far from it. Harriet is a normal young woman with more than her share of intelligence. To a great extent," he said, as if this settled the matter, "I educated her myself. After Pauline saw fit to abandon us, I was both father and mother to my girl. It grieves me to say no to her on this marriage. She's pinned her hopes of heaven to it. But it wouldn't last six months.

"Or rather it would last six months—just long enough for him to get his hands on her money." He propped his head on his fist and peered at me sideways, one of his eyes half closed by the pressure of his hand. "My wife doubtless told you that there is money involved?"

"She didn't say how much."

"My late sister Ada set up a half-million-dollar trust fund for Harriet. She'll come into active control of the money on her next birthday. And she'll have at least as much again when I—pass away."

The thought of his own death saddened him. His sadness changed perceptibly to anger. He leaned forward and struck the top of my desk so hard that the pen-set hopped. "No thief is going to get his paws on it!"

"You're very certain in your mind that Burke Damis is one."

"I know men, Mr. Archer."

"Tell me about the other men Harriet wanted to marry. It may help me to understand the pattern of her behavior." And the pattern of her father's.

"They're rather painful to contemplate. However. One was a man in his forties with two wrecked marriages behind him, and several children. Then there was a person who called himself a folk singer. He was a bearded nonentity. Another was an interior decorator in Beverly Hills—a nancy-boy if I ever saw one. All of them were after her money. When I confronted them with the fact, they bowed out more or less gracefully."

"What did Harriet do?"

"She came around. She sees them now as I saw them from the beginning. If we can keep her from doing something rash, she'll see through Damis eventually, just as I do."

"It must be nice to have X-ray eyes."

He gave me a long black look from under his formidable eyebrow. "I resent that remark. You're not only personally insulting but you seem decidedly lukewarm about my problem. Apparently my wife really got to you."

"Your wife is a very charming woman, and possibly a wise one."

"Possibly, in some situations. But Damis has her hoodwinked —she's only a woman after all. I'm surprised that you should be taken in, however. I was told that you run one of the best one-man operations in Los Angeles County."

"Who told you that?"

"Peter Colton, of the D.A.'s office. He assured me I couldn't find a better man. But I must say you don't exhibit much of the bloodhound spirit."

"You may have enough of it for both of us."

"What is that supposed to mean?"

"You've got the case all wrapped up and tied with a noose before I've started on it. But you haven't given me any concrete evidence."

"Getting the evidence is your job."

"If it's there. I'm not going to cook up evidence, or select it to confirm you in your prejudices. I'm willing to investigate Damis on the understanding that the chips fall where they fall."

He threw his Roman-emperor look around my office. It

bounced off the drab green filing cabinet with the dents in it, riffled the flaking slats of the venetian blind, and found the ugly pin-ups on the wall all guilty as charged.

"You feel you can afford to lay down terms to your prospective clients?"

"Certain terms are always implied. Sometimes I have to spell them out. I have a license to lose, and a reputation."

His face had entered the color cycle again, starting with pink. "If you consider me a threat to your reputation—"

"I didn't say that. I said I had one. I intend to keep it."

He tried to stare me down. He used his face like an actor, making his brow horrendous, converting his eyes into flinty arrowheads pointed at me between slitted lids. But he grew tired of the game. He wanted my help.

"Of course," he said in a reasonable tone, "I had nothing in mind but a fair, unprejudiced investigation. If you got any other impression, you misread me. You realize my daughter is very dear to me."

"I can use a few more facts about her. How long has she been back from Mexico?"

"Just a week."

"This is the seventeenth of July. Does that mean she returned on the tenth?"

"Let me see. It was a Monday. Yes, she flew back on Monday, July tenth. I met them at the airport around lunchtime."

"Damis was with her?"

"He was very much with her. It's what all the trouble is about."

"Just what kind of trouble has there been?"

"Nothing overt, yet. We've had some—ah—discussions in the family. Harriet has been quite obstinate, and Isobel, as you know, is on the side of the lovebirds."

"You've talked to Damis?"

"I have, on two occasions. The three of us had lunch at the airport last Monday. He did a good deal of talking, about theories of painting and the like. Harriet sat there enthralled. I was not impressed.

"But it was the second time we met that I really began to smell a rat. He came to dinner Saturday night. Harriet had already confided to me that they were planning marriage, so I made an occasion to talk to him alone. It was then he gave me all those evasive answers. On one point at least he wasn't evasive. He admitted that he didn't have a dime. At the same time he was ogling around my house as if he already owned it. I told him that would happen only over my dead body."

"You told him that?"

"Later," he said. "After dinner. He'd made himself highly obnoxious at the table. I mentioned that the Blackwell family name embodies three centuries of tradition, going back to the early days of the Massachusetts colony. Damis seemed to think it was funny. He made a satiric remark about the Colonial Dames—my mother was one, as it happens—and announced that he was bored by such traditions. I said in that case he would certainly be bored as my son-in-law, and he agreed.

"But later I surprised the fellow in my bedroom. He was actually fingering through my wardrobe. I asked him what he thought he was doing there. He answered flippantly that he was making a study of how the other half lives. I said that he would never find out, not at my expense or the expense of any member of my family. I invited him to leave my house and while he was at it to vacate my other house which he is occupying. But Harriet came rushing in and made me countermand—withdraw the suggestion."

"Damis is living in a house that belongs to you?"

"Temporarily. Harriet talked me into it the first day. He needed a place to paint, she said, and I agreed to let him use the beach house."

"And he's still there?"

"I assume he is. They're not even married, and he's already

scrounging on us. I tell you, the man's an operator."

"He doesn't sound like a very smooth one to me. I've known a few painters. The young unrecognized ones have a special feeling about accepting things from other people. They live off the country while they do their work. All most of them want is a north light and enough money to buy paints and eat."

"That's another thing," he said. "Harriet's given him money. I happened to glance through her checkbook yesterday, shortly after I phoned you." He hesitated. "I don't normally pry, but when it's a question of protecting her—"

"Just what are you trying to protect her from?"

"Disaster." His voice sank ominously. "Complete and utter personal disaster. I've had some experience of the world, and I know what can come of marrying the wrong person."

I waited for him to explain this, wondering if he meant his first wife. But he failed to satisfy my curiosity. He said: "Young people never seem to learn from their parents' experience. It's a tragic waste. I've talked to Harriet until I was blue in the face. But the fellow's got her completely under his thumb. She told me Saturday night that if it came to a showdown between me and Damis, she would go with him. Even if I disinherited her."

"The subject of disinheritance came up?"

"I brought it up. Unfortunately I have no ultimate control over the money she has coming from her aunt. Ada would have been well advised to leave the money permanently in my keeping."

This struck me as a doubtful proposition. Blackwell was a sad and troubled man, hardly competent to play God with anybody's life. But the sadder and more troubled they were, the more they yearned for omnipotence. The really troubled ones believed they had it.

"Speaking of money," I said.

We discussed my fee, and he gave me two hundred dollars' advance and the addresses of his houses in Bel Air and Malibu. He gave me something else I hadn't thought of asking for: a key to the beach house, which he detached from his key ring.

chapter 3

IT WAS IN a small isolated settlement north of Malibu. Far down below the highway under the slanting brown bluffs, twelve or fifteen houses huddled together as if for protection against the sea. It was calm enough this morning, at low tide, but the overcast made it grey and menacing.

I turned left off the highway and down an old switchback blacktop to a dead end. Other cars were parked here against a white rail which guarded the final drop to the beach. One of them, a new green Buick Special, was registered to Harriet Blackwell.

A wooden gangway ran from the parking area along the rear of the houses. The ocean glinted dully through the narrow spaces between them. I found the one I was looking for, a grey frame house with a peaked roof, and knocked on the heavy weathered door.

A man's voice grunted at me from inside. I knocked again, and his grudging footsteps padded across the floorboards.

"Who is it?" he said through the door.

"My name is Archer. I was sent to look at the house."

He opened the door. "What's the matter with the house?"

"Nothing, I hope. I'm thinking of renting it."

"The old man sent you out here, eh?"

"Old man?"

"Colonel Blackwell." He pronounced the name very distinctly, as if it was a bad word he didn't want me to miss.

"I wouldn't know about him. A real-estate office in Malibu

put me onto this place. They didn't say it was occupied."

"They wouldn't. They're bugging me."

He stood squarely in the doorway, a young man with a ridged washboard stomach and pectorals like breastplates visible under his T-shirt. His black hair, wet or oily, drooped across his forehead and gave him a low-browed appearance. His dark blue eyes were emotional and a bit sullen. They had a potential thrust which he wasn't using on me.

The over-all effect of his face was that of a boy trying not to be aware of his good looks. Boy wasn't quite the word. I placed his age around thirty, a fairly experienced thirty.

He had wet paint on his fingers. His face, even his bare feet, had spots of paint on them. His jeans were mottled and stiff with dried paint.

"I guess he has a right, if it comes down to that. I'm moving out any day." He looked down at his hands, flexing his colored fingers. "I'm only staying on until I finish the painting."

"You're painting the house?"

He gave me a faintly contemptuous look. "I'm painting a picture, *amigo*."

"I see. You're an artist."

"I work at the trade. You might as well come in and look around, since you're here. What did you say your name was?"

"Archer. You're very kind."

"Beggars can't be choosers." He seemed to be reminding himself of the fact.

Stepping to one side, he let me into the main room. Except for the kitchen partitioned off in the corner to my left, this room took up the whole top floor of the house. It was spacious and lofty, with a raftered ceiling and a pegged oak floor that had been recently polished. The furniture was made of rattan and beige-colored leather. To my right as I went in, a carpeted flight of steps with a wrought iron railing descended to the lower floor. A red brick fireplace faced it across the room.

At the far end, the ocean end, on the inside of the sliding

glass doors, an easel with a stretched canvas on it stood on a paint-splashed tarpaulin.

"It's a nice house," the young man said. "How much rent do they want from you?"

"Five hundred for the month of August."

He whistled.

"Isn't that what you've been paying?"

"I've been paying nothing. *Nada.* I'm a guest of the owner." His sudden wry grin persisted, changing almost imperceptibly to a look of pain. "If you'll excuse me, I'll get back to work. Take your time, you won't disturb me."

He walked the length of the room, moving with careful eagerness like an animal stalking prey, and planted himself in front of the easel. I was a little embarrassed by his casual hospitality. I'd expected something different: another yelling match, or even a show of violence. I could feel the tension in him, as it was, but he was holding it.

A kind of screaming silence radiated from the place where he stood. He was glaring at the canvas as if he was thinking of destroying it. Stooping quickly, he picked up a traylike palette, squizzled a brush in a tangle of color, and with his shoulder muscles bunched, stabbed at the canvas daintily with the brush.

I went through the swinging doors into the kitchen. The gas stove, the refrigerator, the stainless steel sink were all sparkling clean. I inspected the cupboards, which were well stocked with cans of everything from baked beans to truffles. It looked as though Harriet had been playing house, for keeps.

I crossed to the stairway. The man in front of the easel said: "Augh!" He wasn't talking to me. He was talking to his canvas. Stepping softly, I went down the stairs. At their foot a narrow door opened onto outside steps which led down to the beach.

There were two bedrooms, a large one in front and a smaller one in the rear, with a bathroom between them. There was nothing in the rear bedroom but a pair of twin beds with bare

mattresses and pillows. The bathroom contained a pink washbowl and a pink tub with a shower curtain. A worn leather
shaving kit with the initials B.C. stamped on it in gold lay on
the back of the washbowl. I unzipped it. The razor was still
wet from recent use.

The master bedroom in front, like the room above it, had
sliding glass doors which opened onto a balcony. The single
king-sized bed was covered with a yellow chenille spread on
which women's clothes had been carefully folded: a plaid
skirt, a cashmere sweater, underthings. A snakeskin purse
with an ornate gold-filled clasp that looked Mexican lay on top
of the chest of drawers. I opened it and found a red leather
wallet which held several large and small bills and Harriet
Blackwell's driving license.

I looked behind the louvered doors of the closet. There were
no women's clothes hanging in it, and very few men's. The
single lonesome suit was a grey lightweight worsted number
which bore the label of a tailor on Calle Juares in Guadalajara.
The slacks and jacket beside it had been bought at a chain
department store in Los Angeles, and so had the new black
shoes on the rack underneath. In the corner of the closet was a
scuffed brown samsonite suitcase with a Mexicana Airlines
tag tied to the handle.

The suitcase was locked. I hefted it. It seemed to have nothing inside.

The door at the foot of the stairs opened behind me. A
blonde girl wearing a white bathing suit and dark harlequin
glasses came in. She failed to see me till she was in the room
with me.

"Who are you?" she said in a startled voice.

I was a little startled myself. She was a lot of girl. Though
she was wearing flat beach sandals, her hidden eyes were almost on a level with my own. Smiling into the dark glasses, I
gave her my apologies and my story.

"Father's never rented the beach house before."

"He seems to have changed his mind."

"Yes, and I know why." Her voice was high and small for so large a girl.

"Why?"

"It doesn't concern you."

She whipped off her glasses, revealing a black scowl, and something else. I saw why her father couldn't believe that any man would love her truly or permanently. She looked a little too much like him.

She seemed to know this; perhaps the knowledge never left her thoughts. Her silver-tipped fingers went to her brow and smoothed away the scowl. They couldn't smooth away the harsh bone that rose in a ridge above her eyes and made her not pretty.

I apologized a second time for invading her privacy, and for the unspoken fact that she was not pretty, and went upstairs. Her fiancé, if that is what he was, was using a palette knife to apply cobalt blue to his canvas. He was sweating and oblivious.

I stood behind him and watched him work on his picture. It was one of those paintings concerning which only the painter could tell when it was finished. I had never seen anything quite like it: a cloudy mass like a dark thought in which some areas of brighter color stood out like hope or fear. It must have been very good or very bad, because it gave me a *frisson*.

He threw down his knife and stood back jostling me. His gymnasium smell was mixed with the sweeter smell of the oils. He turned with a black intensity in his eyes. It faded as I watched.

"Sorry, I didn't know you were there. Have you finished looking around?"

"Enough for now."

"Like the place?"

"Very much. When did you say you were moving?"

"I don't know. It depends." A troubled expression had taken

the place of the singleness that was his working look. "You
don't want it before August, anyway."

"I might."

The girl spoke from the head of the stairs in a carrying
voice: "Mr. Damis will be out of here by the end of the week."

He turned to her with his wry, self-mocking smile. "Is that
an order, Missy Colonel?"

"Of course not, darling. I never give orders. But you know
what our plans are."

"I know what they're supposed to be."

She came toward him in a flurried rush, her plaid skirt swinging, the way a child moves in on a loved adult. "You can't
mean you've changed your mind again?"

He lowered his head, and shook it. The troubled expression
had spread from his eyes to his mouth.

"Sorry, kid, I have a hard time making decisions, especially
now that I'm working. But nothing's changed."

"That's wonderful. You make me happy."

"You're easily made happy."

"You know I love you."

She had forgotten me, or didn't care. She tried to put her
arms around him. He pushed her back with the heels of his
hands, holding his fingers away from her sweater.

"Don't touch me, I'm dirty."

"I like you dirty."

"Silly kid," he said without much indulgence.

"I like you, love you, eat-you-up, you dirty."

She leaned toward him, taller in her heels than he was, and
kissed him on the mouth. He stood and absorbed her passion,
his hands held away from her body. He was looking past
her at me. His eyes were wide open and rather sad.

chapter 4

HE SAID WHEN she released him: "Is there anything else, Mr. Archer?"

"No. Thanks. I'll check back with you later."

"If you insist."

Harriet Blackwell gave me a peculiar look. "Your name is Archer?"

I acknowledged that it was. She turned her back on me, in a movement that reminded me of her father, and stood looking out over the grey sea. Like a man stepping under a bell jar which muffled sound and feeling, Damis had already returned to his painting.

I let myself out, wondering if it had been a good idea to put in a personal appearance at the beach house. I found out in a moment that it hadn't been. Before I reached my car, Harriet came running after me, her heels rat-tat-tatting on the wooden gangway.

"You came here to spy on us, didn't you?"

She took hold of my arm and shook it. Her snakeskin bag fell to the ground between us. I picked it up and handed it to her as a peace offering. She snatched it out of my hand.

"What are you trying to do to me? What did I ever do to you?"

"Not a thing, Miss Blackwell. And I'm not trying to do anything to you."

"That's a lie. Father hired you to break it up between me and Burke. I heard him talk to you yesterday, on the telephone."

"You don't have very good security at your house."

"I have a right to protect myself, when people connive against me."

"Your father thinks he's protecting you."

"Oh, certainly. By trying to destroy the only happiness I'll ever know or want." There was a lilt of hysteria in her voice. "Father pretends to love me, but I believe in his secret heart of hearts he wishes me ill. He *wants* me to be lonely and miserable."

"That's not very sensible talk."

She shifted her mood abruptly. "But what you're doing is very sensible, I suppose. Sneaking around other people's houses pretending to be something different from what you are."

"It wasn't a good idea."

"So you admit it."

"I should have gone about it in a different way."

"You're *cynical*." She curled her lips at me youngly. "I don't know how you can bear to live with yourself."

"I was trying to do a job. I bungled it. Let's start over."

"I have nothing to say to you whatever."

"I have something to say to you, Miss Blackwell. Are you willing to sit in the car and listen to me?"

"You can say it right out here."

"I don't want interruptions," I said, looking back toward the beach house.

"You don't have to be afraid of Burke. I didn't tell him who you are. I don't like to upset him when he's working."

She sounded very much like a young wife, or almost-wife. I made a comment on this. It seemed to please her.

"I love him. It's no secret. You can write it down in your little black book and make a full report of it to Father. I love Burke, and I'm going to marry him."

"When?"

"Very soon now." She hid her secret behind a hushed mysterious look. Perhaps she wasn't sure she had a secret to hide. "I wouldn't dream of telling you when or where. Father would call out the National Guard, at least."

"Are you getting married to please yourself or spite your father?"

She looked at me uncomprehendingly. I had no doubt it was a relevant question, but she didn't seem to have an answer to it.

"Let's forget about Father," I said.

"How can I? There's nothing he wouldn't do to stop us. He said so himself."

"I'm not here to stop your marriage, Miss Blackwell."

"Then what are you trying to do?"

"Find out what I can about your friend's background."

"So Father can use it against him."

"That's assuming there's something that can be used."

"Isn't that your assumption?"

"No. I made it clear to Colonel Blackwell that I wouldn't go along with a smear attempt, or provide the material for any kind of moral blackmail. I want to make it clear to you."

"And I'm supposed to believe you?"

"Why not? I have nothing against your friend, or against you. If you'd co-operate—"

"Oh, very likely." She looked at me as though I'd made an obscene suggestion. "You're a brash man, aren't you?"

"I'm trying to make the best of a bad job. If you'd co-operate we might be able to get it over with in a hurry. It's not the kind of a job I like."

"You didn't have to take it. I suppose you took it because you needed the money." There was a note of patronage in her voice, the moral superiority of the rich who never have to do anything for money. "How much money is Father paying you?"

"A hundred a day."

"I'll give you five hundred, five days' pay, if you'll simply go away and forget about us."

She took out her red wallet and brandished it.

"I couldn't do that, Miss Blackwell. Besides, it wouldn't do you any good. He'd go and hire himself another detective. And if you think I'm trouble, you should take a look at some of my colleagues."

She leaned on the white guard rail and studied me in silence. Behind her the summer tide had begun to turn. The rising surge slid up the beach, and sanderlings skimmed along its wavering edges. She said to an invisible confidant located somewhere between me and the birds: "Can the man be honest?"

"I can and am. I can, therefore I am."

No smile. She never smiled. "I still don't know what I'm going to do about you. You realize this situation is impossible."

"It doesn't have to be. Don't you have any interest in your fiancé's background?"

"I know all I need to know."

"And what is that?"

"He's a sweet man, and a brilliant one, and he's had a very rough time. Now that he's painting again, there's no limit to what he can accomplish. I want to help him develop his potential."

"Where did he study painting?"

"I've never asked him."

"How long have you known him?"

"Long enough."

"How long?"

"Three or four weeks."

"And that's long enough to make up your mind to marry him?"

"I have a right to marry whom I please. I'm not a child, and neither is Burke."

"I realize *he* isn't."

"I'm twenty-four," she said defensively. "I'm going to be twenty-five in December."

"At which time you come into money."

"Father's briefed you very thoroughly, hasn't he? But there

are probably a few things he left out. Burke doesn't care about
money, he despises it. We're going to Europe or South America
and live very simply, and he will do his work and I will help
him and that will be our life." There were stars in her eyes,
dim and a long way off. "If I thought the money would prevent
me from marrying the man I love, I'd *give* it away."

"Would Burke like that?"

"He'd love it."

"Have you discussed it with him?"

"We've discussed everything. We're very frank with each
other."

"Then you can tell me where he comes from and so on."

There was another silence. She moved restlessly against the
guard rail as though I had backed her into a corner. The
chancy stars in her eyes had dimmed out. In spite of her protestations, she was a worried girl. I guessed that she was main-
lining on euphoria, which can be as destructive as any drug.

"Burke doesn't like to talk about the past. It makes him unhappy."

"Because he's an orphan?"

"That's part of it, I think."

"He must be thirty. A man stops being an orphan at twenty-
one. What's he been doing since he gave up being a full-time
orphan?"

"All he's ever done is paint."

"In Mexico?"

"Part of the time."

"How long had he been in Mexico when you met him?"

"I don't know. A long time."

"Why did he go to Mexico?"

"To paint."

We were going around in circles, concentric circles which
contained nothing but a blank. I said: "We've been talking
for some time now, and you haven't told me anything that
would help to check your friend out."

"What do you expect? I haven't pried into his affairs. I'm not a detective."

"I'm supposed to be," I said ruefully, "but you're making me look like a slob."

"That could be because you are a slob. You could always give up and go away. Go back to Father and tell him you're a failure."

Her needle failed to strike a central nerve, but I reacted to it. "Look here, Miss Blackwell. I sympathize with your natural desire to break away from your family ties and make a life of your own. But you don't want to jump blindly in the opposite direction—"

"You sound exactly like Father. I'm sick of people breathing in my face, telling me what to do and what not to do. You can go back and tell him that."

She was getting terribly restless. I knew I couldn't hold her very much longer. Her body mimed impatience in its awkward gangling attitude, half sitting on the rail, with one foot kicking out spasmodically. It was a fine big body, I thought, not meant for spinsterhood. I had serious doubts that Harriet and her fine big body and her fine big wad of money were meant for Burke Damis, either. The little love scene I'd witnessed between them had been completely one-sided.

Her face had darkened. She turned it away from me. "Why are you looking at me like that?"

"I'm trying to understand you."

"Don't bother. There's nothing to understand. I'm a very simple person."

"I was thinking that, too."

"You make it sound like an insult."

"No. I doubt that your friend Burke is quite so simple. That isn't an insult, either."

"What is it?"

"Call it a warning. If you were my daughter, and you're young enough to be, I'd hate to see you fling yourself into this thing in a frantic hurry—merely because your father is against it."

"That isn't my reason. It's a positive thing."

"Whatever your reasons are, you could find yourself in water over your head."

She looked out past the kelp beds where the ocean went dark and deep and the sharks lived out of sight.

"'Hang your clothes on a hickory limb,'" she quoted, "'but don't go near the water.' I've heard that before."

"You could even keep your clothes on."

She gave me another of her looks, her black Blackwell looks. "How dare you speak to me in that way?"

"The words came out. I let them."

"You're an insufferable man."

"While I'm being insufferable, you may be able to clear up a small discrepancy for me. I noticed that the shaving kit in the bathroom has the initials B.C. on it. Those initials don't go with the name Burke Damis."

"I never noticed it."

"Don't you find it interesting?"

"No." But the blood had drained out of her face and left it sallow. "I imagine it belonged to some previous guest. A lot of different people have used the beach house."

"Name one with the initials B.C."

"Bill Campbell," she said quickly.

"Bill Campbell's initials would be W.C. Who is Bill Campbell, by the way?"

"A friend of Father's. I don't know if he ever used the beach house or not."

"Or if he ever existed?"

I'd pressed too hard, and lost her. She dismounted from the rail, smoothing down her skirt, and started away from me toward the beach house. I watched her go. No doubt she was a simple person, as she said, but I couldn't fathom her.

chapter 5

I drove back up to the highway. Diagonally across the intersection, a large fading sign painted on the side of a roadside diner advertised Jumbo Shrimp. I could smell grease before I got out of the car.

The stout woman behind the counter looked as though she had spent her life waiting, but not for me. I sat in a booth by the front window, partly obscured by an unlit neon beer sign. She brought me a knife and fork, a glass of water, and a paper napkin. I was the only customer in the place.

"You want the shrimp special?"

"I'll just have coffee, thanks."

"That will cost you twenty cents," she said severely, "without the food to go with it."

She picked up the knife and fork and the paper napkin. I sat and nursed the coffee, keeping an eye on the blacktop road that led up from the beach.

The overcast was burning off. A sun like a small watery moon appeared behind it. The muffled horizon gradually cleared, and the sea changed from grey to greyish blue. The surf had begun to thump so hard I could hear it.

Two or three cars had come up from the cluster of beach houses, but there had been no sign of Harriet's green Buick. I started in on my second cup of coffee. Refills were only ten cents.

A zebra-striped hearse with a broken headlight came in off the highway. It disgorged, from front and rear, four boys and two girls who all looked like siblings. Their hair, bleached by sun and peroxide, was long on the boys and short on the girls so that it was almost uniform. They wore blue sweatshirts over bathing suits. Their faces were brown and closed.

They came in and sat in a row at the counter, ordered six
beers, drank them with hero sandwiches which the girls made
out of French loaves and other provisions brought in in paper
bags. They ate quietly and voraciously. From time to time, between bites, the largest boy, who carried himself like their
leader, made a remark about big surf. He might have been
talking about a tribal deity.

They rose in unison like a platoon, and marched out to their
hearse. Two of the boys got into the front seat. The rest of
them sat in the back beside the surfboards. One of the girls,
the pretty one, made a face at me through the side window.
For no good reason, I made a face back at her. The hearse
turned down the blacktop toward the beach.

"Beach bums," the woman behind the counter said.

She wasn't talking to me. Having nursed two coffees for an
hour, I may have been included in her epithet. The coffee, or
the waiting, was beginning to make me nervous. I ordered a
therapeutic beer and turned back to the window.

The woman went on talking to herself. "You'd think they'd
have more respect, painting a hearse in stripes like that. They
got no respect for the living or the dead. How they expect me
to make a living, bringing in their own food? I don't know
what the world is coming to."

Harriet's car appeared, coming out of a tight curve, halfway up the slope. I saw when it reached the highway that she
was driving and that her friend was in the seat beside her. He
was wearing his grey suit, with a shirt and tie, and he bore a
curious resemblance to those blank-faced dummies you see in
the windows of men's clothing stores. They turned south, toward Los Angeles.

I followed them down the highway. Malibu slowed them,
and I was close on their tail as they passed through the shabby
fringes of Pacific Palisades. They made a left turn onto Sunset.
The light had changed when I reached the corner. By the time

it changed in my favor, the Buick was far out of sight. I tried
to make up the minutes I had lost, but the squealing curves of
the Boulevard kept my speed down.

I remembered that the Blackwells lived in the hills off Sunset. On the chance that Harriet was on her way home, I
turned in through the baronial gates of Bel Air. But I couldn't
find the Blackwell house, and had to go back to the hotel to
ask directions.

It was visible from the door of the hotel bar. The white-
coated barman pointed it out to me: a graceful Spanish man-
sion which stood at the top of the terraced slope. I gave the
barman a dollar of Blackwell's money and asked him if he
knew the Colonel.

"I wouldn't say I *know* him. He isn't one of your talkative
drinkers."

"What kind of a drinker is he?"

"The silent type. My favorite type."

I went back to my car and up the winding road to the hilltop house. The rose garden in front of it was contained like a
conflagration by a clipped boxwood hedge. Harriet's Buick
was standing in the semicircular gravel drive.

I could see her father's white head over the roof of the car.
His voice carried all the way out to the road. I caught isolated
words like sneak and scrounger.

When I got nearer I could see that Blackwell was carrying
a double-barreled shotgun at the hip. Burke Damis got out of
the car and spoke to him. I didn't hear what he said, but the
muzzle of the shotgun came up to the level of his chest. Damis
reached for it.

The older man fell back a step. The level gun rested firmly
at his shoulder. Damis took a step forward, thrusting out his
chest as if he welcomed the threat of the gun.

"Go ahead and shoot me. It would fix you at least."

"I warn you, you can press me so far and no farther."

Damis laughed. "You ain't seen nothing yet, old man."

These things were being said as I climbed out of my car
and walked toward them, slowly. I was afraid of jarring the
precarious balance of the scene. It was very still on the hilltop.
I could hear the sound of their breathing and other things besides: my feet crunching in the gravel, the low call of a
mourning dove from the television antenna on the roof.

Neither Blackwell nor Damis looked at me as I came up
beside them. They weren't in physical contact, but their faces
were contorted as though their hands had death grips on each
other. The double muzzle of the shotgun dominated the
scene like a pair of empty insane eyes.

"There's a dove on the roof," I said conversationally. "If you
feel like shooting something, Colonel, why don't you take a
shot at it? Or is there a law against it in these parts? I seem to
remember something about a law."

He turned to me with a grimace of rage stamped in the
muscles of his face. The gun swung with his movement. I took
hold of the double barrel and forced it up toward the unoffend-
ing sky. I lifted it out of Blackwell's hands, and broke open
the breach. There was a shell in each chamber. I tore a fingernail unloading them.

"Give me back my shotgun," he said.

I gave it to him empty. "Shooting never solved a thing.
Didn't you learn that in the war?"

"The fellow insulted me."

"The way I heard it, insults were traveling in both directions."

"But you didn't hear what he said. He made a filthy accusation."

"So you want big black filthy headlines, and a nice long filthy
trial in Superior Court."

"The filthier the better," Damis said.

I turned on him. "Shut up."

His eyes were somber and steady. "You can't shut me up.
Neither can he."

"He almost did, boy. Twelve-gauge shotgun wounds at this range ruin you for keeps."

"Tell *him*. I couldn't care less."

Damis looked as though he didn't care, for himself or anyone. But he seemed to feel exposed under my eyes. He got into the passenger's seat of Harriet's car and pulled the door shut. The action, all his actions, had something bold about them and something secretive.

Blackwell turned toward the house and I went along. The veranda was brilliant with fuchsias growing out of hanging redwood tubs. To my slightly jittered vision, they resembled overflowing buckets of blood.

"You came near committing murder, Colonel. You should keep your guns unloaded and locked up."

"I do."

"Maybe you ought to throw the key away."

He looked down at the gun in his hands as if he didn't remember how it had got there. Sudden pockets had formed under his eyes.

"What led up to this?" I said.

"You know the long-term part of it. He's been moving in on me and my household, robbing me of my most precious possession—"

"A daughter isn't exactly a possession."

"I have to look out for her. Someone has to. She announced a few minutes ago that she was going away to marry the fellow. I tried to reason with her. She accused me of being a little Hitler who had hired a private Gestapo. That accusation hurt, from my own daughter, but the fellow"—he shot an angry glance toward the car—"the fellow made a worse one."

"What did he say?"

"I wouldn't repeat it, to anyone. He made a filthy allegation about me. Of course there's nothing to it. I've always been upright in my dealings with others, especially my own daughter."

"I don't doubt that. I'm trying to find out what kind of thinking goes on in Damis's head."

"He's a mixed-up young man," Blackwell said. "I believe he's dangerous."

That made two of them, in my opinion.

A screen door slammed, and Harriet appeared behind the hanging red and purple fuchsias. She had changed to a light sharkskin suit and a hat with a little grey veil fluttering from it. The little veil bothered me, perhaps because it short-circuited the distance between brides and widows. She was carrying a blue hatbox and a heavy blue case.

Her father met her on the steps and reached for the blue case. "Let me help with that, dear."

She swung it away from him. "I can handle it myself, thank you."

"Is that all you have to say to me?"

"Everything's been said. We know what you think of us. Burke and I are going away where you won't be tempted to —harass us." Her cold young eyes rested on me, and then on the shotgun in her father's hand. "I don't even feel physically safe."

"The gun's empty," I said. "Nobody got hurt and nobody's going to. I wish you'd reconsider this move, Miss Blackwell. Give it a day's thought, anyway."

She wouldn't speak directly to me. "Call off your dogs," she said to Blackwell. "Burke and I are going to be married and you have no right to stop us. There must be legal limits to what even a *father* can do."

"But won't you listen to me, dear? I have no desire to do anything—"

"Stop doing it then."

I'd been surprised by his quiet reasonableness. He didn't have the self-control to sustain it. The sudden yelling demon took possession of him again. "You've made your choice, I wash my hands of you. Go off with your filthy little miracle

man and roll in the mire with him. I won't lift a finger to
rescue you."

She said from the height of her pale cold anger: "You're talking foolishly, Father. What is the matter with you?"

She strode on to the car, swinging her bags like clumsy
weapons. Damis took them from her and put them in the
trunk, beside his own suitcase.

Isobel Blackwell had come out of the house and down the
veranda steps. As she passed between me and her husband,
she pressed his shoulder in sympathy and perhaps in admoni-
tion. She went up to Harriet.

"I wish you wouldn't do this to your father."

"I'm not doing anything *to* him."

"He feels it that way. He loves you, you know."

"I don't love him."

"I'm sure you'll regret saying that, Harriet. When you do,
please let him know."

"Why should I bother? He has you."

Isobel shrugged, as though the possession of herself was no
great boon to anyone. "You're more important to him than I
am. You could break his heart."

"He's going to have to get over it then. I'm sorry if you feel
badly." In a quick uprush of feeling, Harriet embraced the
older woman. "You've been the best to me—better than I deserve."

Isobel patted her back, looking past her at Damis. He had
been watching the two of them like a spectator at a game on
which he had placed a moderate bet.

"I hope you'll take good care of her, Mr. Damis."

"I can try."

"Where are you taking her?"

"Away from here."

"That isn't very informative."

"It wasn't intended to be. This is a big country, also a free
one. Let's go, Harriet."

She disengaged herself from her stepmother and got into the driver's seat of her car. Damis climbed in beside her. I made a note of the license number as they drove away. Neither of them looked back.

Blackwell approached us, walking rather uncertainly in the gravel. His body seemed to have shrunk some more in his clothes, while his large face had grown larger.

"You let them go," he said accusingly.

"I had nothing to stop them with. I can't use force."

"You should have followed them."

"What for? You said you'd washed your hands of them."

His wife spoke up: "Perhaps it would be better if you did that, Mark. You can't go on in this fashion, letting the situation drive you crazy. You might as well accept it."

"I refuse to accept it, and it's not driving me crazy. I've never been saner in my life. I resent the implication that I'm not."

The ranting rhythm was taking over his voice again. She laid her gentle admonishing hand on his arm.

"Come into the house. You need to relax, after all you've been through."

"Leave me alone." He flung her hand off and said to me: "I want Damis put in jail, do you hear me?"

"To do that, you'd have to prove that he's committed a jailable offense."

"What about taking a girl across a state line for immoral purposes?"

"Has he done that?"

"He transported my daughter from Mexico—"

"But marriage isn't considered an immoral purpose under the law."

Isobel Blackwell tittered unexpectedly.

He turned on her. "You think it's funny, do you?"

"Not particularly. But it's better to laugh than to weep. And better to marry than to burn. I'm quoting your own words to me, remember?"

Her tone was serious, but there was irony in it. Blackwell stalked toward the house, picking up his shotgun on the way. He slammed the front door so violently that the dove flew up with whistling wings from the television antenna. Isobel Blackwell spread her arms as though a larger bird had escaped from them.

"What am I going to do with him?"

"Give him a tranquilizer."

"Mark has been *eating* tranquilizers all week. It doesn't seem to help his nerves. If he goes on at this rate, I'm afraid he'll shake himself to pieces."

"It's other people I'm worried about."

"You mean the young man—Damis?"

"I mean anyone who crosses him."

She touched me lightly on the arm. "You don't think he's capable of doing actual harm to anyone?"

"You know him better than I do."

"I thought I knew Mark very well indeed. But he's changed in the last year. He's always been a gentle man. I never thought he belonged in the military profession. The Army came to agree with me, as it happened. They retired him after the war, very much against his will. His first wife, Pauline, divorced him about the same time."

"Why, if you don't mind my asking?"

"You'd have to ask her. She went to Nevada one day and got a divorce and married another man—a retired dentist named Keith Hatchen. They've lived in Mexico ever since. I suppose Pauline and her dentist have a right to whatever happiness they can muster. But it left poor Mark with nothing to fill his life but his guns and his sports and the Blackwell family history which he has been trying to write for lo these many years."

"And Harriet," I said.

"And Harriet."

"I'm beginning to get the picture. You say he's changed in the past year. Has anything special happened, besides Harriet's taking up with Damis?"

"Mark took up with me last fall," she said with a one-sided smile.

"You don't strike me as a malign influence."

"Thank you. I'm not."

"I had the impression that you'd been married longer than that." It was partly a question and partly an expression of sympathy.

"Did you now? Of course I've been married before. And I've known Mark and Harriet for a great many years, practically since she was a babe in arms. You see, my late husband was very close to Mark. Ronald was related to the Blackwells."

"Then you probably know a lot of things you haven't told me," I said.

"Every woman does. Isn't that your experience, Mr. Archer?"

I liked her dry wit, even if it was cutting me off from further information. I made a gesture that took in the big house and the roses and the gap in the boxwood hedge where Harriet's car had last been seen.

"Do you think I should go on with this?"

She answered deliberately: "Perhaps you had better. Mark certainly needs another man to guide his hand and advise him—not that he's terribly good at taking advice. I liked the way you handled this crisis just now. It could have erupted into something terrible."

"I wish your husband realized that."

"He does. I'm sure he does, though he won't admit it." Her dark eyes were full of feeling. "You've done us all a good turn, Mr. Archer, and you'll do us another by staying with us in this. Find out what you can about Damis. If you can give him a clean bill of health, morally speaking, it should do a lot to reconcile Mark to the marriage."

"You're not suggesting a whitewash job on Damis?"

"Of course not. I'm interested in the truth, whatever it may turn out to be. We all are. Now if you'll excuse me I think I'd better go in and look after my husband. Holding his hand seems to be my function in life these days."

She wasn't complaining, exactly, but I detected a note of resignation. As she turned away, very slim in her linen sheath, I caught myself trying to estimate her age. If she had known the Blackwells since Harriet was a baby, and had come to know them through her first husband, she must have married him more than twenty years ago. Which suggested that she was over forty.

Well, so was I.

chapter 6

I USED BLACKWELL'S KEY to let myself into the beach house. Nothing had changed in the big upstairs room, except that there were black paper ashes in the fireplace. They crumbled when I tried to pick them up on the fire shovel. The painting hung on its easel, still gleaming wet in places. In the light that slanted through the glass doors, the spot of cobalt blue which Damis had added last glared at me like an eye.

I backed away from the picture, trying to understand it, and went down the stairs to the master bedroom. The louvered doors of the closet were swinging open. It had been cleared out. There was nothing in the chest of drawers, nothing in the bathroom but some clean towels. The back bedroom was empty.

I moved back into the front bedroom and went through it carefully. The wastebasket had been emptied, which probably accounted for the burned paper in the upstairs fireplace. Damis had gone to a lot of trouble to cover his traces.

But he had overlooked one piece of paper. It was jammed between the sliding glass door and its frame, evidently to keep the door from rattling. It was thick and yellowish paper, folded small. When I unfolded it, I recognized it as one of those envelopes that airlines give their passengers to keep their tickets in.

This was a Mexicana Airlines envelope, with flight instructions typed inside the flap. Mr. Q. R. Simpson, the instructions said, was to leave the Guadalajara airport at 8:40 A.M. on July 10 and arrive at Los Angeles International at 1:30 P.M. the same day.

I messed around in the bedroom some more, discovered only some dust mice under the bed, and went upstairs. The painting drew me back to it. It affected me differently each time. This time I saw, or thought I saw, that it was powerful and ugly—an assault of dark forces on the vision. Perhaps I was reading my fantasy into it, but it seemed to me that its darkness was the ultimate darkness of death.

I had an impulse to take it along and find an expert to show it to. If Damis was a known artist, his style should be recognizable. But I couldn't move the thing. The oils were still wet and would smear.

I went out to the car to get my camera. The zebra-striped hearse was standing empty beside it. The sky had cleared, and a few sun-bathers were lying around in the sand like bodies after a catastrophe. Beyond the surf line the six surfers waited in prayerful attitudes on their boards.

A big wave rose toward them. Five of the surfers rode it in, like statues on a traveling blue hillside. The sixth was less skillful. The wave collapsed on her. She lost her board and swam in after it.

Instead of taking it out to sea again, she carried it up the beach on her head. She left it on the sand above the tide line and climbed the rocky bank to the parking space. She had the bust and shoulders of a young Amazon, but she was shivering and close to tears.

It was the girl who had made the face at me, which gave us something in common. I said: "You took quite a spill."

She looked at me as if she had never seen me before, almost as if she wasn't seeing me now. I was a member of another tribe or species. Her eyes were wet and wild, like the eyes of sea lions.

She got a man's topcoat out of the back of the hearse and put it on. It was good brown tweed which looked expensive, but there were wavy white salt marks on it, as if it had been immersed in the sea. Her fingers trembled on the brown leather buttons. One of the buttons, the top one, was missing. She turned up the collar around the back of her head where the wet hair clung like a golden helmet.

"If you're cold I have a heater in my car."

"Blah," she said, and turned her tweed back on me.

I loaded the camera with color film and took some careful shots of Damis's painting. On my way to the airport I dropped the film off with a photographer friend in Santa Monica. He promised to get it developed in a hurry.

The very polite young man at the Mexicana desk did a few minutes' research and came up with the information that Q. R. Simpson had indeed been on the July 10 flight from Guadalajara. So had Harriet Blackwell. Burke Damis hadn't.

My tentative conclusion, which I kept to myself, was that Damis had entered the United States under the name of Simpson. Since he couldn't leave Mexico without a non-transferable tourist card or enter this country without proof of citizenship, the chances were that Q. R. Simpson was Damis's real name.

The polite young Mexican told me further that the crew of the July 10 flight had flown in from Mexico again early this afternoon. The pilot and copilot were in the office now, but they wouldn't know anything about the passengers. The steward and stewardess, who would, had already gone for the day. They were due to fly out again tomorrow morning. If I came out to the airport before flight time, perhaps they would have a few minutes to talk to me about my friend Señor Simpson.

Exhilarated by his Latin courtesy, I walked back to the Immigration and Customs shed. The officers on duty took turns looking at my license as if it was something I'd found in a box of breakfast cereal.

Feeling the need to check in with some friendly authority, I drove downtown. Peter Colton was in his cubicle in the District Attorney's office, behind a door that said Chief Criminal Investigator.

Peter had grown old in law enforcement. The grooves of discipline and thought were like saber scars in his cheeks. His triangular eyes glinted at me over half-glasses which had slid down his large aggressive nose.

He finished reading a multigraphed sheet, initialed it, and scaled it into his out-basket.

"Sit down, Lew. How's it going?"

"All right. I dropped by to thank you for recommending me to Colonel Blackwell."

He regarded me quizzically. "You don't sound very grateful. Is Blackie giving you a bad time?"

"Something is. He handed me a peculiar case. I don't know whether it's a case or not. It may be only Blackwell's imagination."

"He never struck me as the imaginative type."

"Known him long?"

"I served under him, for my sins, in Bavaria just after the war. He was in Military Government, and I was in charge of a plain-clothes section of Military Police."

"What was he like to work for?"

"Tough," Colton said, and added reflectively: "Blackie liked command, too much. He didn't get enough of it during the fighting. Some friend in Washington, or some enemy, kept him in the rear echelons. I don't know whether it was for Blackie's own protection or the protection of the troops. He was bitter about it, and it made him hard on his men. But he's a bit of an ass, and we didn't take him too seriously."

"In what way was he hard on his men?"

"All the ways he could think of. He went in for enforcement of petty rules. He was very keen on the anti-fraternization policy. My men had murder and rape and black-marketeering to contend with. But Blackie expected us to spend our nights patrolling the cabarets suppressing fraternization. It drove him crazy to think of all the fraternization that was going on between innocent American youths and man-eating *Fräuleins*."

"Is he some kind of a sex nut?"

"I wouldn't put it that strongly." But Colton's grin was wolfish. "He's a Puritan, from a long line of Puritans. What made it worse, he was having fraternization problems in his own family. His wife was interested in various other men. I heard later she divorced him."

"What sort of a woman is she?"

"Quite a dish, in those days, but I never knew her up close. Does it matter?"

"It could. Her daugher Harriet went to Mexico to visit her a few weeks ago and made a bad connection. At least it doesn't look too promising. He's a painter named Burke Damis, or possibly Q. R. Simpson. She brought him back here with her, intends to marry him. Blackwell thinks the man is trying to take her for her money. He hired me to investigate that angle, or anything else that I can find on Damis."

"Or possibly Q. R. Simpson, you said. Is Damis using an alias?"

"I haven't confirmed it. I'm fairly sure he entered the country a week ago under the Q. R. Simpson name. It may be his real name, since it isn't a likely alias."

"And you want me to check it out."

"That would be nice."

Colton picked up his ball-point pen and jabbed with it in my direction. "You know I can't spend public time and money on a private deal like this."

"Even for an old friend?"

"Blackwell's no friend of mine. I recommended you to get him out of my hair in one quick easy motion."

"I was referring to myself," I said, "no doubt presumptuously. A simple query to the State Bureau of Criminal Investigation wouldn't take much time, and it might save trouble in the long run. You always say you're more interested in preventing crime than punishing it."

"What crime do you have in mind?"

"Murder for profit is a possibility. I don't say it's probable. I'm mainly concerned with saving a naïve young woman from a lot of potential grief."

"And saving yourself a lot of potential legwork."

"I'm doing my own legwork as usual. But I could knock on every door from here to San Luis Obispo and it wouldn't tell me what I need to know."

"What, exactly, is that?"

"Whether Q. R. Simpson, or Burke Damis, has a record."

Colton wrote the names on a memo pad. I'd succeeded in arousing his curiosity.

"I suppose I could check with Sacramento." He glanced at the clock on the wall. It was nearly four. "If the circuits aren't too loaded, we might get an answer before we close up for the night. You want to wait outside?"

I read a law-enforcement trade journal in the anteroom, all the way through to the advertisements. Police recruits were being offered as much as four hundred and fifty dollars a month in certain localities.

Peter Colton opened his door at five o'clock on the nose and beckoned me into his office. A teletype flimsy rustled in his hand.

"Nothing on Burke Damis," he said. "Quincy Ralph Simpson

is another story: he's on the Missing Persons list, has been for a couple of weeks. According to his wife, he's been gone much longer than that."

"His wife?"

"She's the one who reported him missing. She lives up north, in San Mateo County."

chapter 7

IT WAS CLEAR late twilight when the jet dropped down over the Peninsula. The lights of its cities were scattered like a broken necklace along the dark rim of the Bay. At its tip stood San Francisco, remote and brilliant as a city of the mind, hawsered to reality by her two great bridges—if Marin and Berkeley were reality.

I took a cab to Redwood City. The deputy on duty on the ground floor of the Hall of Justice was a young man with red chipmunk cheeks and eyes that were neither bright nor stupid. He looked me over noncommittally, waiting to see if I was a citizen or one of the others.

I showed him my license and told him I was interested in a man named Quincy Ralph Simpson. "The Los Angeles D.A.'s office says you reported him missing about two weeks ago."

He said after a ruminative pause: "Have you spotted him?"

"I may have."

"Where?"

"In the Los Angeles area. Do you have a picture of Simpson?"

"I'll see." He went into the back of the office, rummaged through a drawerful of bulletins and circulars, and came back empty-handed. "I can't find any, sorry. But I can tell you what he looks like. Medium height, about five-nine or -ten; medium build, one-sixty-five or so; black hair; I don't know the color of his eyes; no visible scars or other distinguishing marks."

"Age?"

"About my age. I'm twenty-nine. Is he your man?"

"It's possible." Just barely possible. "Is Simpson wanted for anything?"

"Non-support, maybe, but I don't know of any complaint. What makes you think he's wanted?"

"The fact that you can describe him."

"I know him. That is, I've seen him around here."

"Doing what?"

He leaned on the counter with a kind of confidential hostility. "I'm not supposed to talk about what I see around here, friend. You want to know anything about that, you'll have to take it up with the boys upstairs."

"Is Captain Royal upstairs?"

"The Captain's off duty. I wouldn't want to disturb him at home. You know him well?"

"We worked together on a case."

"What case was that?"

"I'm not supposed to talk about it, friend. Can you give me Mrs. Simpson's address?"

He reached under the counter and produced a phone book which he pushed in my direction. Q. R. Simpson was listed, at 2160 Marvista Drive. My taxi driver told me that this was in a tract on the far side of Skyline, toward Luna Bay: a five-dollar run.

We drove through darkening hills and eventually turned off the road past a tattered billboard which announced: "No Down Payment. No Closing Costs." The tract houses were new and small and all alike and already declining into slums. Zigzagging through the grid of streets like motorized rats in a maze, we found the address we were looking for.

It stood between two empty houses, and had a rather abandoned air itself. The tiny plot of grass in front of it looked brown and withered in the headlights. A 1952 Ford convertible with the back window torn out was parked in the carport.

I asked the driver to wait, and rang the doorbell. A young woman answered. The door was warped, and she had some trouble opening it all the way.

She was a striking brunette, very thin and tense, with a red slash of mouth and hungry dark eyes. She had on a short black tight dress which revealed her slender knees and only half concealed her various other attractions.

She was aware of these. "This isn't free show night. What is it you want?"

"If you're Mrs. Simpson, I'd like to talk about your husband."

"Go ahead and talk about him. I'm listening." She cocked her head in an angry parody of interest.

"You reported him missing."

"Yes, I reported him missing. I haven't set eyes on him for two whole months. And that suits me just fine. Who needs him?" Her voice was rough with grief and resentment. She was looking past me across the scraggy untended lawn. "Who's that in the taxi?"

"Just the driver. I asked him to wait for me."

"I thought it might be Ralph," she said in a different tone, "afraid to come in the house and all."

"It isn't Ralph. You say he's been gone a couple of months, but you only reported him missing two weeks ago."

"I gave him all the leeway I could. He's taken off before, but never for this long. Mr. Haley at the motel said I ought to clue in the cops. I had to go back to work at the motel. Even with that I can't keep up the house payments without some help from Ralph. But a lot of good it did telling the cops. They don't do much unless you can prove foul play or something." She wrinkled her expressive upper lip. "Are you one?"

"I'm a private detective." I told her my name. "I ran into a man today who could be your missing husband. May I come in?"

"I guess so."

She moved sideways into her living room, glancing around as if to see it through a visitor's eyes. It was tiny and clean and poor, furnished with the kind of cheap plastic pieces that you're still paying installments on when they disintegrate. She turned up the three-way lamp and invited me to sit at one end of the chesterfield. She sat at the other end, hunched forward, her sharp elbows resting on her knees.

"So where did you see him?"

"Malibu."

I wasn't paying much attention to what I said. There was a framed oil painting on the wall above the television set. Though it was recognizable as a portrait of Mrs. Simpson, it looked amateurish to me. I went over and examined it more closely.

"That's supposed to be me," she said behind me.

"It's not a bad likeness. Did your husband do it?"

"Yeah. It's a hobby he has. He wanted to take it up seriously at one time but a man he knew, a real painter, told him he wasn't good enough. That's the story of his life, hopeful beginnings and nothing endings. So now he's living the life of Riley in Malibu while I stay here and work my fingers to the bone. What's he doing, beachcombing?"

I didn't answer her question right away. A dog-eared paperback entitled *The Art of Detection* lay on top of the television set. It was the only book I could see in the room. I picked it up and riffled through the pages. Many of them were heavily underlined; some of them were illustrated with bad cartoons penciled in the margins.

"That was another one of Ralph's big deals," she said. "He was going to be a great detective and put us on easy street. Naturally he didn't get to first base. He never got to first base with any of his big wheels and deals. A man he knows on the cops told him with his record—" She covered her mouth with her hand.

I laid the book down. "Ralph has a record?"

"Not really. That was just a manner of speaking." Her eyes had hardened defensively. "You didn't tell me what he was doing in Malibu."

"I'm not even certain it was your husband I saw there."

"What did he look like?"

I described Burke Damis, and thought I caught the light of recognition in her eyes. But she said definitely: "It isn't him."

"I'd like to be sure about that. Do you have a photograph of Ralph?"

"No. He never had his picture taken."

"Not even a wedding picture?"

"We had one taken, but Ralph never got around to picking up the copies. We were married in Reno, see, and he couldn't hold on to the twenty dollars long enough. He can't keep away from the tables when he's in Reno."

"Does he spend much time in Reno?"

"All the time he can get away from work. I used to go along with him, I used to think it was fun. I had another think coming. It's the reason we never been able to save a nickel."

I moved across the room and sat beside her. "What does Ralph do for a living, Mrs. Simpson?"

"Anything he can get. He never finished high school, and that makes it tough. He's a pretty good short-order cook, but he hated the hours. Same with bartending, which he did for a while. He's had some good-paying houseboy jobs around the Peninsula. But he's too proud for that kind of work. He hates to take orders from people. Maybe," she added bitterly, "he's too proud for any kind of work, and that's why he ran out on me."

"How long ago did he leave?"

"Two months ago, I told you that. He left here on the night of May eighteen. He just got back from Nevada that same day, and he took right off for Los Angeles. I think he only came home to try and talk me out of the car. But I told him he wasn't going to leave me marooned without a car. So he finally broke down and took a bus. I drove him down to the bus station."

"What was he planning to do in Los Angeles?"

"I don't know. He told me this story, when he was trying to talk me out of the car, but I didn't believe it. He said he was doing undercover work. I heard the same story from him before, when he was working in a drive-in on Camino Real. He claimed the cops were paying him to give them tips."

"Tips about what?"

"Kids smoking reefers, stuff like that. I didn't know whether to believe him or not. I thought maybe he was just talking to make himself feel important. He always wanted to be a cop himself."

"But his record wouldn't let him."

"He has no record."

"You said he had."

"You must have been hearing things. Anyway, I'm getting tired. I've had enough of this."

She rose in a sudden thrust of energy and stood by the door, inviting me to leave. I stayed where I was on the plastic chesterfield.

"You might as well leave," she said. "It isn't Ralph you saw in Malibu."

"I'm not so sure of that."

"You can take my word."

"All right, I take your word." It doesn't pay to argue with a source of information. "But I'm still interested in Ralph. Aren't you?"

"Naturally I am. I'm married to him. At least I'm supposed to be married to him. But I got a funny feeling, here." Her left hand moved up her body to her breast. "I got a feeling he traded me in on a new model, and *that's* the undercover work."

"Do you know who the other woman might be?"

"No. I just got a feeling. Why would a man go away and not come back?"

I could think of various answers to that, but I didn't see much point in spelling them out. "When Ralph took the bus south, did he say anything about going to Mexico?"

"Not to me he didn't."

"Has he ever been there?"

"I don't think so. He would of told me if he had."

"Did he ever talk about leaving the country?"

"Not lately. He used to talk about going back to Japan someday. He spent some time there in the Korean War. Wait a minute, though. He took his birth certificate with him, I think. That could mean he was planning to leave the States, couldn't it?"

"It could. He took his birth certificate to Los Angeles?"

"I guess he did, but it was a couple of weeks before that he had me looking for it. It took me hours to find it. He wanted to take it along to Nevada with him. He said he needed it to apply for a job."

"What kind of a job?"

"He didn't say. He was probably stringing me, anyway." She moved restlessly and stood over me. "You think he left the country?"

Before I could answer her, a telephone rang in another part of the house. She stiffened, and walked quickly out of the room. I heard her voice: "This is Vicky Simpson speaking."

There was a long pause.

"I don't believe it," she said.

Another pause.

"It can't be him," she said. "He can't be dead."

I followed the fading sound of her voice into the kitchen. She was leaning on the yellow formica breakfast bar, holding the receiver away from her head as if it was a dangerous yellow bird. The pupils of her eyes had expanded and made her look blind.

"Who is it, Mrs. Simpson?"

Her lips moved, groping for words. "A caw—a policeman

down south. He says Ralph is dead. He can't be."

"Let me talk to the man."

She handed me the receiver. I said into the mouthpiece: "This is Lew Archer. I'm a licensed private detective working in co-operation with the Los Angeles District Attorney's office."

"We had a query from them this evening." The man's voice was slow and uncertain. "We had this body on our hands, unidentified. Their chief investigator called—fellow named Colton, maybe you know him."

"I know him. Who am I talking to?"

"Leonard, Sergeant Wesley Leonard. I do the identification work for the sheriff's department here in Citrus County. We use the L.A. facilities all the time, and we had already asked for their help on this body. Mr. Colton wanted to know if maybe it was this certain Ralph Simpson who is missing. We must have mislaid the original missing report," he added apologetically, "or maybe we never got it in the first place."

"It happens all the time."

"Yeah. Anyway, we're trying to get a positive identification. What's the chances of Mrs. Simpson coming down here?"

"Pretty good, I think. Does the body fit the description?"

"It fits all right. Height and weight and coloring and estimated age, all the same."

"How did he die?"

"That's a little hard to say. He got pretty banged up when the bulldozer rooted him out."

"A bulldozer rooted him out?"

"I'll explain. They're putting in this new freeway at the west end of town. Quite a few houses got condemned to the state, they were standing vacant you know, and this poor guy was buried in back of one of them. He wasn't buried very deep. A 'dozer snagged him and brought him up when they razed the houses last week."

"How long dead?"

"A couple of months, the doc thinks. It's been dry, and he's in pretty fair condition. The important thing is who he is. How soon can Mrs. Simpson get down here?"

"Tonight, if I can get her on a plane."

"Swell. Ask for me at the courthouse in Citrus Junction. Sergeant Wesley Leonard."

She said when I hung up: "Oh no you don't, I'm staying here."

She retreated across the kitchen, shocked and stumbling, and stood in a corner beside the refrigerator.

"Ralph may be dead, Vicky."

"I don't believe it. I don't want to see him if he is."

"Somebody has to identify him."

"*You* identify him."

"I don't know him. You do."

Her mascara had started to dissolve. She dashed murky tears from her eyes. "I don't *want* to see him dead. I never saw anybody dead before."

"Dead people won't hurt you. It's the live ones that hurt you."

I touched her goosefleshed arm. She jerked it away from me.

"You'll feel better if you have a drink," I said. "Do you have anything to drink in the house?"

"I don't drink."

I opened a cupboard and found a glass and filled it at the tap. Some of it spilled down her chin. She scrubbed at it angrily with a dish towel.

"I don't want to go. It'll only make me sick."

But after a while she agreed to get ready while I phoned the coastal airlines. There was room for us on a ten-thirty flight to Los Angeles. By midnight we were approaching Citrus Junction in the car I had left at International Airport.

The road was walled on each side by thick orange groves. It

emerged into a desolate area rimmed with houses, where highway construction had been under way. Earth movers hulked in the darkness like sleeping saurians.

The road became the main street of the town. It was a back-country town, in spite of its proximity to Los Angeles. Every-thing was closed for the night, except for a couple of bars. A few men in working clothes wandered along the empty pave-ments, staggering under the twin burdens of alcohol and loneliness.

"I don't like it here," Vicky said. "It looks like hicksville."

"You won't have to stay long."

"How long? I'm stony until payday."

"The police will probably make arrangements for you. Let's wait and see how it falls."

The metal cupola of the courthouse swelled like a tarnished bubble under the stars. The building's dark interior smelled mustily of human lives, like the inside of an old trunk. I found the duty deputy in an office on the first floor. He told me that Sergeant Leonard was at the mortuary, just around the corner.

It was a three-storied white colonial building with a sign on the lawn in front of it: "Norton's Funeral Parlors." Vicky hung back when we got out of the car. I took her arm and walked her down a hall through the odor of carnations to a lighted doorway at the end of the hall and through it into the odor of formaldehyde.

She dragged on my arm. "I can't go through with it."

"You have to. It may not be Ralph."

"Then what am I doing here?"

"It may be Ralph."

She looked wildly around the room. It was bare except for a grey coffin standing on trestles against the wall.

"Is he in that?"

"No. Get yourself under control, Vicky. It will only take a minute and then it will be over."

"But what am I going to do afterward?"

It was a question I couldn't attempt to answer. A further door opened, and a deputy with sergeant's stripes on his arm came through toward us. He was a middle-aged man with a belly overlapping his gunbelt, and slow friendly eyes that went with his voice on the telephone.

"I'm Leonard."

"Archer. This is Mrs. Simpson."

He bowed with exaggerated courtliness. "I'm pleased to know you, ma'am. It was good of you to make the journey."

"I had to, I guess. Where is he?"

"The doctor's working on him."

"You mean he's still *alive?*"

"He's long dead, ma'am. I'm sorry. Dr. White is working on his internal organs, trying to find out what killed him."

She started to sit down on the floor. I caught her under the arms. Leonard and I helped her into an adjoining room where a night light burned and the smell of carnations was strong. She half lay on an upholstered settee, with her spike heels tucked under her.

"If you don't mind waiting a little, ma'am, Doc White will get him ready for your inspection." Leonard's voice had taken on unctuous intonations from the surroundings. He hovered over her. "Maybe I could get you a drink. What would you like to drink?"

"Embalming fluid."

He made a shocked noise at the back of his palate.

"Just go away and leave me alone. I'm all right."

I followed Leonard into the autopsy room. The dead man lay on an enameled table. I won't describe him. His time in the earth, and on the table, had altered him for the worse. He bore no great resemblance to Burke Damis, and never had.

Dr. White was closing a butterfly incision in the body. His rubber-gloved hands looked like artificial hands. He was a bald-headed man with hound jowls drooping from under a tobacco-stained mustache. He had a burning cigarette in his mouth, and wagged his head slowly from side to side to keep the smoke out of his eyes. The smoke coiled and drifted in the brilliant overhead light.

I waited until he had finished what he was doing and had drawn a rubberized sheet up to the dead man's chin.

"What did you find out, Doctor?"

"Heart puncture, in the left ventricle. Looks like an icepick wound." He stripped off his rubber gloves and moved to the sink, saying above the noise of running water: "Those contusions on the head were inflicted after death, in my opinion— a long time after death."

"By the bulldozer?"

"I assume so."

"Just when was he dug up?"

"Friday, wasn't it, Wesley?"

The Sergeant nodded. "Friday afternoon."

"Did you make a preliminary examination then?"

Dr. White turned from the sink, drying his hands and arms. "None was ordered. The D.A. and the Sheriff, who's also Coroner, are both in Sacramento at a convention."

"Besides," Leonard put in, eager to save face, "the icepick wound didn't show from the outside hardly at all. It was just a little nick under the left breast."

It wasn't for me to tell them their business. I wanted cooperation. "Did you find the icepick?"

Leonard spread his hands loosely. "You couldn't find anything out there after the 'dozers went through. Maybe you saw the mess on your way into town?"

"I saw it. Are you ready for Mrs. Simpson now?"

I was talking to the doctor and the Sergeant, but the question hung in the air as though it belonged to the dead man on the table. I even had a feeling that he might answer me. The room was getting me down.

I brought Vicky Simpson into it. The time by herself had calmed her. She had strength enough to walk across the room and stand by the table and look down at the ruined head for a minute, for minutes on end.

"It's him. It's Ralph."

She proved it by stroking his dusty hair.

She looked up at Leonard. "What happened to him?"

"He was icepicked, ma'am, a couple of months ago."

"You mean he's been dead all this time?"

"A couple of months."

The two months of waiting seemed to rush across her eyes like dizzy film. She turned blindly. I took her back to the room where the night light burned.

"Do you know who killed him, Vicky?"

"How would I know? I've never even been in Citrus Junction—is that what they call this hole?"

"You mentioned that Ralph was paid by the police to gather information."

"That's what he said. I don't know if it was true or not. Anyway, it was a long time ago."

"Did Ralph have criminal connections?"

"No. He wasn't that kind of a man."

"You said he had a record."

She shook her head.

"You might as well tell me, Vicky. It can't hurt him now."

"It didn't amount to anything," she said. "He was just a kid. He got in with a bad crowd in high school and they got caught smoking reefers one time and they all got sent to Juvie. That was all the record Ralph had."

"You're certain?"

"I'm not lying."

"Did he ever speak of a man named Burke Damis?"

"Burke Damis?"

"Damis is the man I met in Malibu, the one I described to you. He's an artist, a painter, who apparently has been using your husband's name."

"Why would he do that?"

"Perhaps because he's ashamed of his own name. I believe he used Ralph's name to cross the border from Mexico last week. You're sure the name Burke Damis rings no bell?"

"I'm sure."

"And you don't recognize the description?"

"No. At this point I wouldn't recognize my own brother if he walked in the door. Aren't you ever going to leave me alone?"

Leonard came into the room. I suspected that he had been listening outside the door, and chose this moment to break up the interview. He was a kind man, and he said that he and his wife would look after Vicky for the balance of the night.

I drove home to Los Angeles, home to a hot shower and a cold drink and a dark bed.

chapter 8

I HAD A DREAM which I'd been dreaming in variant forms for as long as I could remember. I was back in high school, in my senior year. The girl at the next desk smiled at me snootily.

"Poor Lew. You'll fail the exams."

I had to admit to myself that this was likely. The finals loomed up ahead like the impossible slopes of purgatory, guarded by men with books I hadn't read.

"*I'm* going to college," she said. "What are you going to do?"

I had no idea. I knew with a part of my dreaming mind that I was a grown man in my forties. There wasn't anything more that high school could do to me. Yet here I was, back in Mr. Merritt's classroom, dreading the finals and wondering what I would do when I had failed them.

"You'll have to learn a trade," the snooty one said.

So far it was more or less the dream I had always had.

Then something different happened. I said to the girl, rather snootily: "I have a trade, kiddo. I'm a detective. You'll be reading about me in the papers."

I woke up with a warm feeling in my chest and the small birds peeping outside the pale grey rectangle of the window. The dream had never ended this way before. Did it mean that I had made it? That didn't seem likely. You went on making it, or trying to, all your life—working your way up the same old terraced slopes with different street names on them.

The Blackwell case came back on my mind, muffling the bird sounds and draining the last of the warm feeling from my chest. There were two cases, really. One belonged to me and one belonged to the authorities, but they were connected. The link between them was small but definite: the airline envelope with Q. R. Simpson's name on it which Burke Damis, or possibly someone else, had left in the beach house. I wanted to explore the connection further, without too much interference from the police. The possibility existed that Damis had come by the envelope, or even used the name, quite innocently.

It was broad daylight and the birds had finished their matins when I went back to sleep. I slept late into the morning. Perhaps I was hoping for another good dream. More likely I was fixing my schedule so that I wouldn't have time to report in to Peter Colton.

I had become a great frequenter of airports. Before I set out this time, I dug my birth certificate out of the strongbox in the bedroom closet. I had no definite plan to use it. I just thought it would be nice to have along.

The polite young man at the Mexicana desk greeted me like a long-lost brother. The crew I was interested in had already checked in for their flight, and the steward and stewardess had gone up to the restaurant for coffee. He was tall and dark; she was short and plump and pretty, with red hair. They both had on Mexicana uniforms, and I surely couldn't miss them.

I picked them out in the murmurous cavern of the restaurant, hunched over coffee cups at one of the long counters. The girl had an empty stool beside her, and I slid onto it. She was certainly pretty, though the red hair that curled from under her overseas-type cap had been dyed. She had melting dark eyes and a stung-cherry mouth. Like American airline hostesses, she had on enough make-up to go on the stage.

She was talking in Spanish with the steward, and I waited for a pause in their conversation.

"Miss Gomez?"

"Yessir, what can I do for you?" she said in a pleasantly accented voice.

"I'm looking for a little information. A week ago yesterday, a man and woman I know took your flight from Guadalajara to Los Angeles. That was Monday, July the tenth. You may remember them, or one of them. The woman is quite tall, about your age, blonde. She often wears dark glasses, and she probably had on expensive clothes. Her name is Harriet Blackwell."

She nodded her head emphatically. "I remember Miss Blackwell, yes—a very nice lady. The lady across from her was sick —we had some rough air out of Mazatlán—and she took care of the sick lady's baby for her." She said to the steward beside her: "You remember the tall lady who was so nice with the baby?"

"Sí."

"Is Miss Blackwell all right?" she asked me solicitously.

"I think so. Why do you ask?"

"I thought of her afterward, after we landed. And now you are inquiring about her."

"What did you think about her after you landed?"

"I thought—do you speak Spanish? I express myself better in Spanish."

"Your English is ten times better than my Spanish will ever be."

"*Gracias, señor.*" She gave me a full dazzling smile. "Well, I saw her after we landed, going through Customs. She looked very—excited. I thought she was going to faint. I approached her and inquired if she was all right. The man with her said that she was all right. He didn't like—he didn't want me asking questions, so I went away."

"Can you describe the man?"

"Yes." She described Burke Damis. "A very beautiful young man," she added with a trace of satire in her voice.

"What was his name?"

"I don't remember."

She turned to her companion and spoke in rapid Spanish. He shrugged. He didn't remember either.

"Who would know?"

"You, perhaps," she said pertly. "You said they were your friends."

"I said I knew them."

"I see. Are they in trouble?"

"That's an interesting question. What brings it up?"

"You," she said. "You look like trouble for them."

"For him, not for her. Did they sit together on the plane?"

"Yes. They embarked together at Guadalajara. I noticed them, I thought they were *recién casados*—honeymooners. But they had different names."

"What was his name?"

"I said I don't remember. If I can find the passenger list—"

"Try and do that, will you?"

"You are a policeman?"

"An investigator."

"I see. Where will I see you?"

"On the plane, if they have a seat for me." I looked at my watch. I had half an hour till flight time.

"We are never crowded in the middle of the week."

She turned out to be right. I bought a return ticket to Guadalajara from my courteous friend, leaving the date of my return open. At another desk in the same building I applied for a Mexican tourist card. The hurried clerk who took my application barely glanced at my birth certificate.

"I'll type up your card *pronto.* Your plane will take off soon."

In the time I had left, I made the necessary call to Colonel Blackwell. He picked up the phone on the first ring, as if he had been waiting there beside it.

"Mark Blackwell speaking."

"This is Archer. Have you heard anything from Harriet?"

"No. I don't expect to." His voice rose shakily from the depths of depression. "You haven't either, I take it."

"No. I have been busy on the case. It took me to the Bay area last night."

"Is that where they've gone?"

"It's possible, but it's not why I went up there. To make a long story short, I stumbled on a murder which Damis may be involved in."

"A murder?" His voice sank almost out of hearing. He said in a rustling whisper: "You're not trying to tell me that Harriet has been murdered?"

"No. It's a man named Simpson, icepicked in Citrus Junction two months ago. I'm trying to trace his connection with Damis, and get a line on Damis's identity and background. The next logical step, as I see it, is to go back to the point where Harriet met him and work forward from there. If it's all right with you, I intend to fly down to Mexico."

There was a long silence on the line. Outside the telephone booth, I could hear my flight being announced over the loudspeakers.

"Are you there, Colonel?"

"I'm here. You're planning to go to Mexico, you say. When?"

"In about five minutes. It's going to cost you a couple of hundred dollars—"

"Money is no object. By all means go if you think it will help."

"I can't guarantee any results, but it's worth trying. Can you give me your ex-wife's address in Ajijic?"

"She doesn't have an address. But any member of the American community should be able to tell you where she lives. Pauline was never one to hide her light under a bushel."

"Her last name is Hatchen?"

"That is correct. Good luck." He sounded as though his own had run out.

The plane was barely half full. I had a window seat over the left wing. As the redheaded stewardess placed me in it, I noticed that she looked at me in a peculiar way.

The broken jigsaw of Los Angeles tilted and drifted backward into brownish smog. When the plane had leveled out at cruising altitude, the stewardess slipped into the empty seat beside me. She held a folded newspaper in the hand away from me. Under the make-up, her color wasn't good.

"I found the seating chart for July—July ten. The man with Miss Blackwell, his name was Simpson, Q. R. Simpson."

"I thought so."

"You thought so?" Her look was accusing. "Why didn't you tell me, then, that Señor Simpson is dead?"

"I wasn't aware of it." It was a half truth, or a half lie, according to which version of Simpson we were talking about. "How do you know he is, Miss Gomez?"

She held the morning *Times* under my nose, jabbing the late bulletins at the bottom of the front page with a chipped carmine fingernail.

"Slain Man Identified," one of the items said.

The body of Quincy R. Simpson, found icepicked in a shallow grave in Citrus Junction last Friday, was positively identified late last night by his widow. The victim, missing for the past two months, was a resident of San Mateo County. Police suspect a gang killing, according to Sergeant Wesley Leonard of the Citrus County Sheriff's office.

"You see," Miss Gomez insisted, "he is dead. Murdered."

"I see."

"You said you are an investigator. Are you investigating his murder?"

"It's beginning to look like it, isn't it?"

"And you suspect someone from Mexico?" she said in a nationalistic way.

"Someone from the United States."

This relieved her, but not for long. "Poor Miss Blackwell, she was so crazy about him. All the time, even when she was holding the lady's baby, she kept looking at him like"—she searched for a phrase—"like he was a saint."

"He was no saint."

"Was he a *rufian*—a gangster?"

"I doubt it."

"It says in the paper that it was a gang killing."

"Gangsters kill citizens, too."

She wrinkled her dark brows over this idea. The doubleness of the conversation was getting on my nerves; or perhaps it was the doubleness of my attitude toward Damis. In spite of the evidence tightening around him, I was trying to keep an open mind.

I was glad when the girl went to attend to her duties. She stayed away. When she passed me in the aisle, she carefully avoided meeting my eyes. I think she was afraid of the contagion I carried from Simpson's death.

We were flying over the sea within sight of land. The air was perfectly transparent. Baja California passed under the wing like the endless harsh shores of hell, its desolation unbroken by tree or house or human being.

As the sun declined, the shadows of the yellow hills lengthened into the dry valleys. The first green and brown checker-board of cultivated fields came as a relief to the eye and the mind. The desolation didn't go on forever.

Miss Gomez unbent a little when she brought me my dinner. "Are you enjoying the flight, sir?"

I said yes.

We circled in over Mazatlán in a red sunset. The three rocky islands offshore jutted up angrily out of a streaked purple sea. A single freighter lay in the harbor with the fishing boats. At the other end of the town, beyond the airport where we landed, new apartment buildings stood along the sea like a miniature Copacabana.

We were herded into the terminal building, to have our tourist cards checked, it was explained. A boy was selling, or trying to sell, costumed puppets which he manipulated on a string. His bare arms were almost as thin as the wooden arms of his dolls.

The line of passengers moved forward slowly in steamy heat. I got my turn at the battered rostrumlike desk where a man in an open-necked white shirt presided. He had pockmarks on his face, and they gave special emphasis to his question: "Certificado de vacunacion, señor?"

I had none. No one had told me. That was a silly thing to say, but I said it. He leaned toward me not so much in anger as in sorrow.

"You must have the vacunacion. I cannot permit you to enter—"

"How do I get one?"

"They will vacunate you ahora, now, here."

He summoned an attendant in olive whipcord who escorted me to an office at the far end of the building. A dark and dumpy woman in white was waiting at the desk with a maternal smile. The white masonry wall behind her had jagged cracks in it.

"Vaccination?"

"I'm afraid so."

She took my name and home address on a filing card. "Don't worry, it won't hurt, I never hurt 'em. Jacket off and roll up your left sleeve, please."

She struck my arm smartly as the needle went in.

"You took it well," she said. "Some of them keel over."

"You speak good English."

"Why not? I was a nurse's aide in Fresno six years before I went into training. I got a married daughter in Los Angeles. You can roll down your sleeve now. You'll probably have a reaction by tomorrow."

I buttoned the cuff of my shirt and put on my jacket. "Do you give many of these impromptu vaccinations?"

"Two or three a day, at least, since the government clamped down. People are always forgetting their certificates, or else they didn't get the word in the first place. They process so many at the L.A. airport that they get careless."

I said, on the off-chance of learning something: "A man I know passed through here from L.A. some time in the last two months. I'm wondering if you had to vaccinate him."

"What does he look like?"

I described Burke Damis.

She twisted her mouth to one side. "I think I do remember him. He had big fat biceps, like yours. But he didn't like the needle. He tried to talk himself out of it."

"When was this?"

"I couldn't say exactly. A couple of months ago, like you said. I could look it up if you'll give me his name."

"Quincy Ralph Simpson."

She opened one of the desk drawers, went through a filing box of cards, and picked out one of them.

"*Here* it is, Simpson. I gave him his shot on May twenty."

It meant that Burke Damis had entered Mexico two days after the original Simpson left home for the last time. It probably meant that Simpson had been murdered between May

18 and May 20, more likely than not by the man who had stolen his name.

"A very nice-appearing young man," the woman was saying. "We had a nice chat after we got the vaccination out of the way."

"Chat about what?"

"My daughter in Los Angeles. And he wanted to know if that was earthquake damage." She waved her hand toward the cracks in the masonry.

"I was asking myself the same thing."

"It was no earthquake. The hurricane did it. It practically tore out the whole end of the building. You'd never know it was built in the last ten years."

The man in the whipcord uniform came back. He had two more victims with him, a young couple who were explaining that they had been assured that these formalities could be taken care of when they got to Mexico City. The nurse smiled at them maternally.

chapter 9

IT WAS RAINING HARD when we put down at Guadalajara, as if our descent had ruptured a membrane in the lower sky. In spite of the newspaper tent I held over my head, the short walk from the plane to the terminal pasted my clothes to my back.

I exchanged some damp dollars for some dry pesos and asked the cashier to get me an English-speaking taxi driver, if possible. The porter he dispatched reappeared with a man in a plastic raincoat who grinned at me from under his dripping mustache.

"Yessir, where you want to go?"

"Ajijic, if they have a hotel there."

"Yessir, they have a very nice *posada.*"

He led me across the many-puddled parking lot to a fairly new Simca sedan. I climbed squishing into the front seat.

"Wet night."

"Yessir."

He drove me through it for half an hour, entertaining me with fragments of autobiography. Like the nurse who had vaccinated me in Mazatlán, he had learned his English in the Central Valley.

"I was a wetback," he said with some pride. "Three times I walked across the border. Two times they picked me up on the other side and hauled me back on a bus. The third time, I made it, all the way to Merced. I worked around Merced for four years, in the fields. You know Merced?"

"I know it. How were working conditions?"

"Not so good. But the pay, it was very good. I made enough to come back home and go into business." He slapped the wheel of his Simca.

We emerged from between steep black hills onto a lakeshore road. I caught pale glimpses of ruffled water. A herd of burros crossed the headlights and galloped away into darkness. Through the streaming windshield they looked like the grey and shrunken ghosts of horses.

Church towers, buttressed by other buildings, rose from the darkness ahead. The rain was letting up, and had stopped by the time we reached the village. Though it was past ten o'clock, children swarmed in the doorways. Their elders were promenading in the steep cobbled streets, which had drained already.

At the corner of the central square an old woman in a shawl had set up a wooden table on the sidewalk. She was serving some kind of stew out of a pot, and I caught a whiff of it as we went by. It had a heady pungency, an indescribable smell which aroused no memories; expectation, maybe, and a smattering of doubt. The smell of Mexico.

I felt closer to home when we reached the *posada*. The night clerk was a big middle-aged American named Stacy, and he was glad to see me. The pillared lobby of the place had a deserted air. Stacy and I and my driver, who was waiting for me just inside the entrance, were the only human beings within sight or sound.

Stacy fussed over me like somebody trying to give the impression that he was more than one person. "I can certainly fix you up, Mr. Archer. I can give you your choice of several nice private cottages."

"Any one of them will do. I think I'll only be staying one night."

He looked disappointed. "I'll send out the *mozo* for your luggage."

"I have no luggage."

"But you're all *wet*, man."

"I know. Luckily this is a drip-dry suit."

"You can't let it dry right on you." He clucked sympathetically. "Listen, you're about my size. I'll lend you some slacks and a sweater if you like. Unless you're thinking of going right to bed."

"I wasn't intending to. You're very kind."

"Anything for a fellow American," he said in a mocking tone which was half serious after all.

He took me through a wet garden to my cottage. It was clean and roomy; a fire was laid in the fireplace. He left me with instructions to use the bottled water, even for cleaning my teeth. I lit the fire and hung up my wet suit on a wall bracket above the mantel.

Stacy came back after a while with an armful of dry clothes. His large rubbery face was flushed with generosity and a meantime drink. The flannel slacks he gave me were big in the waist. I cinched them in with my belt and pulled on his blue turtleneck sweater. It had a big monogrammed "S" like a target over the heart, and it smelled of the kind of piny scent they foist off on men who want to smell masculine.

"You look very nice," Stacy declared.

He stood and watched me in wistful empathy. Perhaps he saw himself with ten pounds shifted from his waistline to his shoulders, and ten lost years regained. He got a bit flustered when I told him I was going out. He may have been looking forward to an intimate conversation by the fire: *And what is your philosophy of life?*

Keep moving, amigo.

Stacy knew where the Hatchens lived, and passed the word in rapid Spanish to my driver. We drove to a nameless street. The only sign at the corner had been painted on a wall by an amateur hand: *"Cristianismo sí, Comunismo no."* A church tower rose on the far side of the wall.

The Hatchens' gate was closed for the night. I knocked for some time before I got a response. My knocking wasn't the only sound in the neighborhood. Up the street a radio was going full blast; hoofs clip-clopped; a burro laughed grotesquely in the darkness; the bell in the church tower rang the three-quarter hour and then repeated it for those who were hard of hearing; a pig squealed.

A man opened the upper half of the wicket gate and flashed a bright light in my face. *"Quien es?* Are you American?"

"Yes. My name is Archer. You're Mr. Hatchen?"

"Dr. Hatchen. I don't know you, do I? Is there some trouble?"

"Nothing immediate. Back in the States, your wife's daughter, Harriet, has run off with a young man named Burke Damis whom you may know. I came here to investigate him for Colonel Blackwell. Are you and Mrs. Hatchen willing to talk to me?"

"I suppose we can't refuse. Come back in the morning, eh?"

"I may not be here in the morning. If you'll give me a little time tonight, I'll try to make it short."

"All right."

I paid off my driver as Hatchen was opening the lower gate. He led me up a brick walk through an enclosed garden. The flashlight beam jumped along in front of us across the uneven bricks. He was a thin aging man who walked with great strenuosity.

He paused under an outside light before we entered the house. "Just what do you mean when you say Harriet's run off with Damis?"

"She intends to marry him."

"Is that bad?"

"It depends on what I find out about him. I've already come across some dubious things."

"For instance?" He had a sharp wizened face in which the eyes were bright and quick.

"Apparently he came here under an alias."

"That's not unusual. The Chapala woods are full of people living incognito. But come in. My wife will be interested."

He turned on a light in a screened portico and directed me through it to a further room. A woman was sitting there on a couch in an attitude of conscious elegance. Masses of blondish hair were arranged precariously on her head. Her black formal gown accentuated the white puffiness of her shoulders. The classic lines of her chin and throat were a little blurred by time.

"This is Mr. Archer, Pauline. My wife," Hatchen said proudly.

She took my hand with the air of a displaced queen and held onto it in a subtle kind of Indian wrestling until I was sitting beside her on the couch.

"Sit down," she said unnecessarily. "To what do we owe the pleasure?"

"Mr. Archer is an emissary from dear old Mark."

"How fascinating. And what has dear old Mark been up to

now? Wait, don't tell me. Let me guess." She held a fore-finger upright in front of her nose. "He's worried about Harriet."

"You're a good guesser, Mrs. Hatchen."

She smiled thinly. "It's the same old story. He's always brooded over her like a father hen."

"Mother hen," Hatchen said.

"*Father* hen."

"At any rate, she's run off and married that Damis chap," he said.

"I'm not surprised. I'm glad she had it in her. All Harriet ever needed was a little of her mother's spirit and fortitude. Speaking of spirits, Mr. Archer"—she waved her finger— "Keith and I were just about to have a nightcap. Won't you join us?"

Hatchen looked at her brightly. He was still on his feet in the middle of the room. "You've had your ration, dear one. You know what the doctor said."

"The doctor's in Guad and I'm here."

"I'm here, too."

"So be a sport and get us all a drink. You know what I like."

He shrugged and turned to me. "What will you have?"

"Whisky?"

"I can't recommend the whisky. The gin's okay."

"Gin and tonic will be fine."

He left the room with a nervous glance at his wife, as if she might be contemplating elopement. She turned the full panoply of her charm on me.

"I know you must think I'm a strange sort of mother, totally unconcerned with my daughter's welfare and so on. The fact is I'm a kind of refugee. I escaped from Mark and his ménage long long ago. I haven't even seen him for thirteen years, and for once that's a lucky number. I turned over a fresh page and started a new chapter—a chapter dedicated to love and freedom." Romanticism soughed in her voice like a loosely strung Aeolian harp.

"It isn't entirely clear to me why you left him."

She took the implied question as a matter of course. "The marriage was a mistake. We had really very little in common. I love movement and excitement, interesting people, people with a sense of life." She looked at me sideways. "You seem to be a man with a sense of life. I'm surprised that you should be a friend of Mark's. He used to spend his spare time doing research on the Blackwell genealogy."

"I didn't say I was a friend of Mark's."

"But I understood he sent you here."

"I'm a private detective, Mrs. Hatchen. He hired me to look into Damis's background. I was hoping you could give me some assistance."

"I barely knew the fellow. Though I sensed from the beginning that Harriet was smitten with him."

"When was the beginning?"

"A few days after she got here. She came a little over a month ago. I was really glad to see her." She sounded surprised. "A little disappointed, perhaps, but glad."

"Why disappointed?"

"I had various reasons. I'd always sort of hoped that she'd outgrow her ugly-duckling phase, and she did to some extent, of course. After all she is my daughter." Her active forefinger went to her brow and moved down her nose to her mouth and chin, which she tilted up. "And I was disappointed that we didn't really have anything in common. She didn't take to our friends or our way of life. We did our best to make her comfortable, but she moved out before the end of the first week."

"And moved in with Damis?"

"Harriet wouldn't do that. She's quite a conventional girl. She rented a studio down near the lake. I think he had one somewhere in the neighborhood. I have no doubt they spent a lot of time together. More power to them, I thought."

"Did you know Burke Damis before she met him?"

"No, and she didn't meet him in our *casa*. We'd seen him around, of course, but we'd never met him till Harriet introduced him. That was a few days after she got here, as I said."

"Where did you see him around?"

"At the *Cantina* mostly. I think that's where Harriet picked —where Harriet met him. A lot of arty young people hang out there, or used to."

"You saw him there before she met him?"

"Oh, yes, several times. He's rather conspicuously good-looking, don't you think?"

"Was he using the name Burke Damis?"

"I suppose so. You could always ask the *Cantina* people. It's just down the street."

"I'll do that. Before Harriet arrived, did Damis ever try to contact you?"

"Never. We didn't know him from Adam." Her eyes narrowed. "Is Mark trying to pin the blame on me for something?"

"No, but it occurred to me that Damis might have had her spotted before she got here."

"Spotted?"

"As a girl with money behind her."

"He didn't learn it from us, if that's what you're thinking."

"And there was nothing to show that he deliberately planned to meet her?"

"I doubt it. He picked her up in the *Cantina* and she was dazzled with gratitude, poor girl."

"Why do you say 'poor girl'?"

"I've always felt that way about Harriet. She had a rough deal, from both of us. I realize I appear to be a selfish woman, leaving her and Mark when she was just a child. But I had no choice if I wanted to save my soul."

I sat there wondering if she had saved it and waiting for

her to elaborate. Her eyes had the hardness that comes from seeing too many changes and not being changed by them.

"To make a long story short, and a sordid one, I moved into the Tahoe house and got a Reno divorce. I didn't want to do it. It broke my heart to turn my back on Harriet. But she was very much her father's daughter. There was nothing I could do to break that up, short of murder. And don't think I haven't contemplated murder. But a Nevada divorce seemed more civilized. Keith"—she gestured toward the kitchen, where ice was being picked—"Keith was in Nevada on the same errand. What's keeping him out there so long?"

"He may be giving us a chance to talk."

"Yes, he's a very thoughtful man. I've been very happy with Keith, don't think I haven't." There was a hint of defiance in her voice. "On the other hand, don't think I haven't felt guilty about my daughter. When she visited us last month the old guilt feelings came back. It was so obvious that she wanted —that she needed something from me. Something I couldn't give, and if I could, she couldn't have taken it. She still blamed me for deserting her, as she put it. I tried to explain, but she wouldn't listen to any criticism of her father. He's always dominated her every thought. She went into hysterics, and so did I, I suppose. We quarreled, and she moved out on *me*."

"It looks as though that made her ripe for Damis. I've known other men like him. They prey on girls and women who step outside the protection of their families."

"You make him sound like a very devious type."

"He's devious. Does the name Q. R. Simpson mean anything to you? Quincy Ralph Simpson?"

She shook her head and her hairdo slipped. It made her entire personality seem held in place by pins. "Should I know the name?"

"I didn't really expect you to."

"What name?" her husband said from the doorway. He came in carrying a hammered brass tray with three pale drinks placed geometrically on it.

"The name that Burke Damis used to cross the border, coming and going. Quincy Ralph Simpson."

"I've never heard it."

"You will if you take the California papers."

"But we don't." He passed the drinks around with a flourish. "We are happy fugitives from the California papers, and from nuclear bombs and income taxes—"

"And the high cost of liquor," his wife chimed in like the other half of a vaudeville team.

"This gin costs me forty American cents a liter," he said, "and I don't believe you can top it at any price. Well, *salud*." He lifted his glass.

I drank from mine. The gin was all right, but it failed to warm me. There was something cold and lost about the room and the people in it. They had roosted like migrant birds that had lost their homing instincts, caught in a dream of perpetual static flight. Or so it seemed through the bottom of my glass.

I set it down and got up. Hatchen rose, too.

"What was that about this man Simpson and the newspapers?"

"Simpson was stabbed with an icepick a couple of months ago. His body was found last week."

"And you say Damis was using his name?"

"Yes."

"Is he suspected of Simpson's murder?"

"Yes. By me."

"Poor Harriet," Mrs. Hatchen said over her drink.

chapter **10**

THE *Cantina* had several interconnected public rooms, and looked as though it had once been a private house. At eleven-thirty on this Tuesday night it had just about reverted to privacy. A single drinker, a big man with streaked yellow hair that hung down to his collar, sat in a corner behind the deserted bandstand. There was no one else in the place.

A number of small oil paintings hung on the walls. Their blobs and blocks and whorls and scatterations reminded me of the shapes that dissolve on the retina between sleeping and waking. I felt that I was getting closer to Burke Damis, and I moved from picture to picture looking for his style or his signature.

"*Las pinturas,* they are for sale, señor," a mild voice said behind me.

It belonged to a Mexican youth in a waiter's apron. He had a broken nose and a mouth that had been hurt both physically and morally. Intelligence burned like fever in his black eyes.

"Sorry, I don't buy pictures."

"Nobody buys them. No more. 'Quoth the Raven, "Nevermore." ' "

"You read Poe?"

"In school, señor," he said smiling. " 'My beautiful Annabel Lee, . . . in this kingdom by the sea.' I studied to be a professor but my father lost his nets, I had to give it up. There is very little money, and work is not easy to find. Tourism is slow this summer."

"Why?"

He shrugged. "Who understands the migration of the birds? I only know it is hard to make an honest living. I tried boxing, but it is not for me." He touched his nose.

His story had come fast and slick, and I was expecting a touch. I liked him anyway. His battered face had an incandescence, as if the scattered lights of the dark town had gathered and were burning in him. "Something to drink, señor?"

"I guess a beer."

"Dark or light?"

"Light."

"*Bueno,* we have no dark. We have three bottles of light beer, one *litro* of tequila, and no ice. The beer is cold, however. I borrowed it."

Smiling intensely, he went into a side room and came back with a bottle and a glass. He poured the contents of the one into the other.

"You pour beer well."

"Yessir. Also I can make martinis, margueritas, any kind of drink. I work at parties sometimes, which is how I speak English so good. Please to tell your friends, when they need a first-class *cantinero,* José Perez of the *Cantina* is at your service."

"I'm afraid I have no friends in these parts."

"You are a tourist?"

"Sort of. I'm just passing through."

"An artist, *por ventura?*" he said with an eye on Stacy's sweater. "We used to have many artists here. My boss himself is an artist." He glanced across the room to the solitary drinker in the corner.

"I'd like to talk to him."

"I will tell him, señor."

José darted across the room and said something in Spanish to the long-haired man. He picked up his drink and plodded toward me as if the room was hip-deep in water, or eye-deep in tequila. A woven belt with an amethyst-studded silver buckle divided his globular stomach into two hemispheres.

"Aha," he said. "I spy with my little eye a customer and a fellow American."

"Your eye is sound. My name is Archer, by the way."

He stood over me tall and leaning, a Pisan tower of flesh.

"Why don't you sit down?"

"Thank you." He subsided into a chair. "I am Chauncey Reynolds, no kin to Sir Joshua Reynolds, though I do dabble in paint. I've always considered Sir Joshua a better critic than he was a painter. Or don't you share my opinion?" He hunched forward with a touch of belligerence.

"I wouldn't know, Mr. Reynolds. I'm not too hep artistically."

"I thought you were, since you were looking at the paintings. No matter. It's a pleasure to have a customer."

"What happened to all the other customers?"

"*Où sont les neiges d'antan?* This place was jumping, honestly, when I took over the lease. I thought I had a gold mine on my hands." He looked down into his pudgy hands as if he was surprised by their emptiness. "Then people stopped coming. If the drought of customers persists, I'll close up and go back to work." He seemed to be delivering an ultimatum to himself.

"You paint for a living?"

"I paint. Fortunately I have a small private income. Nobody paints for a *living*. You have to die before you make a living out of painting. Van Gogh, Modigliani, all the great ones had to die."

"What about Picasso?"

"Picasso is the exception that proves the rule. I drink to Pablo Picasso." He raised his glass and drank from it. "What do you do for a living, Mr. Archer?"

"I'm a detective."

He set down his glass with a rap. His bloodshot eyes watched me distrustfully, like a wounded bull from his *querencia*. "Did Gladys send you to ferret me out? She isn't supposed to know where I am."

"I don't know any Gladys."

"Honestly?"

"And I never heard of you until now. Who's Gladys?"

"My ex-wife. I divorced her in Juarez but the New York courts don't recognize it. Which is why, my friend, I am here. Forever." He made it sound like a long time.

"The one I'm interested in," I said, "is a young man named Burke Damis."

"What's he wanted for?"

"He isn't wanted."

"Kid me not. I read a great deal of mystery fiction in the long night watches, and I recognize that look you have on your face. You have the look of a shamus who is about to put the arm on a grifter."

"How well you express yourself. I take it you know Damis."

"In a casual way. He used to pass the time here, mainly before I took over the leash—the lease." He leaned forward over the table, and his long hair flopped like broken wings. "Why do you suppose they all stopped coming? Tell me— you're a trained objective observer—do I have an offensive personality?"

"José tells me business is slow all over," I said noncommittally. "It's like the migrations of the birds."

He looked around for José, who was leaning against the wall, and called for another drink. José replenished his glass from a bottle of tequila.

"Did you ever talk to Damis?"

"Not what you'd call intimately. He's an attractive chap but I never got to know him. He was usually with other people. Do you know if he's still in Ajijic?"

"No. Can you name some of the other people?"

"The one I saw him with most often was Bill Wilkinson."

"How can I get in touch with Wilkinson?"

"You might find him at The Place. I hear he's taking most of his business there since we had our little run-in."

"Run-in?"

"Actually, it was Mrs. Wilkinson I had the run-in with. She's one of those Southern California types who fancies herself as an art collector simply because she has money. I told her what she could do with her money, and Bill would be better off if he did the same. I'm not a woman hater—"

"Neither is Damis, I understand. Did you ever see him with women?"

"Almost invariably. He spent a lot of time with Annie Castle. That was before he took up with the blonde girl, what was her name?" He sat locked in combat with his memory.

"It doesn't matter. Who is Annie Castle?"

"She runs an artsy-craftsy shop on the other side of the plaza. As a matter of fact, Damis has or had his studio on the same premises. No doubt propinquity did its deadly work. Annie's a cute enough kid if you like them dark and serious. But he dropped her when the big little blonde showed up."

"What do you mean, 'big little' ? "

"*Quien sabe?* Big girl, little ego, maybe. She hasn't made the breakthrough, into womanhood, you know." He refreshed his alcoholic insight from his glass. "Whenas she ever does, she could be quite a thing. Beauty isn't in the features so much as in the spirit, in the eyes. That's why it's so hard to paint."

"You're quite an observer," I encouraged him.

"I'm a people watcher, my friend. If you're a detective, as you say, you must be something of a people watcher yourself."

"I'm a walking field guide," I said. "You seem to have paid pretty close attention to the blonde girl."

"Oh, I did. What was her name? Miss Blackstone, I believe. Her mother introduced us some time ago. I haven't seen her lately. I tend to take special notice of the tall ones, being rather outsize myself. Gladys is nearly six feet, *mirabile dictu.* She was once a burlesque queen on the Bowery, whence I rescued her and made a model of her, foolish man. With the consequence that I am here on my personal Bowery." His eyes strayed around the empty rooms.

I got up. "Thanks for all the information. Can you tell me how to get to The Place?"

"I can, but look here, man, I'm enjoying this. Drink up your beer, and I'll have José make you a proper drink. Where is José? José!"

"Don't bother. I have to see Bill Wilkinson."

He rose cumbrously. "Whatever you say. Do you feel like telling me what this is all about?"

"I could make up a story for you. But that would be a waste of time." I got out my wallet. "How much do I owe you for the beer?"

"Nothing." He fanned his arm in a lordly gesture which threatened to overbalance him. "You're a stranger within my gates, I couldn't possibly accept your money. Besides, I have a feeling you're going to bring me luck."

"I never have yet, Mr. Reynolds."

He told me how to get to The Place and I set out through the midnight streets. The children had been swallowed up by the doorways. Some men and a very few women were still out. Wrapped in blankets, with faces shadowed by volcano-shaped hats, the men had a conspiratorial look. But when I said *"Buenas noches"* to one small group, a chorus of *"Buenas noches"* followed me.

chapter 11

THE PLACE was closed for the night. Steering a course by dead reckoning and the sound of the town clock chiming the quarter, I made my way back to the central square. It was abandoned except for one lone man locked behind the grille of the unicellular jail.

Followed by his Indian gaze, I took myself for a walk

around the perimeter of the square. Seven eighths of the way around, I was stopped by a sign in English hand-lettered on wood: "Anne's Native Crafts." The shutters were up but there was light behind them, and the thump and clack of some rhythmic movement.

The noise stopped when I knocked on the door beside the shutters. Heels clicked on stone, and the heavy door creaked open. A smallish woman peered out at me.

"What do you want? It's very late."

"I realize that, Miss Castle. But I'm hoping to fly out of here in the morning, and I thought since you were up—"

"I know who you are," she said accusingly.

"News travels fast in Ajijic."

"Does it not? I can also tell you that you're here to no purpose. Burke Damis left Ajijic some time ago. It's true I sublet a studio to him for a brief period. But I can tell you nothing whatever about him."

"That's funny. You know all about me, and you never even saw me before."

"There's nothing funny about it. The waiter at the *Cantina* is a friend of mine. I taught his sister to weave."

"That was nice of you."

"It was part of the normal course of my life and work. You are distinctly not. Now if you'll take your big foot out of my doorway, I can get back to my weaving."

I didn't move. "You work very late."

"I work all the time."

"So do I when I'm on a case. That gives us something in common. I think we have something else in common."

"I can't imagine what it would be."

"You're concerned about Burke Damis, and so am I."

"Concerned?" Her voice went tinny on the word. "I don't know what you mean."

"I don't either, Miss Castle. You would have to tell me."

"I'll tell you nothing."

"Are you in love with Burke Damis?"

"I certainly am not!" she said passionately, telling me a great deal. "That's the most absurd statement—question, that anyone ever asked me."

"I'm full of absurd questions. Will you let me come in and ask you some of them?"

"Why should I?"

"Because you're a serious woman, and serious things are happening. I didn't fly down from Los Angeles for fun."

"What *is* happening then?"

"Among other things," I said, "Burke has eloped with a young woman who doesn't know which end is up."

She was silent for a long moment. "I know Harriet Blackwell, and I quite agree with your description of her. She's an emotionally ignorant girl who threw—well, she practically threw herself at his head. There's nothing I can do about it, or want to."

"Even if she's in danger?"

"Danger from Burke? That's impossible."

"It's more than possible, in my opinion, and I've been giving it a good deal of thought."

She moved closer to me. I caught the glint of her eyes, and her odor, light and clean, devoid of perfume. "Did you really come all the way from the States to ask me about Burke?"

"Yes."

"Has he—done something to Harriet Blackwell?"

"I don't know. They've dropped out of sight."

"What makes you suspect he's done something?"

"I'll tell you if you'll tell me. We both seem to have the same idea."

"No. You're putting words into my mouth."

"I wouldn't have to, if you'd talk to me."

"Perhaps I had better," she said to me and her conscience. "Come in, Mr. Archer." She even knew my name.

I followed her into the room behind her shop. A wooden

hand loom stood in one corner, with a piece of colored fabric growing intricately on it. The walls and furniture were covered with similar materials in brilliant designs.

Anne Castle was quite brilliant in her own way. She wore a multicolored Mexican skirt, an embroidered blouse, in her ears gold hoops that were big enough to swing on. Black hair cut short emphasized her petiteness and the individuality of her looks. Her eyes were brown and intelligent, and warmer than her voice had let me hope.

She said when we were seated on the divan: "You were going to tell me what Burke has done."

"I'd rather have your account of him first, for psychological reasons."

"You mean," she said carefully, "that I may not want to talk after you've done your talking?"

"Something like that."

"Is it so terrible?"

"It may be quite terrible. I don't know."

"As terrible as murder?" She sounded like a child who names the thing he fears, the dead man walking in the attic, the skeleton just behind the closet door, in order to be assured that it doesn't exist.

"Possibly. I'm interested in your reasons for suggesting it."

"Well," she hedged, "you said Harriet Blackwell was in danger."

"Is that all?"

"Yes. Of course." The skeleton had frightened her away from the verge of candor. She covered her retreat with protestations: "I'm sure you must be mistaken. They seem fond of each other. And you couldn't describe Burke as a violent man."

"How well did you know him, Miss Castle?"

She hesitated. "You asked me, before, if I was in love with him."

"I apologize for my bluntness."

"I don't care. Is it so obvious? Or has Chauncey Reynolds been telling tales out of school?"

"He said that you were seeing a lot of Burke, before Harriet Blackwell entered the picture."

"Yes. I've been trying ever since to work him out of my system. With not very striking success." She glanced at the loom in the corner. "At least I've gotten through a lot of work."

"Do you want to tell me the story from the beginning?"

"If you insist. I don't see how it can help you."

"How did you meet him?"

"In a perfectly natural way. He came into the shop the day after he got here. His room at the *posada* didn't suit him, because of the light. He was looking for a place to paint. He said he hadn't been able to paint for some time, and he was burning to get at it. I happened to have a studio I'm not using, and I agreed to rent it to him for a month or so."

"Is that how long he wanted it for? A month?"

"A month or two, it wasn't definite."

"And he came here two months ago?"

"Almost to the day. When I think of the changes there have been in just two months—!" Her eyes reflected them. "Anyway, the day he moved in, I had to make a speed trip to Guad. One of my girls has a rheumatic heart and she needed emergency treatment. Burke came along for the ride, and I was impressed by his kindness to the girl—she's one of my best students. After we took her to the hospital we went to the *Copa de Leche* for lunch and really got to know each other.

"He talked to me about his plans as an artist. He's still caught up in abstraction but he's trying to use that method to penetrate more deeply into life. It's his opinion that the American people are living through a tragedy unconsciously, suffering without knowing that we are suffering or what the source of the suffering may be. He thinks it's in our sexual life." She flushed suddenly. "Burke is very verbal for a painter."

"I hadn't noticed," I said. "Who paid for the lunch?"

Her flush deepened. "You know quite a bit about him, don't you? I paid. He was broke. I also took him to an artists' supply house and let him charge four hundred pesos' worth of paints on my account. It was my suggestion, not his, and I don't regret it."

"Did he pay you back?"

"Of course."

"Before or after he attached himself to Harriet Blackwell?"

"Before. It was at least a week before she got here."

"What did he use for money?"

"He sold a picture to Bill Wilkinson, or rather to his wife—she's the one with the money. I tried to persuade him not to sell it or, if he insisted, to sell it to me. But he was determined to sell it to her, and she was determined to have it. She paid him thirty-five hundred pesos, which was more than I could afford. Later on he regretted the sale and tried to buy the picture back from the Wilkinsons. I heard that they had quite a ruction about it."

"When was this?"

"A couple of weeks ago. I only heard about it at second hand. Burke and I were no longer speaking, and I have nothing to do with the Wilkinsons. Bill Wilkinson is a drunk married to a woman older than himself and living on her." She paused over the words, perhaps because they had accidentally touched on her relations with Damis. "They're dangerous people."

"I understand that Wilkinson was Burke's boon companion."

"For a while. Bill Wilkinson is quite perceptive, in the sense that he understands people's weaknesses, and Burke was taken in by him for a while."

"Or vice versa?"

"That was not the case. What would a man like Burke have to gain from a man like Bill Wilkinson?"

"He sold his wife a picture for thirty-five hundred pesos."

"It's a very good picture," she said defensively, "and cheap at the price. Burke isn't ever high on his own work, but even he admitted that it was the kind of tragic painting he was aiming at. It wasn't like his other things, apart from a few sketches. As a matter of fact, it's representational."

"Representational?"

"It's a portrait," she said, "of a lovely young girl. He called it 'Portrait of an Unknown Woman.' I asked him if he'd ever known such a woman. He said perhaps he had, or perhaps he dreamed her."

"What do you think?"

"I think he must have known her, and painted her from memory. I never saw a man work so ferociously hard. He painted twelve and fourteen hours a day. I had to make him stop to eat. I'd walk into the studio with his *comida*, and he'd be working with the tears and sweat running down his face. He'd paint himself blind, then he'd go off on the town and get roaring drunk. I'd put him to bed in the wee hours, and he'd be up in the morning painting again."

"He must have given you quite a month."

"I loved it," she said intensely. "I loved him. I still do."

It was an avowal of passion. If there was some hysteria in it, she had it under control. Everything was under control, except that she worked all the time.

We sat there smiling dimly at each other. She was an attractive woman, with the kind of honesty that chisels the face in pure lines. I recalled what Chauncey Reynolds had said in drunken wisdom about Harriet, that she hadn't made the breakthrough into womanhood. Anne Castle had.

I kept my eyes on her face too long. She rose and moved across the room with hummingbird vitality, and opened a portable bar which stood against the wall:

"May I give you something to drink, Mr. Archer?"

"No, thanks, there's a long night coming up. After you and I have finished, I'm going to try and see the Wilkinsons. I want a look at that portrait they bought, for one thing."

She closed the door of the bar, sharply. "Haven't we finished?"

"I'm afraid not, Miss Castle."

She came back to the divan. "What more do you want from me?"

"I still don't understand Damis and his background. Did he ever talk about his previous life?"

"Some. He came from somewhere in the Middle West. He studied at various art schools."

"Did he name them?"

"If he did, I don't remember. Possibly Chicago was one of them. He knew the Institute collection. But most painters do."

"Where did he live before he came to Mexico?"

"All over the States, I gathered. Most of us have."

"Most of the people here, you mean?"

She nodded. "This is our fifty-first state. We come here when we've run through the other fifty."

"Burke came here from California, we know that. Did he ever mention San Mateo County, or the Bay area in general?"

"He'd spent some time in San Francisco. He was deeply familiar with the El Grecos in the museum there."

"Painting is all he ever talked about, apparently."

"He talked about everything under the sun," she said, "except his past life. He *was* reticent about that. He did tell me he'd been unhappy for years, that I'd made him happy for the first time since he was a boy."

"Then why did he turn his back on you so abruptly?"

"That's a very painful question, Mr. Archer."

"I know it, and I'm sorry. I'm trying to understand how the Blackwell girl got into the picture."

"I can't explain it," she said with a little sigh. "Suddenly there she was, spang in the middle of it."

"Had he ever mentioned her before she arrived?"

"No. They met here, you see."

"And he had no previous knowledge of her?"

"No. Are you implying that he was lying in wait for her or something equally melodramatic?"

"My questions don't imply anything. They're simply questions. Do you happen to know where they first met?"

"At a party at Helen Wilkinson's. I wasn't there, so I can't tell you who introduced whom to whom, or who was the aggressor, shall we say. I do know it was love at first sight." She added dryly: "On her part."

"What about his part?"

Her clear brow knotted, and she looked almost ugly for a moment. "It's hard to say. He dropped me like the proverbial hotcake when she hove into sight. He dropped his painting, too. He spent all his time with her for weeks, and finally went off with her. Yet the few times I saw them together— he was still living here, but I arranged to see as little of him as possible—I got the impression that he wasn't terribly attracted to her."

"What do you base that on?"

"Base is too definite a word for what I have to go on—the way he looked at her and the way he didn't look. He struck me as a man doing a job, doing it with rather cold efficiency. That may be wishful thinking on my part."

I doubted that it was. I'd seen the lack of interest in his face the day before, in the Malibu house, when Harriet ran to him across the room.

"I don't believe you do much wishful thinking, Miss Castle."

"Do I not? But they didn't seem to talk about each other, as people in love are supposed to. As Burke and I did when we were—together." The ugly darkness caught in her brow again. "They talked about how much money her father had, and what a beautiful place he maintained at Lake Tahoe. Things like that," she said contemptuously.

"Just what was said about the place at Tahoe?"

"She described it to him in some detail, as if she was trying to sell a piece of real estate. I know I'm being hard on her, but it was hard to listen to. She went on for some time about the great oaken beams, and the stone fireplace where you could roast an ox if you had an ox, and the picture window overlooking the lake. The disheartening thing was, Burke was intensely interested in her very materialistic little recital."

"Did she say anything about taking him there?"

"I believe she did. Yes, I remember she suggested that it would be an ideally secluded place for a honeymoon."

"This may be the most helpful thing you've told me yet," I said. "How did you happen to overhear it, by the way?"

She tugged at one of her earrings in embarrassment. "I didn't mean to let that slip. I might as well confess, though, while I'm confessing all. I eavesdropped on them. I didn't intend to do it, but he brought her to the studio several nights in a row, and my good intentions broke down. I had to know what they were saying to each other." Her voice took on a satiric lilt: "So she was saying that her father had oodles of money and three houses, and Burke was drinking it in. Maybe he had an underprivileged childhood, who knows?"

"It's a funny thing about con men, they often come from respectable well-heeled families."

"He *isn't* a confidence man. He's a good painter."

"I have to reserve my judgment, on both counts. It might be a good idea for you to reserve yours."

"I've been trying, these last weeks. But it's fearfully hard, when you've made a commitment—" She moved her hands helplessly.

"I'd like to have a look at the studio you rented him. Would that be possible?"

"If you think it will help in any way."

On the far side of the courtyard, where a Volkswagen was parked for the night, a detached brick building with a huge window stood against the property wall. She unlocked the door and turned on a lamp inside. The big bare-walled room smelled of insecticide. Several unsittable-looking pigskin-covered chairs were distributed around the tile floor. A cot with its thin mattress uncovered stood in one corner. The only sign of comfort was the hand-woven drapes at the big window.

"He lived frugally enough here," I said.

"Just like a monk in his cell." Her inflection was sardonic. "Of course I've stripped the place since he moved out. That was a week ago Sunday."

"He didn't fly to Los Angeles until the following day."

"I presume he spent the last night with her."

"They were spending nights together, were they?"

"Yes. I don't know what went on in the course of the nights. You mustn't think I spied on them persistently. I only broke down the once." She folded her arms across her breasts and stood like a small monument, determined never to break down again. "You see me in my nakedness, Mr. Archer. I'm the classic case of the landlady who fell in love with her star boarder and got jilted."

"I don't see you in that light at all."

"What other light could you possibly see me in?"

"You'd be surprised. Have you ever been married, Miss Castle?"

"Once. I left Vassar to get married, to a poet, of all things. It didn't work out."

"So you exiled yourself to Mexico?"

"It's not that simple, and neither am I," she said with a complicated smile. "You couldn't possibly understand how I feel about this place. It's as ancient as the hills and as new as the Garden of Eden—the real New World—and I love to be a part of it." She added sadly, her mind revolving around a single pole: "I thought that Burke was beginning to feel the same."

I moved around the room and in and out of the bathroom

at the rear. It was all bare and clean and unrevealing. I came back to her.

"Did Damis leave much behind him, in the way of things?"

"He left no personal things, if that's what you're interested in. He had nothing when he came here and not much more when he left, except for his brushes."

"He came here with nothing at all?"

"Just the clothes he had on, and they were quite used up. I persuaded him to have a suit made in Guad. Yes, I paid for it."

"You did a lot for him."

"*Nada.*"

"Did he give you anything in return?"

"I didn't want anything from him."

"No keepsakes or mementos?"

She hesitated. "Burke gave me a little self-portrait. It's only a sketch he tossed off. I asked him for it."

"May I see it?"

"If you like."

She locked up the studio and took me back across the courtyard to her bedroom. Framed in bamboo, the small black and white picture hung on the wall above her smooth bed. The sketch was too stylized to be a perfect likeness, and one eye was for some reason larger than the other, but Burke Damis was easily recognizable in it. He glared out somberly from a nest of crosshatched lines.

Anne Castle stood and answered his look with defensive arms folded across her breasts.

"I have a favor to ask you. A big one."

"You want the sketch," she said.

"I promise you'll get it back."

"But you must know what he looks like. You've seen him, haven't you?"

"I've seen him, but I don't know who I've seen."

"You think he's using a false name?"

"I believe he's using at least two aliases. Burke Damis is one. Quincy Ralph Simpson is another. Did he ever use the Simpson name when he was with you?"

She shook her head. The movement left her face loose and expectant.

"He came to Mexico under the Simpson name. He used it again when he left. There's a strange thing about the name Quincy Ralph Simpson. The man who originally owned it is dead."

Her head moved forward on her neck. "How did he die?"

"Of an icepick in the heart, two months ago, in a town near Los Angeles called Citrus Junction. Did Burke ever mention Citrus Junction to you?"

"Never." Her arms had fallen to her sides. She looked at the bed, and then sat down on it. "Are you trying to tell me that Burke killed him?"

"Burke, or whatever his name is, is the leading suspect in my book, so far the only one. He left the United States shortly after Simpson disappeared. It's virtually certain he was using Simpson's papers."

"Who was Simpson?"

"A little man of no importance who wanted to be a detective."

"Was he after Burke for—some crime?"

Her voice had overtones and undertones. The dead man was walking in the attic again. The skeleton hung behind her half-shuttered eyes.

"You brought up the subject of murder before," I said. "Is that the crime you have in mind?"

She looked from me to the picture on the wall and back at me. She said miserably: "Did Burke kill a woman?"

"It's not unlikely," I said in a neutral tone.

"Do you know who she was?"

"No. Do you?"

"He didn't tell me her name, or anything else about her. All he said—" She straightened up, trying to discipline her thoughts. "I'll see if I can reconstruct exactly what he did say. It was our first night together. He'd been drinking, and he was in a low mood. Post-coital *tristesse,* I believe they call it."

She was being cruel to herself. Her fingers worked in the coverlet of her bed. One of her hands, still working, went to her breast. She was no longer looking at me.

"You were going to tell me what he said, Miss Castle."

"I can't."

"You already have, in a sense."

"I shouldn't have spoken. Jilted landlady betrays demon lover. I didn't think that was my style. I'm a hopeless creature," she said, and flung herself sideways with her face in the pillow, her legs dragging on the floor.

They were good legs, and I was aware of it, in the center of my body as well as in my head. A wave of feeling went through me; I wanted to comfort her. But I kept my hands off. She had more memories than she could use, and so had I.

The memory I was interested in came out brokenly, half smothered by the pillow. "He said he was bad luck to his women. I should have nothing to do with him if I liked my neck in one piece. He said that that had happened to his last one."

"What happened to her?"

"She was choked to death. It was why he had to leave the States."

"That implies he was responsible for her death. Did he make a confession to you?"

"He didn't say it outright. It was more of a threat to me, or a warning. I suppose he was bullying me. But he never actually hurt me. He's very strong, too. He could have hurt me."

"Did he ever repeat the confession, or the threat?"

"No, but I often thought of it afterward. I never brought it up, though. I was always a little afraid of him after that. It didn't stop my loving him. I'd love him no matter what he'd done."

"Two murders take a lot of doing, and a very special kind of person to do them."

She detached her face from the comfort of the pillow and sat up, smoothing her skirt and then her hair. She was pale and shaken, as if she'd been through a bout of moral nausea.

"I can't believe that Burke is that kind of person."

"Women never can about the men they love."

"Just what evidence is there against him?"

"What I've told you, and what you've told me."

"But it doesn't amount to anything. He might have been simply *talking*, with me."

"You didn't think so at the time, or later. You asked me right off if murder was involved. And I have to tell you that it certainly is. I saw Ralph Simpson's body just twenty-four hours ago."

"But you don't know who the woman was?"

"Not yet. I have no information on Damis's past life. It's why I came here, and why I want to borrow your picture of him."

"What use will you make of it?"

"An acquaintance of mine is art critic on one of the L.A. papers. He knows the work of a lot of young painters, and quite a few of them personally. I want to show the sketch to him and see if he can put a name to your friend."

"Why do you think Burke Damis isn't his name?"

"If he's on the run, as he seems to be, he wouldn't be using his own name. He entered Mexico under the Simpson alias, as I told you. There's one other little piece of evidence. Did you ever notice a shaving kit he had, in a leather case?"

"Yes. It was just about his only possession."

"Do you recall the initials on it?"

"I don't believe I do."

" 'B.C.,' " I said. "They don't go with the name Burke Damis.

I'm very eager to know what name they do go with. That picture may do it."

"You can have it," she said, "and you don't have to send it back. I shouldn't have hung it here anyway. It's too much like self-flagellation."

She took it off its hook and gave it to me, talking me out of the room and herself out of her embarrassed pain. "I'm a very self-flagellant type. But I suppose it's better than having other people do it to you. And so very much more economical—it saves paying the middlemen."

"You talk a great deal, Anne."

"Too much, don't I? Much too much too much."

But she was a serviceable woman. She gave me a bag of woven straw to carry the picture in, backed her Volkswagen out over my protests, and drove me out to the Wilkinsons' lakefront house. It was past one but the chances were, she said, that Bill and his wife would still be up. They were late risers and late drinkers.

She turned in at the top of their lane and kept her headlights on the barbed-wire gate while I unfastened it and closed it behind me. Then she gave a little toot on her horn and started back toward the village.

I didn't expect to see her again, and I regretted it.

chapter 12

MUSIC DRIFTED from the house. It was old romantic music of the twenties, poignant and sweet as the jasmine on the air. The dooryard was thickly planted with shrubbery and trees. Wide terraces descended from it to the lake, which glimmered faintly in the middle distance.

I bumped my head on a low-hanging fruit which was probably a mango. Above the trees the stars hung in the freshly

cleared sky like clusters of some smaller, brighter fruit too
high to reach.

I knocked on the heavy door. A woman spoke over the
music: "Is that you, Bill?"

I didn't answer. After a minute's waiting she opened the
door. She was blonde and slim in something diaphanous. She
also wore in her right hand a clean-looking .38 revolver pointed
at my stomach.

"What do you want?"

"A little talk. My name is Archer and I'm only here over-
night and I realize this is a poor time to come bothering you—"

"You haven't told me what you want."

"I'm a private detective investigating a crime."

"We don't have crime here," she said sharply.

"This crime occurred up north."

"What makes you think that I know anything about it?"

"I'm here to ask you, is all."

She moved back, and waved the revolver commandingly.
"Come in under the light and let me see you."

I stepped into a room so huge that its far corners were in
darkness. Gershwin spilled in a nostalgic cascade from a mas-
sive hi-fi layout against one wall. The blonde woman was
heavily made up in an old-fashioned way, as if she had been
entertaining ghosts. Her triangular face had the taut immobil-
ity that plastic surgery often leaves behind.

She looked at my feet and swept her eyes up my body like
searchlights, half occulted by eye shadow. I recognized the
way she used her eyes. I'd seen it a dozen times before
through the fallout of old late movies, and earlier still, when
I was a juvenile patron of the Long Beach movie houses and
she was a western leading lady smirking and ogling her way
out of triangular relationships with horses.

I reached deep for her movie name, but I couldn't quite
dredge it up.

"You're fairly pretty," she said. "Isn't that Claude Stacy's sweater you're wearing?"

"He lent it to me. My clothes got rained on."

"I gave him that sweater. Are you a friend of Claude's?"

"Not an intimate one."

"That's good. You don't *look* his type. Do you like women?"

"Put the gun away and I'll give you a truthful answer," I said with the necessary smile.

She responded with a smile of her own, a 1929 smile that rested on her mouth like a footnote to history. "Don't let the gun bother you. I learned to handle a gun when I was playing in westerns. My husband insists I keep it handy when I'm alone at night. Which I usually am."

She laid the revolver down on a table near the door and turned back to me. "You haven't told me if you like women or not."

"I like individual women. I've liked you, for example, for a longer time than either of us would care to admit." The name she had used as an actress had come back to me. "You're Helen Holmes, aren't you?"

She lit up coldly and brightly, like a marquee. "You remember me. I thought everyone had forgotten."

"I was a fan," I said, spreading it not too thick.

"How nice!" She clenched her hands at her shoulders and jumped a few inches off the floor, with both feet, her smile immobile. "For that you may sit you down and I'll pour you a drink and tell you anything you want to know. Except about me. Name your poison."

"Gin and tonic, since you're so kind."

"One gin and tonic coming up."

She turned on a gilt chandelier which hung like a barbaric treasure among the ceiling beams. The room was like an auctioneer's warehouse, crowded with furniture of various periods and countries. Against a distant wall stood an ornately carved bar, backed by shelves of bottles, with half a dozen leather-covered stools in front of it.

"Come sit at the bar. It's cozier."

I sat and watched her mix my drink. For herself she compounded something out of tequila and grenadine, with coarse salt sprinkled around the rim of the glass. She stayed behind the bar to drink it, leaning on her forearms and exposing her bosom like a barmaid favoring a customer.

"I won't waste time beating around the bush. I'm interested in Burke Damis. You know him, Mrs. Wilkinson?"

"Slightly. He is, or was, a friend of my husband's."

"Why do you put it in the past tense?"

"They had a quarrel, some time before Mr. Damis left here."

"What about?"

"You ask very direct questions."

"I don't have time for my usual subtlety."

"*That* must be something to experience."

"Oh, it is. What did they quarrel about?"

"Me, if you have to know. Poor little old me." She fluttered her eyelashes. "I was afraid they were going to kill each other, honestly. But Bill contented himself with burning the picture. That way he got back at both of us." She raised one hand like a witness. "Now don't ask me for doing what. There wasn't any *what*. It's just that Bill is very insecure in our relationship."

"He burned the 'Portrait of an Unknown Woman'?"

"Yes, and I haven't forgiven him for it," she said, as though this were proof of character. "He broke up the frame and tore the canvas and put the whole thing in the fireplace and set fire to it. Bill can be quite violent sometimes."

She sipped her drink and licked the salt from her lips with a pale pointed tongue. She reminded me of a cat, not a domestic cat, but one of the larger breeds that could stalk men. Her bright lips seemed to be savoring the memory of violence.

"Did Damis know the picture was destroyed?"

"I told him. It broke him up. He wept actual tears, can you imagine?"

"I wonder why."

"It was his best picture, he said. I liked it, too."

"I heard he'd tried to buy it back."

"He did, but I wouldn't part with it." Between the shadowed lids her eyes were watchful. "Who else have you been talking to?"

"Various people around the village."

"Claude Stacy?"

"No. Not yet."

"Why are you so interested in that particular picture?"

"I'm interested in everything Damis does."

"You mentioned a crime that occurred up north. Do you want to let down your back hair about it? I've been letting down my back hair."

I told her what had happened to Quincy Ralph Simpson. She looked somehow disappointed, as if she'd been expecting something more lurid.

"This is all new to me," she said. "There's nothing I can tell you about Simpson."

"Let's get back to the picture then. Damis called it a portrait. Did he ever say who the subject of it was?"

"He never did," she said shortly.

"Do you have any ideas?"

She shrugged her shoulders and made a stupid face, with her mouth turned down at the corners.

"You must have had a reason for buying the painting and wanting to keep it. Your husband cared enough about it to burn it."

"I don't know who the woman was," she said, too forcefully.

"I think you do."

"Think away. You're getting rather boring. It's late, and I

have a headache." She drew her fingers across her forehead.
"Why don't you drink up and go?"

I left my drink where it was on the bar between us. "I'm
sorry if I pressed too hard. I didn't mean to—"

"Didn't you?" She finished her drink and came around the
end of the bar, licking her lips. "Come on, I'll let you out."

It had been a very quick party. Reluctantly I followed her
to the door.

"I was hoping to ask you some questions about Harriet
Blackwell. I understand Damis met her here at your house."

"So what?" she said, and pulled the door open. "Out."

She slammed it behind me. In the dooryard I bumped my
head on the same low-hanging fruit. I picked it—it was a
mango—and took it along with me as a souvenir.

It was a long walk back, but I rather enjoyed it. It gave me
a chance to think, among other things about Helen Holmes
Wilkinson. Our rather tenuous relationship, based on Claude
Stacy's sweater and my remembering her movie name, had
broken down over the identity of the woman in the burned
portrait. I would give odds that she knew who the woman was
and what her connection with Damis had been.

I wondered about Helen's own connection with Damis.

Headlights approached me, coming very fast from the direction of the village. They belonged to a beetle-shaped
Porsche which swerved in long arcs from one side of the road
to the other. I had to slide into the ditch to avoid being run
over. As the Porsche went by I caught a glimpse of the driver's
face, pale under flying dark hair. I threw my mango at him.

The clock chimed two quarters—half-past two—as I struggled through the village to the *posada*. In the room behind
the desk, Claude Stacy was sleeping in his clothes on a mohair
couch. It was a couch with one high end, the kind psychia-
trists use, and he was curled up on it in foetal position.

I shook him. He grimaced and snorted like a huge old baby
being born into a world he never made.

"What is it?"

"I met a friend of yours tonight. Helen Wilkinson. She mentioned you."

"Did she now?" He took a comb out of his pocket and ran it through his thinning hair. "I hope it was complimentary."

"Very," I lied.

He basked in the imaginary compliment. "Oh, Helen and I get along. If Bill Wilkinson hadn't got to her first I might have thought of marrying her myself." He thought about it now. "She used to be in pictures, you know, and she saved her money. I did some acting at one time myself. But I didn't hang on to any money."

"What does Bill Wilkinson do for a living?"

"Nothing. He must be twenty years younger than Helen is," he said by way of explanation. "You'd never know it, she's so beautifully preserved. And Bill has let himself go frightfully. He used to be a Greek god, I mean it."

"Have you known him long?"

"Years and years. It's through him I got to know Helen. He married her a couple of years ago, after his folks stopped sending him money. I wouldn't say he married her for her money, but he married where money is. Tennyson." Stacy giggled. "It drives him out of his mind when Helen even *looks* at another man."

"She looks at other men?"

"I'm afraid she does. She was interested in me at one time." He flushed with vanity. "Of course I wouldn't steal another fellow's wife. Bill knows he can trust me. Bill and I have been buddy-buddy for years."

"Have you seen him tonight?"

"No, I haven't. I think he went to a party in Guadalajara. He has some very good connections. His family are very well-known people in Texas."

"Does he drive a Porsche?"

"If you can call it driving. His driving is one reason he had to leave Texas."

"I can believe it. He almost ran me down on the road just now."

"Poor old Bill. Some night he's going to end up in the ditch with a broken neck. And maybe I'll marry Helen after all, who knows?" The prospect failed to cheer him. "I need a drink, old chap. Will you have one with me?"

"All right. Drinking seems to be the favorite indoor sport around here."

He looked at me to see if I was accusing him of being a drunk. I smiled. He gave me a Mexican-type shrug and got a bottle of Bacardi out from under the high end of the couch. He poured some into paper cups from a dispenser that hung on the wall beside the bottled water. I added water to mine.

"*Salud,*" he said. "If you don't mind my asking, how did you happen to run into Helen Wilkinson?"

"I went to see her."

"Just like that?"

"I happen to be a private investigator."

He sat bolt upright. His drink slopped over the rim of the cup. I wondered what old scandal had the power to galvanize him.

"I thought you were a tourist," he said resentfully.

"I'm a detective, and I came here to investigate a man who calls himself Burke Damis. I think he stayed with you for a night or two."

"One night," Stacy said. "So it's really true about him, after all? I hated to believe it—he's such a fine-looking chap."

"You hated to believe what?"

"That he murdered his wife. Isn't that why you're after him?"

With the aid of a little rum and water I made a quick adjustment. "These rumors get around. Where did you happen to pick that one up?"

"It was going the rounds, as you say. I think it started when Bill Wilkinson told somebody at The Place that he was going to report Damis as an undesirable alien." Stacy sounded like a connoisseur of rumors, who collected them as other men collected notable sayings or pictures or women. "The government has been bearing down on undesirables, rounding them up and pushing them back across the border. Takes wetbacks in reverse."

"And Wilkinson turned Damis in?"

"I don't believe he actually did, but he threatened to. Which is probably why Damis got out in a hurry. So he really is one jump ahead of the law?"

"A long jump," I said. "This rumor interests me. What exactly was said?"

"Simply that Damis—which wasn't his real name—was wanted for the murder of his wife."

"How do you know it isn't his real name?"

"I don't know anything. It was all part of the rumor. I pestered Bill and Helen for more details, but they refused to talk—"

"They know more details, do they?"

"I would say so."

"Where did they get them?"

"I've asked myself that question many times. I know they made their border trip last May and spent a week or so in California. That's when the murder occurred, isn't it? Maybe they read about it in the newspapers. But if they knew all about it, I can't understand why they would get chummy with the man. The three of them were very buddy-buddy for a while, before Bill turned against him. Helen got too interested in Damis."

"But Damis had a girl of his own." Or two. Or three.

He smiled indulgently. "That wouldn't stop Helen."

"Do you know the girl he left here with—Harriet Blackwell?"

"I met her once, at a party."

"Where did Damis meet her?"

"Same party, at Helen Wilkinson's. Helen told me he asked her to invite her."

"Damis asked Helen to invite Harriet to the party?"

"That's what I said."

"So that he could meet Harriet?"

"Apparently. I only know what I hear."

The interview was beginning to depress me. Stacy's eyes had a feeding look, as if he lived on these morsels and scraps of other people's lives. Perhaps I feared a similar fate for myself.

He poured himself more Bacardi and offered me some. I turned it down, politely. If I wanted to get back to California tomorrow—and now I was determined to—I had some further legwork to do tonight.

"Tell me, Mr. Stacy, is there a taxi in the village?"

"There's a man who drives people. You'd have a frightful time routing him out at three in the morning. Why?"

"I have to get out to the Wilkinsons, and I don't feel like walking it again."

"I'll drive you."

"You're very hospitable."

"Think nothing of it. This is *exciting* for me. I'll take you on one condition, that you don't tell Bill or Helen I had any part in this. The connection is important to me, you know."

"Sure."

He brought his battered Ford around to the entrance and drove me out the lake road. Roosters were crowing in the dark countryside. Stacy parked at the head of the Wilkinsons' lane and let me go in by myself.

The Wilkinsons were having an argument which was loud enough to penetrate the walls. I stood outside the front door and listened to it.

She called him an alcoholic. He said she couldn't talk to a

Charro like that. She said it took more than a Charro hat to make a Charro, that he was a Charro like she was a member of the DAR.

He called her a sexoholic. She told him if he didn't watch his lip she'd divorce him and turn him loose to beg in the streets. He announced that she'd be doing him a favor, since marriage to her was uphill work at best.

The argument simmered down after a while, so that I could hear the roosters in the distance, yelling with insane glee in the dead dark middle of the night. I balled up the rest of my energy in my fist and knocked on the door.

Wilkinson answered it this time. He was a big man in his thirties who looked older. His Mexican clothes and haircut made him seem to be metamorphosing under my eyes, changing into something that was strange even to himself. He had alcohol in him, red in the eye, sour on the breath, thick on the tongue.

"I don't know you. Go 'way."

"Just give me a minute. I'm a private detective, and I flew down from L.A. to do some checking on Burke Damis. I heard you were a friend of his."

"You heard wrong. He came sucking around for free drinks. Once I caught onto him, I cut him dead. But dead."

Wilkinson had a nasty whining drawl. His red eyes glared with something stronger than drink, perhaps a touch of madness.

"What did you catch on to about Damis?"

"He wormed himself into my good graces so he could get next to my wife. I don't stand for that."

He made a sideways slicing gesture. The edge of his hand struck the doorframe. He put the edge of his hand in his mouth.

"I heard a rumor that he killed his own wife."

"That was no rumor. We were in San Francisco in the spring, and I saw it in the paper with these eyes—the dead woman's picture and all. It said that he shtrangled her. But we didn't know who he was when he came here worming his way. We didn't know till we saw the picture he painted."

"Was it a portrait of his wife?"

"Thass right. Helen reckonized her face, poor little woman. That snake-in-the-grass shtrangled her with his own hands."

Wilkinson made clutching motions, as though he was having a waking dream of strangling or being strangled. His wife called from somewhere out of sight: "Who is it, Bill? Who are you talking to?"

"Man from L.A. He says that he's a detective."

She ran the length of the living room to his side. "Don't talk to him."

"I'll talk to him if I like," he said with the look of a spoiled and sullen child. "I'll put the kibosh on Damis once and for all."

"You stay out of it."

"You were the one that got me into it. If you hadn't tried to blackmail him into—"

"Be quiet. You're a fool."

They faced each other in a rage that created a vacuum around them. He was twice as big as she was, and almost twice as young, but she held her anger better. Her taut and shining face was expressionless.

"Listen to me, Bill. This man was here an hour or so ago. I had to ask him to leave."

"Whaffor?"

"He made a pass at me." Her hooked fingers swept across her bosom.

His attention slopped heavily in my direction. "Izzat true?"

"Don't believe her."

"Now he's calling me a liar." Her white triangular face was at his shoulder. "Are you going to let him get away with it?"

He threw a wild fist at my head. I let it go by and hit him in the body. He sat down holding his belly with both hands. I shouldn't have hit him. He retched.

"Why you dirty lousy son," the woman said.

She picked her revolver off the table and fired it at me. The bullet tugged at a loose fold of Stacy's sweater, close to my side. I turned and ran.

chapter 13

IN THE MORNING, the sudden morning, Stacy drove me to the airport. He wouldn't let me pay him for the service, or for the double hole in his sweater. He said it would make a conversation piece.

But he did ask me when I had the time to call a friend of his who managed a small hotel in Laguna Beach. I was to tell the man that Claude was doing all right, and there were no hard feelings.

I tottered on board the plane and slept most of the way to Los Angeles. We landed shortly after one o'clock. It was hot, hotter than it had been in Mexico. Smog lay over the city like the lid of a pressure cooker.

I immured myself in an outside phone booth and made several calls. Colonel Blackwell had had no word from Harriet since she drove off with Damis the day before yesterday. It was possible, he agreed, that they had gone to Tahoe. His lodge there was situated on the lake, on the Nevada side of State Line.

I cut his anxious questions short with a promise to come and see him at his house. Then I called Arnie Walters in Reno. He ran a detective agency which covered that end of Nevada.

Arnie's wife and partner answered the phone. Phyllis Walters had the official-sounding voice of an ex-policewoman, but it didn't quite hide her exuberant femininity.

"How are you, Lew? Where have you been keeping yourself?"

"All over the map. Last night, for instance, I spent a week in Mexico."

"You do get around. Arnie's out. Is it business or just social?"

"Urgent business. You'd better record this."

"All right. Go ahead."

I gave her a description of Harriet and Damis and asked to have them looked for in the Tahoe and Reno area, with special attention to the Blackwell lodge and the wedding chapels. "If Arnie or one of his men runs into Damis, with or without the girl, I want Damis held."

"We can't detain him, you know that."

"You can make a citizen's arrest and turn him over to the nearest cop. He's a fugitive from a murder rap."

"Who did he murder?"

"His wife, apparently. I expect to get the details this afternoon. In the meantime Arnie should be warned that the man is dangerous."

"Will do."

"Good girl. I'll get back to you later, Phyllis."

I called the photographer with whom I'd left my film of Damis's painting. The slides were ready. Finally, I called the art critic Manny Meyer. He said he'd be home for the next hour, and he was willing to look at my exhibits. I picked up the slides in Santa Monica and drove up Wilshire to Westwood.

Manny lived in one of the big new apartment buildings on the hill. The windows of his front room overlooked the UCLA campus. It was the room of a man who loved art and not much besides. Dozens of books had overflowed from the bookshelves onto the furniture, including the closed top of the baby grand piano. The walls were literally paneled with nineteenth-century reproductions and contemporary originals. Entering the room was like stepping into the interior of Manny's head.

He was a small man in a rumpled seersucker suit. His eyes looked deceptively sleepy behind his glasses. They regarded me with quiet waiting patience, as if I was the raw material of art.

"Sit down, Lew."

He waved his hand at the encumbered chairs. I remained standing.

"You would like me to identify a style, is that the problem? It isn't always so easy. You know how many painters there are? I bet you I could find five hundred within a radius of a mile. A thousand, maybe." He smiled slightly. "All of them geniuses of the first water."

"This particular genius did a self-portrait, which ought to make it easier for you."

"If I have ever seen him."

I got the bamboo-framed sketch out of my straw bag and showed it to Manny. He held it in his hands, studying it with concentration, like a man peering into a mirror for traces of illness.

"I believe I *have* seen him. Let me look at the transparencies."

I slid them out of their envelope. He held them up to the window one at a time.

"Yes. I know him. He has his own style, though there has been some change in it, perhaps some deterioration. That wouldn't be surprising." When he turned from the window his eyes were sorrowful.

"His name is Bruce Campion. I saw some of his work at a showing of young artists in San Francisco last year. I also met him briefly. I hear since then that he has come to grief, that he is wanted by the police, for murdering his wife. It was in the San Francisco papers. I'm surprised you didn't see it."

"I don't take the San Francisco papers."

"Perhaps you should. You could have saved yourself time and trouble." He gathered together the sketch and the slides and handed them back to me. "I suppose you're hot on his heels?"

"On the contrary, the trail is cold."

"I'm glad. Campion is a good painter."

"How good?"

"So good that I don't greatly care what he did to his wife," he said softly. "You live in a world of stark whites and blacks. My world is one of shadings, and the mechanism of punishment is anathema to me. 'An eye for an eye and a tooth for a tooth' is the law of a primitive tribe. If we practiced it to the letter we would all be eyeless and toothless. I hope he eludes you, and goes on painting."

"The danger is that he'll go on killing."

"I doubt it. According to my reading, murderers are the criminals least likely to repeat their offense. Now if you'll excuse me I have a show to cover."

Meyer's parting smile was gentle. He didn't believe in evil. His father had died in Buchenwald, and he didn't believe in evil.

chapter 14

I DROVE ACROSS to Sunset, and up the winding road to Blackwell's house in Bel Air. He opened the front door himself, brushing aside a little maid in uniform. His eyes moved on my face like a blind man's eyes trying to glean a ray of light.

"You've found out something?"

"The news is not good."

His hands came out and clutched both of my arms above the elbows. With the mindless automatism of St. Vitus's dance, he started to shake me. I pushed him away.

"Calm down and I'll tell you about it."

"How can you expect me to be calm? My daughter has been gone for forty-eight hours. I should have used force to stop them. I should have shot him dead at my feet—"

"That's nonsense," I said. "We need to talk. Can we go in and sit down?"

He blinked like a man waking up from troubled sleep. "Yes. Of course."

The drawing room he took me into was furnished with Empire pieces which gave it a museumlike atmosphere. Family portraits looked down their Blackwell noses from the walls. One of them, of an officer in the uniform of the War of 1812, had the weight and finish of a Gilbert Stuart.

Blackwell sat in an armchair under it, as if to call attention to the family resemblance. I parked myself uninvited on a red divan with a curved back, and gave him a brief rundown on my Mexican trip.

"I've put together certain facts I uncovered there with others that cropped up here and come to a definite conclusion about Damis. He's a wanted man traveling under more than one alias. His real name is Bruce Campion, and he's wanted for murder."

Blackwell's jaw moved slackly. I could see the pale insides of his mouth. "What did you say?"

"Damis's real name is Campion. He's wanted in San Mateo County for strangling his wife last spring."

Blackwell's face looked like cracked plaster. Consciousness withdrew from his eyes, leaving them blank as glass. He slipped from the armchair onto his knees, then fell heavily sideways. His white hair spilled like a sheaf on the old rose carpet.

I went to the door and called the maid. She came trotting and skidding on the parquetry, her excited little breasts bobbing under her uniform. She let out a muffled scream when she saw the fallen man.

"Is he dead?"

"He fainted, honey. Bring some water, and a washcloth."

She was back in thirty seconds, half spilling a pan of water on the carpet. I sprinkled some of it on Blackwell's face and swabbed his long forehead. His eyes came open, recognized me, remembered what I had told him. He groaned, and tried to faint again.

I slapped him with the wet cloth. The little maid stood and watched me with wide blue eyes, as if I was committing lese majesty.

"What's your name?" I asked her.

"Letty."

"Where's Mrs. Blackwell, Letty?"

"She does hospital work one day a week. This is the day."

"You'd better try and get in touch with her."

"All right. Should I call the doctor, do you think?"

"He doesn't need a doctor unless he has a heart history."

"Heart history?" she repeated like a lip reader.

"Has he ever had a heart attack, or a stroke?"

Blackwell answered me himself, in a shamed voice: "I've never even fainted before." He sat up laboriously, resting his back against the chair. "I'm not as young as I am—as I was. What you told me came as a fearful shock."

"It doesn't mean that Harriet is dead, you know."

"Doesn't it? I must have jumped to that conclusion." He noticed the young maid standing over him. He smoothed his hair and tried to compose his face. "You may go now, Miss Flavin. Be good enough to take that pot of water with you. It's out of place in here."

"Yessir." She picked it up and marched out.

Blackwell levered himself into the chair. "We have to do something," he said unsteadily.

"I'm glad you feel that way. I've already alerted detectives in the Reno area. I think we should extend the search to the whole Southwest, if not the entire country. That will cost a good deal of money."

He extended his limp fingers. "It doesn't matter. Anything."

"It's time to bring in the police, too, give them all we know and build a fire under them. I suggest you start off by talking to Peter Colton."

"Yes. I'll do that." He rose shakily as if the weight of his years had fallen on him all at once. "Give me a minute. My mind isn't quite clear yet."

"Better get yourself a drink. In the meantime, I have an important call to make. May I use one of your phones?"

"There's one in Isobel's sitting room. You can be private there."

It was a small pleasant room whose French doors opened onto a private terrace. The furniture was well used, shabby rather than antique. It didn't match the nineteenth-century grandeur of the drawing room, and I guessed that Isobel Blackwell had saved it from some less opulent period of her life—a period on which she hadn't turned her back.

I sat at the plain oak desk, called the Hall of Justice in Redwood City, and asked the switchboard operator for Captain Royal. He was San Mateo County's homicide chief, and I had met him on an earlier case.

"What can I do for you?" he said, after a few preliminaries.

"I have some information about Bruce Campion, who is alleged to have strangled his wife last May in your bailiwick. Is that correct?"

"Correct. It happened the night of May fifth. What's your information?"

I heard the small click as Royal switched on his recording machine. There was a second click, that sounded like a receiver being lifted.

"I've been tracing Campion's movements," I said. "He flew from Los Angeles to Guadalajara on May twentieth."

"The airport police were supposed to be watching for him," Royal said impatiently.

"He used false papers and an alias—Quincy Ralph Simpson. Does that name mean anything to you?"

"It does. I found out yesterday that Simpson was icepicked

in Citrus Junction two months ago. You telling me Campion did it?"

"The possibility suggests itself," I said. "He must have been carrying Simpson's identification when he crossed the border. Simpson was almost certainly dead by then."

"Is Campion still in Mexico?"

"No. He spent two months there under the name Burke Damis, in Ajijic on Lake Chapala, where he was eventually recognized as a wanted man. In the meantime he'd got a visiting American girl named Harriet Blackwell to fall for him. Nine days ago the two of them flew back to Los Angeles. Campion used the Simpson alias again. Then he switched back to Damis, and spent a week as a guest in the Blackwell's beach house near Malibu. It's possible the Blackwell girl knows something about his past and is protecting him. Campion has her hypnotized, but she could hardly miss the change of names."

"Is she with him now?"

"I hope not. But she probably is. The two of them left her father's house forty-eight hours ago after a serious altercation which involved threats of shooting. They took off in her car, a new green Buick Special." I gave him the license number.

"Who did the threatening?"

"Her father, Mark Blackwell. He's only a retired Colonel but he has money, and I imagine he pulls weight in some circles. I'm calling from his house in Bel Air now."

"Is Blackwell your client?"

"Yes. My immediate job is to find the girl and get her out of danger. She should be easy to spot. She's a big blonde, short-haired, aged twenty-four, about six feet in her shoes, with a tall girl's stoop. Expensively dressed, good figure, but face a little disfigured by a bony protuberance over the eyes. It's a genetic defect—"

"What?"

"The bony eyebrows are a family trait. The old man has

'em, and all the ancestors. Harriet wears dark glasses part of
the time. I assume you know what Campion looks like."

"I have him memorized," Royal said.

"Picture?"

"No picture. That's how he got across the border."

"I have one. I'll try to get a copy of it into your hands today. Now there's a possibility that Campion and the girl have
doubled back toward Mexico. Nevada is another possibility.
They were talking about getting married, and it's an easy state
to get married in. They may be married now, or representing
themselves as married."

"The girl must be crazy," Royal said, "if she knows what he
did to his wife and still wants to marry him."

"I'm not suggesting she knows about the wife. He probably faked a story to explain the aliases, and she would be
easily taken in. She's crazy in the sense that she's crazy about
him. Also, she's in active revolt against her father. She's twenty-
four, as I said, and he treats her as if she was four."

"Isn't twenty-four a little late for the big rebellion?"

"Harriet has been living under military occupation. She's
a fugitive from injustice."

"So she takes up with a fugitive from justice. I've seen it
happen before." Royal paused. "How much danger do you
think she's in?"

"You'd know more about that than I do, Captain. It depends
on Campion's motivation. Harriet's due to come into money on
her twenty-fifth birthday, so if it's money he's after, she's safe
for the next six months. Did Campion kill his wife for money?"

"There wasn't any money, so far as we know. We haven't
been able to uncover any motive at all. Which means he could
be off his rocker. A lot of these creeps who call themselves
artists are nuts. He lived like a bum in a remodeled garage
near Luna Bay, everything in one room." Royal's voice was
scornful.

"Did he have a record of irrational behavior?"

"I wouldn't know. He has a record, period. A year's hard labor and a dishonorable discharge for assaulting an officer during the Korean War. That's all we've been able to dig up on him, but it shows a history of violence. Also he wasn't get-ting along with his wife. Put the two together, it's all you need in the way of motive."

"Tell me about the wife."

"That can wait, can't it, Archer? I want to get your info out on the wires."

"You could give me a quick rundown."

Royal said in a clipped, toneless voice: "Her name was Dolly Stone Campion, age about twenty, pretty little blonde, not so pretty when we found her. According to our info, Cam-pion picked her up on the South Shore of Tahoe last summer, and married her in Reno in September. It must have been a marriage of inconvenience—Dolly was three months pregnant at the time. At least their child was born in March, six months after the wedding. Two months after that he knocked her off."

"Tahoe keeps cropping up," I said. "The Blackwells have a lodge there, and Q. R. Simpson spent some time at the lake in May, shortly before he was murdered."

"What was he doing there?"

"I have a hunch he was working on the Dolly Campion case. What happened to her baby, by the way?"

"Her mother took him. Look, Archer, this could go on all day, and I have work to do. A lot more work than I had be-fore," he added wryly. "Will you be coming up this way?"

"As soon as I can make it."

Which wasn't soon. I made a second call to Arnie Walters's office in Reno. I wanted to pass the word on Campion and ask Arnie to add more men to the search. He already had, Phyllis told me, because Campion and Harriet Blackwell had been seen in State Line the previous night. That was all so far.

I dropped the receiver into its cradle. When I picked it up, it felt appreciably heavier. I called the airport and made a reservation on the next flight to Reno. They were going to have to give me flying pay.

As I was getting up from the desk, I noticed a folded newspaper which lay on the back of it. "San Mateo Man," I spelled out upside down. I unfolded the paper.

It was yesterday's issue of the *Citrus Junction News-Beacon*. The full headline ran across the top of the page: "San Mateo Man Killed Here: Police Suspect Gang Murder." The story under it was poorly written and poorly printed, and it told me nothing I didn't already know.

I still had the paper in my hands when Blackwell came into the room. He looked like the ghost of one of his ancestors.

"What are you doing with that newspaper?"

"I was wondering how it got into your house."

"That's no concern of yours, I should think." He snatched it away from me and rolled it up small. "A number of things are no concern of yours. For example, I'm not paying out good money to have myself and my daughter slandered to policemen."

"I thought I heard somebody on another extension. Does everyone in your household eavesdrop on everyone else?"

"That's an insulting remark. I demand that you withdraw it."

Blackwell was shaking with another bout of uncontrollable anger. The rolled newspaper vibrated in his hand. He slapped his thigh with it, as if it was a swagger stick or a riding crop. He looked ready to strike me with it, and challenge me to a duel.

"I can't change facts, Colonel. If you don't like what you heard, you could have stopped listening."

"Are you telling me what to do in my own house?"

"It does sound like it, doesn't it?"

"Then get out of my house. Get out, do you hear?"

"They hear you in Tarzana. Don't you want your daughter found?"

"We'll find her without your help. You're fired."

"You've already had my help," I said. "You owe me three hundred and fifty dollars for time and expenses."

"I'll write you a check, now."

"You can stop payment on a check. I need cash."

I was playing for time in the faint hope that Blackwell would come to his senses, as he had once before. Though I couldn't knuckle under to him, I was eager to hold on to the case. It was beginning to break, and a breaking case to a man in my trade is like a love affair you can't stay away from, even if it tears your heart out daily.

"I don't have that much in the house," he was saying. "I'd have to cash a check at the hotel."

"Do that. I'll wait here."

"Outside," he said in a monitory tone. "I don't want you prying around in here. You can wait in your car."

I went down the hall and out, with Blackwell making shooing motions at my kidneys. He backed his black Cadillac out of the garage and drove away down the hill. I put in a bad ten minutes deciding where to go from here. It would have to be Tahoe, though I hated to make the trip on my own time.

The mourning dove had returned to the television antenna. He sat there still and perfect as a heraldic bird. I said hoohoo to him and got a response, hoo-hoo, and I felt better.

Isobel Blackwell, driving a small foreign car, came into the driveway from the road. I got out of my car to meet her. Her face looked wan in the sunlight, but she made herself smile at me.

"Mr. Archer! What a pleasant surprise."

"Didn't Letty get in touch with you?"

"I left the hospital early. I've been concerned about Mark."

"You have some reason to be. He had a fainting spell a while ago. Then he had a yelling spell."

"Mark fainted?"

"I gave him some information that hit him hard."

She ducked out of her little car and thrust her face up toward mine. "Something has happened to Harriet."

"We don't know that. But something could happen to her any time. She's wandering around Nevada with the man who calls himself Damis. His actual name is Bruce Campion, and he's wanted in Redwood City for murdering his wife."

It took her a minute to absorb this. Then she turned toward the house and noticed the empty garage. "Where is Mark?"

"He went down to the hotel to get some money to pay me off. He fired me."

"What on earth for?"

"The Colonel and I have had it, I'm afraid. We've both had too much Army, in different ways—the worm's-eye view and the god's-eye view."

"But I don't understand. You mean you won't go on with him?"

"I'd have to be asked. Which isn't very likely."

"I know how difficult he can be," she said in a rush of feeling. "Tell me exactly what the trouble was."

"He listened in on a telephone conversation I had with a police officer. I made some critical remarks about his treatment of Harriet. He didn't like them."

"And that's all?"

"All there is on the surface. Of course he was thrown by the information I gave him on Damis-Campion. He couldn't handle it, so he threw it back. He thinks that I'm what hurts him."

She nodded. "That's his standard pattern. It's been getting worse since this began. I'm worried about him, Mr. Archer. I don't know how he's going to survive."

"It's Harriet's survival I'm worried about. She and Campion were seen at State Line last night, and I have some Reno detectives on their trail. We have a chance to take him and rescue her, if we can stay with it."

Her whole body reacted to my words. She clutched her handbag to her breast as if it was a child she could protect. "The man is a murderer, you say?"

"It's a matter of police record."

She moved closer to me. Her hand lit on my wrist, and she said in a voice as low as a mourning dove's: "You said you'd have to be asked. I'm asking you. Will you take me for a client?"

"Nothing would suit me better."

"Then it's a contract." Her hand slid from my wrist to my fingers, and squeezed them. "It would be a good idea to let me tell Mark about this. In my own time, in my own way."

"I agree."

She went into the house and came out and gave me money and went in again. Blackwell's Cadillac rolled into the drive. He climbed out and gave me money. His color was better, and I could smell fresh whisky on him. He must have had a quick one or two at the hotel.

He looked at me as though he wanted to speak, but he didn't say a word.

chapter 15

ARNIE WALTERS met me at the Reno airport. He was a short broad man in his early fifties who looked like somebody you'd see selling tips at a race track. But he had the qualities of a first-rate detective: honesty, imagination, curiosity, and a love of people. Ten or twelve years in Reno had left him poor and uncorrupted.

On the way to State Line he filled me in on the situation there. A handyman named Sholto, who kept an eye on several lakeside houses for their absentee owners, had talked to Harriet the night before. She had come to Sholto's house to get the key to her father's lodge, and specifically asked him not to tell her father she was there. Campion had been with her, but stayed in the car, her car.

"Apparently," Arnie went on, "they spent the night, or part of the night, in the lodge. There's some dirty dishes on the sinkboard, recently used. Also there's some indication they're coming back, or planned to. He left his suitcase in the entrance hall. I have the place staked out."

"What about her suitcase?"

"Gone. So is her car."

"I don't like that."

Arnie shifted his eyes from the road to my face. "You seriously think he brought her up here to do her in?"

"It's a possibility that can't be ruled out."

"What were the circumstances of the other killing? The wife."

"He strangled her. I don't have the details yet."

"Did he stand to gain by her death?"

"The San Mateo police think not. The only motive they've come up with is incompatibility, or words to that effect. Evidently it was a forced marriage: the girl was about three months pregnant at the time. He married her in Reno last September, by the way, which means that this isn't new territory to Campion."

"You think he's repeating a pattern?"

"Something like that."

"What kind of a character is he?"

"He has me baffled."

"I never heard you say that before, Lew. Not out loud."

"Maybe I'm slipping. I don't pretend to be attuned to the artistic mind. Campion is a good painter, according to a critic who knows what he's talking about."

"You think he could be psycho? A lot of psychos magnetize the broads."

"The psycho broads," I said. "It's hard to tell about Campion. He had himself in control both times I saw him. The second time was under severe provocation. Harriet's father threatened him with a shotgun, and he stood up to it like a little man. But then psychos can be actors."

"Bad actors. Is he as good-looking as the description says?"

"Unfortunately yes. I brought along a picture of him. It's a self-sketch, not a photograph, but it's a good-enough likeness to circularize. I want it back after you have it photographed."

"Sure. Leave it in the car. I'll get it around to our informers and have it posted in the lookout galleries in the clubs. Sooner or later he'll show, if he's hiding out in this area. You realize he could be long gone by now, and so could the girl."

We drove in silence for a while, through country wooded with evergreens. The trees parted at one point, and I caught a first glimpse of the lake. It was the height of the season, and outboards were rioting in the afternoon sun. Skiers drove their plows of spray in eccentric furrows. I couldn't help remembering that Tahoe was deep and cold. Harriet could be long gone, far down, sheathed in black bottom water.

Her father's lodge stood among dense trees at the end of a frost-cracked asphalt lane. It was an imposing timbered building with half-walls of native stone. Concrete steps with iron railings zigzagged down from the terrace to the shore.

A man stepped out of the trees. He had the stubborn thick-bodied presence of an old cop. Arnie introduced him as Jim Hanna, one of his men. The three of us went inside.

Campion's brown suitcase was standing in the hallway under a moose head. I reached for it, but Arnie stopped me.

"It's a waste of time, Lew. Nothing in it but some painting equipment and shaving kit and some old clothes. He was hungry."

The great front room was furnished with handsome rustic pieces, Navajo rugs, animal skins, animal heads staring down at us with sad glass eyes. The picture window that Harriet had described to Campion framed blue sky and blue lake. Her pitch had been too successful, I was thinking.

We went through the other rooms, including the six upstairs bedrooms. Their mattresses lay bare. A closet in the hallway was full of sheets and pillow slips and towels, none of which had been used.

I left Arnie and Hanna in the house and went down the concrete steps to the shore. The lake had been pulling at me since my first sight of it. It was very low this year, and a swath of gravel sloped down from the foot of the steps.

I took a walk along the edge of the gravel. Speedboat waves lapped at the stones and brightened them. I was looking for some trace of Harriet; yet I was shocked when I found it. It was something that looked like a scrap of grey fishnet tangled with some floating sticks about fifty feet offshore.

I stripped to my shorts behind a tree and went in after it. The lake was icy after the summer air. The thing in the nest of sticks did nothing to warm me. It was her hat, with its little veil fluttering in the sun.

I disentangled it and held it out of the water in my left hand as I side-stroked back to shore. There I discovered that the hat had more than the veil attached to it. In the damp silk lining there was a smear of coagulated blood about the size of a thumbnail. Adhering to this was a thin lock of hair about six inches long. It was fair and straight, like Harriet's, and it had been torn out by the roots.

I dressed and went up to the lodge on cold and heavy legs and showed the other men what I had found.

Arnie whistled softly, on a diminuendo. "Looks like we're too late."

"That remains to be proved. How good is the law around here?"

"Spotty. It's been improving, but there's six or seven different jurisdictions around the lake. It spreads the money thin, and also the responsibility."

"Can you bring the Reno P.D. in on this? It needs lab work."

"And a dragging operation. It's not their territory, but I'll see what I can do. You want to come back to town with me?"

"I should talk to Sholto. Does he live in this neighborhood?"

"A couple of miles from here, on the road to State Line. I'll drop you."

Sholto's boxlike little house stood in a clearing far back from the road. Chickens scratched around it. The young woman who answered the door had a baby on her hip and a slightly larger child hanging onto her skirt. She pushed back her hair and gave Arnie a wide slack smile.

"Hank is out back, Mr. Walters. He's building a hutch for the rabbits. Come through the house if you want."

A third child, a girl of eight or nine, was reading a comic book at the kitchen table, simultaneously drinking chocolate milk through a straw. Her bare toes were curled with concentrated pleasure. She regarded us blankly, as though we were less vivid than the characters in her book. I paid particular attention to the child because her towhead was the same color as Harriet's.

A boy of twelve or so was helping his father in the back yard. That is, he sat on a board laid across wooden horses while Sholto used a handsaw on the board. He was a wiry man of indeterminate age, hipless in faded blue levis. His sun wrinkles gave his jay-blue eyes a fiercely questioning look.

"Hi, Mr. Walters. You find her all right?"

"Not yet. This is my associate Lew Archer. He has some more questions to ask you."

Sholto laid down his saw and gave me a wide hard hand. "Shoot away."

"Before you men talk," Arnie said, "I want to show you a picture, Henry."

He produced the self-sketch of Campion which he had

brought from the car. "Is this the man you saw with Harriet?"

"Sure looks like him. Something funny about the eyes, though. How come one of 'em is bigger than the other?"

"He drew it that way," I said.

"He drew this himself?"

"That's right."

"Why did he do that to the eyes? It makes him look cock-eyed. He's a real nice-lookin' fellow in real life."

Arnie lifted the picture from his hands. "Thanks, Henry. I needed a positive identification."

"Is the guy some kind of a crook?"

"He has a record," I said. "Maybe you'd better send the boy inside."

"I don't wanna go inside."

"Inside," Sholto said.

The boy climbed off his board and went. Arnie followed him into the house, with a curt flick of the hand to us. Sholto said to me: "I hope Miss Blackwell isn't in trouble. She's a nervous young lady, jumpy as a filly. She wouldn't take trouble too well."

"Was she nervous last night when you talked to her?"

He propped one foot up on a sawhorse and rested his arm on his knee. "I'd say she was. Mostly I think she was nervous on account of her father—you know, the young fellow, and them using the lodge. But she had a perfect right—I told Mr. Walters that. And I told her I wouldn't breathe a word to the old man. After all, she's used it before when he wasn't here."

"With men?"

"I dunno about that. This is the first man she ever brought up here, leastways that I saw. What did the two of them have in mind?"

"They talked about getting married."

"Is that a fact?"

"You sound surprised."

"It's just that I never thought of her as the marrying type. I got a sister teaches school in Porterville, she's the same way. She's still living at home."

"Miss Blackwell isn't. How were the two of them getting along when you saw them?"

"I didn't see them together. She came up to the door by herself, wanting the key to the lodge. He stayed in the car." Sholto pushed back his cap and scratched his freckled hairline, as though to promote the growth of an idea. "They did sit out in the car for quite a while after. The wife thought they were having an argument."

"Did you hear any of it?"

"I didn't like to listen," he said delicately. "Besides, I had the radio on."

"Did your wife hear any of it?"

"She must of, or how would she know it was an argument?" He raised his voice: "Molly!"

The woman appeared at the back door with the baby on her hip. From the cover of her other hip, the twelve-year-old peered out resentfully.

"What is it, Hank?"

"Last night, when Miss Blackwell came for the key, and they were sitting out in the car after—did you hear anything they said?"

"Yeah. I told you they were having a battle."

I moved to the foot of the back steps. "Did he hit her?"

"Not that I saw. It was just talk. She didn't want to go to the lodge. He did."

"*She* didn't want to go?"

"That's what she said. She said he was trying to use her or something, said he was taking advantage of her love. He said he wasn't. He said that he was working out his des—destry?"

"Destiny?"

"Yeah, destiny. He said he was working out his destiny or

something. I dunno what he meant when he said that. They were talkin' pretty high-falutin'."

"How did his voice sound? Was he excited?"

"Naw, he was real cool and cold. She was more hysterical like."

"Did he threaten her, Mrs. Sholto?"

"I wouldn't say he threatened her. More like he soothed her down. She was okay when they drove off."

"Who was driving?"

"He was. She was at the wheel when they were sitting there, but he changed places with her. He did the driving."

"What time did they leave?"

"I dunno. The clock broke. When are you going to get me a new clock, Hank?"

"Saturday."

"I bet," she said serenely, and retreated into the house.

Sholto turned to me. "It was twilight when they left here, nearly night, I'd say around eight o'clock. I didn't know there was nothin' wrong or I'd of phoned her father. You think the guy did something to her, eh?"

"We have some evidence that points that way. Was Miss Blackwell wearing a hat when you saw her last night?"

"Yeah, a little hat with a veil. I noticed it because the girls don't go in for hats around here much."

"I found her hat in the lake just now," I said. "With blood and hair on it."

His eyes went almost out of sight in their twin nests of wrinkles.

"The man she was with, Campion, is implicated in two other murders. One was his wife. Her maiden name was Dolly Stone, and she's supposed to have spent some time here last summer. Did you ever hear of a Dolly Stone, or Dolly Campion?"

"No, sir. No siree."

"What about Q. R. Simpson?"

"Come again."

"Quincy Ralph Simpson. His wife told me he was up here a couple of months ago."

"Yeah," he said matter-of-factly, "I knew Ralph. He worked for the Blackwells for a little while, in May I think it was. The Colonel opened the lodge early this year, in April. He told me he wanted to give his new little wife a chance to watch the spring come on." He paused, and glanced at the declining sun as though to reorient himself in the present day. "Did something happen to Ralph Simpson?"

"He's the other murder victim. We don't know for certain that Campion was responsible. The chances are he was. What sort of work was Simpson doing for the Blackwells?"

"Chief cook and bottlewasher, while he lasted. He didn't last long."

"Why not?"

Sholto kicked at one of the sawhorses. "I don't like to pass it on about a dead man. There was talk around that Ralph took something. I didn't put much stock in it myself. Ralph may have been a gamblin' fool, but that don't make him no thief."

"He was a gambler?"

"Yeah, he can't stay away from the tables. It was my belief he gambled away his money and got stuck here and had to take any job he could get. He must of had some reason for hiring himself out for a cook—a young fellow with his brains. Now you tell me he's dead," he said with some resentment.

"Did you know him well, Mr. Sholto?"

"We shot the breeze a couple of times when I was doing repair work at the lodge. The kitchen linoleum buckled, and I had to piece it. Ralph Simpson was a likable fellow, full of ideas."

"What kind of ideas?"

"All kinds. Man in space, the atom bomb, he had an opinion on everything. Reincarnation and the hereafter. He had a great understanding. Also, he had a system to beat the tables, for which he was trying to raise the capital."

"How?"

"He didn't say."

"What is he supposed to have stolen from the Blackwells?"

"I dunno. I never got it straight."

"Who did you hear it from?"

"Kito. He's houseboy in one of the other lodges. But you can't always trust these Orientals."

"Still I'd like to talk to Kito."

"He isn't around any more. The family closed the place up last month and went back to Frisco."

"Do you know their address in Frisco?"

"I have it written down in the house."

"Get it for me, will you?"

He went in and came out with a Belvedere address written in childish longhand on the back of an envelope. I transcribed it in my notebook.

"Is there anything else you can tell me about Simpson?"

"I can't think of anything."

"Or anyone else who can?"

"Well, he did have a girl friend. It wouldn't be fair to pass that on to his wife. Matter of fact, he never mentioned a wife. I thought he was a single man."

"It hardly matters now," I said, with my ball-point poised over the open notebook. "What's the girl friend's name?"

"He called her Fawn. I don't rightly know her last name. I saw her a couple of times in the clubs with Ralph, and once or twice since." He added, with a rueful glance at the house: "I don't go there to gamble. I can't afford to gamble, with my family. But I like to stand around and watch the excitement."

"Can you describe the girl?"

"She's a pretty little thing. She looks something like a real fawn—she has those big brown eyes."

"What color hair?"

"Light blonde, palomino color."

That didn't make it easier. Palomino fillies browsed in herds on the Tahoe shores.

"You say she's little?"

"Yeah, about five foot two or three." He held out a hand at shoulder level. "I call that little in a woman."

"What does she do for a living?"

"I dunno where she works, or if she works. She may not even be here any more. We have a floating population. They drift in and out. I been here for years myself, come here from Porterville when State Line was nothin' more than a wide place in the road."

"When did you last see Fawn?"

"A couple weeks ago, I *think* it was at the Solitaire. She had some older fellow on the string and they were playing the machines, leastways *she* was. He kept buying silver dollars for her. Yeah, I'm pretty certain it was the Solitaire."

chapter 16

SHOLTO DEPOSITED ME in front of the club and bumped away in his pickup. The main street of State Line was an unstable blend of small-time frontier settlement and big-time carnival. The lake seemed artificial seen from here: a man-made lake dyed a special shade of blue and surrounded by papier-mâché mountains. In this setting it was hard to believe in death, and life itself was denatured.

I went inside the club, where the late afternoon crowd were enjoying themselves, if gamblers can be said to enjoy themselves. They wheedled cards or dice like sinners praying to heaven for one small mercy. They pulled convulsively at the handles of one-armed bandits, as if the machines were computers that would answer all their questions. Am I getting old?

Have I failed? Am I immature? Does she love me? Why does he hate me? Hit me, jackpot, flood me with life and liberty and happiness.

A number of men and a few women were hanging around the bar. I waited my turn with one of the overworked bartenders and asked him where the security officer was.

"I saw Mr. Todd on the floor a minute ago." He scanned the big room. "There he is, talking to the character in the hat."

I made my way down one of the aisles of slot machines. Todd was an athletic-looking man in an open-necked shirt. He had iron-grey hair, iron-grey eyes, a face that had been humanized by punishment. The other man, who wore a white Stetson with a rolled brim, was drunk and fat and furious. He had been robbed, the machines were fixed, he'd see the management, invoke his influence with the governor.

With gentle firmness Todd steered him to the front door. I stepped out after Todd, away from the din of the gamblers, and showed him my photostat. He smiled as he handed it back.

"I used to be with the California Highway Patrol. Looking for somebody?"

"Several people." I gave him full descriptions of Campion and Harriet.

"I don't believe I've seen 'em, at least not together. I can't be certain. The turnover in this place is something for the book. Sometimes I think it's the bottleneck where the whole country passes through sooner or later." His eyes were on the drunk, who was weaving across the street through light traffic.

"Try something easier," I said. "A girl named Fawn something. She's a small girl with beautiful brown eyes, I'm told, pale blonde hair. Fawn has been seen in your place."

Todd said with more interest: "What do you want with her?"

"I have some questions to ask her. She knew a man who was murdered in California."

"She involved?"

"I have no reason to think so."

"That's good. She's a nice kid."

"You know her, do you?"

"Sure. She's in and out. Her last name's King, I think, if she hasn't remarried."

"Has she been in today?"

"Not yet. She probably sleeps in the daytime."

"Where?"

"I don't know her that well. She used to work in the beauty parlor down the street. Try there. You'll see it on the left a couple of blocks from here."

He pointed west toward California. I went that way, past gambling houses that resembled supermarkets with nothing to sell. The first effects of night were coming on. Though everything was clearly visible, the fronts of the buildings were stark in their nakedness, as if the light had lost its supportive quality.

Marie's Salon de Paris was closed. I knocked on the glass door. After a while a large woman emerged from a room at the back and minced toward me through the twilit shop.

She turned on a light before she opened the door. Her hair was the color of a spectacular sunset, and she wore it low on her forehead in curled bangs, a dubious advertisement for her trade. Warm air smelling of chemicals and women drifted out past her.

"I'm looking for a woman named Fawn King."

"You're not the first. I hope you'll be the last. Mrs. King doesn't work here any more."

"Where can I put my hands on her?"

It was a bad choice of expression. Her pouched eyes went over me coldly, including my hands. I tried again: "I happen to be a detective—"

"She in trouble?" Marie said hopefully.

"A friend of hers is in the worst kind of trouble. He's dead. Stabbed with an icepick."

She brightened up alarmingly. "Why didn't you say so? Come in. I'll get you King's address."

Fawn lived in an apartment house a mile or so west on the same road. I started to walk, but on the way I noticed a U-drive sign at a gas station. I rented a new-looking Ford that sounded elderly. The attendant said it was the altitude.

The apartment house had a temporary atmosphere, like a motel. It was U-shaped and two-storied. The U enclosed the tenants' parking lot, with its open end facing the street. I drove in and left the Ford in one of the white-marked slots.

Fawn's apartment was number twenty-seven on the second floor. I went up the outside steps and along the railed gallery till I found her door. There was music behind it, the sound of a woman singing a blues. It wasn't quite good enough to be a record, and there was no accompaniment.

The song broke off when I knocked. She appeared at the door, her face still softened by music. Her brown eyes held a puzzled innocence. Perhaps she was puzzled by her body and its uses. It was full and tender under her sweater, like fruit that has ripened too quickly. She held it for me to look at and said in a semiprofessional voice: "Hello. I was just practicing my blues style."

"I heard. You have a nice voice."

"So they all tell me. The trouble is, the competition here is terrif. They bring in recording stars, and it isn't fair to the local talent."

"You're a local girl?"

"This is my third season. My third fabulous season. Which makes me an old-timer."

"And you want to be a singer?"

"Anything," she said. "Anything to get out of the rat race. Do you have any suggestions?"

My usual line was ready, the one I used on aspiring starlets and fledgling nightingales and girls who hoped to model their way into heaven: I was from Hollywood, knew movie people, could help. Her puzzled innocence stopped me.

"Just keep trying."

She regarded me suspiciously, as though I had flubbed my cue. "Did somebody send you?"

"Ralph Simpson."

"What do you know? I haven't heard from Ralph for it must be at least two months." She stepped aside in a quick dancer's movement. "Come in, tell me about him."

It was a hot-plate apartment containing a studio bed that hadn't been made, an open portable record player, a dressing table loaded with cosmetic jars and bottles and a few paperbacked novels with young women like Fawn portrayed on their covers. The calendar on the wall hadn't been changed since April.

I sat on the studio bed. "When did you last hear from Ralph?"

"Couple of months, like I said. He spent the night with me," she went on routinely, "it must of been sometime around the middle of May. That was when he lost his job and didn't have no place—any place to go. I lent him bus fare in the morning, haven't seen him since."

"He must be a good friend of yours."

"Not in the way you think. It's a brother-and-sister act between Ralph and me. We batted around together ever since we were kids in South San Francisco. He was like a big brother to me. Anyway, I wouldn't take a married man away from his wife."

But she posed in front of me as if she was testing out her power to do this.

"I'm not married," I said.

"I was wondering." She sat on the bed beside me, so close I could feel her heat. "You don't talk like a married man and you don't look like a bachelor."

"I had a wife at one time. She looked something like you."

"What was her name?"

"I forget." There was too much pain in the word, and this was no place to deposit it.

"I don't believe you. What happened to your wife?" Her brown eyes were attentive on my face. You'd have thought I was about to tell her fortune.

"Nothing bad happened to her. She left me, but that wasn't bad for her. It was bad for me. Eventually she married somebody else and had some kids and lived happily ever after."

She nodded, as if the story's happy ending might somehow apply to her. "She left you on account of another woman, I bet."

"You'd lose your bet. I treated her badly, but not in that way." The pain stirred like a Santa Ana wind in the desert back reaches of my mind. I'd begun to talk to the girl because she was there. Now I was there, too, more completely than I wanted to be. "Also," I said, "she didn't like my trade. At the moment I'm not too crazy about it myself."

"I wouldn't care what a man did for a living. My ex was just a bookie, but I didn't care. What do you do for a living?"

"I'm a detective."

"How interesting." But her body tensed, and her eyes glazed with distrust.

"Relax," I said. "If I was the kind of detective you're afraid of, I wouldn't be telling you about it, would I?"

"I'm not afraid."

"Good. You have no reason. I'm a private detective from Los Angeles."

"Ralph is interested in that kind of work, too. Is that how you know him?"

"In a way. Let's talk about Ralph. Can you tell me anything about that job he lost?"

"He was a houseboy, more or less. He took jobs like that

when he couldn't get anything else. He worked for a mucky-muck up the lake. He showed me the house one night when the family was out. It was quite a layout."

"I've seen the Blackwell place."

"Blackwell. That was the name."

"How long did Ralph work for the Blackwells?"

"A week or so. I didn't keep tabs on him." She smiled in her puzzled way. "I have enough trouble keeping tabs on myself."

"Why did they fire him?"

"He didn't tell *me* he was fired. He said he quit because he had what he wanted. Anyway, the family was going back down south."

"I don't understand."

"They closed the lodge and went back to L.A. or wherever they live. Ralph thought they were going to stay longer, but they changed their minds."

"I mean I don't understand about Ralph getting what he wanted."

"Neither do I. You know Ralph, he likes to act mysterious. Ralph Simpson, boy detective. It's kind of cute."

"Was Ralph doing some sort of detective work at the Blackwell place?"

"So he said. I don't always buy a hundred per cent of what Ralph says. He goes to a lot of movies and sometimes he gets them mixed up with the things he does himself." She added, with an indulgent glance at the paperbacks on the dressing table: "I do the same thing with stories sometimes. It makes life more exciting."

I brought her back to the subject: "Tell me what Ralph said."

"I couldn't—my memory isn't that good. The way he talked, it was all mixed up with the tragedy that happened to Dolly. That hit Ralph hard. He was very fond of Dolly."

"Are you talking about the Dolly who married Bruce Campion?"

The force of the question pushed her off the bed away from me. She went to the far side of the room, which wasn't very far, and stood beside the dressing table in a defensive posture.

"You don't have to shout at a girl. I have neighbors, remember. The management's always breathing down my back."

"I'm sorry, Fawn. The question is important."

"I bet you're working on Dolly's murder, aren't you?"

"Yes. Was Ralph?"

"I guess he thought he was. But Ralph is no great operator. It's time somebody with something on the ball did something. Dolly was a sweet kid. She didn't deserve to die."

She looked up at the low ceiling, as if Dolly's epitaph was also a prayer for herself. Tentatively, almost unconsciously, she drifted back across the room, stood over me with eyes like brimming pools.

"It's a terrible world."

"There are terrible people in it, anyway. Do you know Bruce Campion?"

"I wouldn't say I *know* him. Ralph took me out to their place once, when Dolly was living with him. *She* was crazy about him at that time. She followed him around like a little poodle."

"How did Campion treat her?"

"All right. Actually he didn't pay too much attention to her. I think he kept her around because he needed a model. He wanted me to model for him, too. I told him I hadn't sunk that low yet, to pose for dirty pictures."

"He painted dirty pictures?"

"It sounded like it to me. Dolly said he made her take her clothes off." Her nostrils flared with righteous indignation. "I only know one good reason a girl should uncover herself in front of a man."

"Why did Campion marry her if all he wanted was a model?"

"Oh, he wanted more. They always do. Anyway, he had to marry her. He got her pregnant."

"Did Dolly tell you this?"

"She didn't have to tell me. I could see it already when Ralph and I were out there."

"Do you remember when that was?"

"It was along toward the end of last summer, late August or early September. They weren't married yet, but they were talking about it, at least she was. Ralph brought along a bottle, and we drank a toast to their happiness. It didn't do much good, did it? She's dead, and he's on the run." She touched my shoulder. "Did he really kill her?"

"All the evidence seems to point to him."

"Ralph said that isn't so. He said there was other evidence, but the cops held back on it. He may have been telling the truth, or having one of his movie spells. You never can tell about Ralph, 'specially where one of his friends is concerned." She drew a deep breath.

"When did Ralph say these things to you?"

Using her hand on my shoulder as a pivot, she sat down beside me. "The last night he was here. We sat up talking, after I got in."

"Did he tell you what the other evidence was?"

"No. He kept his lips buttoned. The man of mystery."

"Did he show you anything?"

"No."

"What did he have with him when he left here?"

"Just the clothes that he stood up in. When he came up here he wasn't planning to stay, but then he got this job." She hesitated. "I almost forgot the bundle. He dropped this bundle off with me a day or two before his job folded. I wasn't supposed to open it, he said. I *felt* it, though. It felt like it had clothes in it."

"What kind of clothes?"

"I wouldn't know. It was a great big bundle." She opened her arms. "I tried to ask Ralph about it, but he wasn't talking."

"Was it stolen goods, do you think?"

She shook her head. "Of course not. Ralph's no thief."

"What sort of a man is he?"

"I thought you knew him."

"Not as well as you do."

She answered after a little thought: "I *like* Ralph. I don't want to criticize him. He has a lot of good ideas. The trouble is, he never follows through on them. He keeps changing, because he can't make up his mind what he wants to be. I can remember, when we were kids, Ralph was always talking about how he was going to be a big criminal lawyer. But then he never even made it through high school. It's been like that all his life."

"How long has he known Campion?"

"It goes 'way back," she said. "Ten years or more. I think they were Army buddies in Korea. They did some talking about Korea the day Ralph took me out to the cabin."

"I'm interested in that cabin. Do you think you could find it again?"

"Now?"

"Now."

She looked at the leatherette-covered traveling clock on the dressing table. "I have a date. He's due here any time."

"Stand him up."

"I got rent to pay, mister. Anyway, you won't find Bruce Campion there. He only had the cabin for a while last summer. Somebody lent him the use of it."

"I still want to see it."

"Tomorrow. Buy me brunch tomorrow, and I'll show you where it is. It's real wild on that side of the lake. Buy some sandwiches and we'll have a picnic."

"I like night picnics."

"But I have a date."

"How much do you expect to make out of him?"

She frowned. "I don't think of it that way. They give me money to gamble, that's their business. Nobody says I have to throw it all away."

"I'm asking you how much a couple of hours of your time is worth."

She blinked her innocent eyes. "Twenty?" she said. "And dinner?"

We set out in the rented Ford, along a road which branched north off the highway through thickening timber. Above the broken dark lines of the trees there were almost as many stars as I had seen in Mexico. The night was turning colder, and the girl moved over against me.

"Turn on the heater, will you, mister? I don't even know your name."

"Lew Archer." I switched on the blower.

"That's a nice name. Is it your real one?"

"Naturally not. My real name is Natty Bumpo."

"You're kidding me."

"It's a free country."

"Is there any such person as Natty What'shisname?"

"Bumpo. He's a character in a book. He was a great rifle-man and a great tracker."

"Are you?"

"I can shoot a rifle but as for tracking, I do my best work in cities."

"Tracking men?"

"Tracking men."

She huddled closer. "Do you have a gun?"

"Several, but not with me. I wish I had."

"Do you think that Campion is hiding out in the cabin?"

"He may be, and he may be dangerous."

She giggled nervously. "You're trying to scare me. I thought he was kind of a sissy, with that little beret he wears, and all his arty talk."

"He's no sissy. He's something more complicated than that."

"How do you mean?"

"It's time I told you, Fawn. Dolly isn't the only one who was killed. Ralph Simpson was icepicked last May, soon after you saw him last. Campion is the prime suspect."

She had drawn in her breath sharply, and now she was holding it. I could feel her body tighten against my flank. Her breath came out in gusts around her words.

"You must be mistaken. Maybe Bruce Campion did kill Dolly—you never can tell what a man will do to his wife. But he would never do anything like that to Ralph. Ralph idolized him, he thought he was the greatest."

"How did Campion feel about Ralph?"

"He *liked* him. They got along fine. Ralph was proud to have a real artist for a friend. It was one of the things he wanted to be himself."

"I've known a few artists. They can make difficult friends."

"But they don't stick icepicks in people." For the first time, the full meaning of what I had said struck the girl. I could feel it pass through her body, a shuddering aftershock. "Is Ralph really dead?"

"I saw him in the morgue. I'm sorry, Fawn."

"Poor Ralph. Now he'll never make it."

We rode in silence for a time. She began to cry, almost inaudibly. At one point she said to the moving darkness: "All my friends are dying off. I feel like an old woman."

I had starred glimpses of the lake between the trees, like polished steel catching the droppings of infinity.

I said when her grief had subsided: "Tell me more about Dolly."

"What's to tell?" Her voice was hoarse. "She came up here last spring to get a job. She made change at one of the clubs for a while, but her subtraction wasn't too hot, so she got herself a man. It's the same old story."

"This time the ending was different. Did you know her well?"

"There wasn't much to know. She was just a country girl from the sticks. I sort of befriended her when she lost her job. Then Ralph introduced her to Campion, and that was that."

"You said Ralph had a crush on her."

"I wouldn't put it that strong. Dolly was a beautiful kid, but he never made a play for her. He just wanted to look after her. She was pretty helpless. She didn't belong up here."

"Where did she belong?"

"Let's see, she told me once where she came from. It was some place down in the orange belt. She used to talk about the orange blossoms."

"Citrus Junction?"

"Yeah. How did you know?"

"Ralph was murdered in Citrus Junction."

chapter 17

THE CABIN STOOD on a wooded point which projected into the lake below the road. I left the car at the top of the lane and told Fawn to stay in it, out of sight. She crouched down in the front seat, peering like a frightened bush-bunny over the edge of the door.

I made my way down the rutted dirt lane, walking quietly, like Natty Bumpo. Starshine filtering down between the black conifers hung in the air like the ghost of light. A ramp of solider light slanted from the window of the cabin.

I approached it from the side and looked in. A man who wasn't Campion was standing in front of the stone fireplace, in which a low fire burned. He was talking to somebody or something.

"Eat it up, Angelo. Enjoy yourself. We've got to keep your weight up, old boy."

Unless there was someone in the shadowed bunks against

the far wall, he seemed to be alone in the room. He was a
small man with a dark head and a thin neck like a boy's. He
wore a plaid shirt under a sleeveless red vest.

I saw when he moved that he was holding a young hawk,
perched on the knuckles of his gauntleted left hand. The
brown bird was tearing with its beak at something red held between the man's thumb and forefinger.

"Gorge yourself," he said indulgently. "Daddy wants you to
be a big, healthy boy."

I waited until the bird had finished his red meal. Then I
knocked on the door. The small man unlatched it and looked
out curiously through rimless spectacles. The hawk's flecked
golden eyes were impassive. I was just another human being.

"I'm sorry to trouble you," I said to both of them. "I was told
a man named Bruce Campion lived here at one time."

His eyes hardened perceptibly behind the glasses. He said
in a careful, cultivated voice: "That's true enough. Last summer before I went to Europe I lent Campion the use of my
place. He spent August and part of September here, he told
me. Then he got married and moved out."

"Do you know what happened to him after that?"

"No. I've been on my sabbatical, and rather completely out
of touch with my friends in this country. I spent the entire
year in Europe and the Near East."

"Campion is a friend of yours?"

"I admire his talent." He was weighing out his words. "I try
to be useful to talent when I can."

"Have you seen Campion recently?"

The question seemed to disturb him. He looked sideways at
the hawk perched on his upright fist, as if the bird might provide an answer or an augury. The bird sat unblinking, its
great eyes bright and calm.

"I don't wish to be rude," the bird man said. "But I'd certainly feel more comfortable if I knew you had authority to
ask me questions."

"I'm a private detective co-operating with several law-enforcement agencies." I gave him my name.

"Co-operating in what?"

"The investigation of a pair of murders, possibly three murders."

He swallowed and grew pale, as though he had swallowed the blood out of his face. "In that case, come in. Don't mind Michelangelo. He's completely indifferent to people."

But the hawk jumped straight up when I entered the room. Held by the leather jesses on its legs, it hung in the air for a moment beating its wings and fanning wind into my face. Then its master thrust his fist up, and the bird returned to its perch.

We sat facing each other with the bird between us.

"I'm Dr. Damis," he said. "Edmund B. Damis. I teach at Berkeley, in the art department." He seemed to be marshaling his professional defenses.

"Is that how you happen to know Campion?"

"I met him some years ago, in Chicago. I was a docent at the Art Institute while he was studying there. I admired his painting, as I said, and I've kept in touch with him. Or rather he has kept in touch with me."

It was a cold account. He was preserving his distance from Campion.

"He's a good painter, I've heard. Is he a good man?"

"I wouldn't care to pass judgment on him. He lives as he can. I took the easy way, myself."

"I'm afraid I don't understand."

"I teach for a living and do my painting, such as it is, on Sundays and on sabbaticals. Campion lives for his work. He cares for nothing else," he said with some feeling.

"You sound almost as though you envied him."

"I almost do."

"It may be a two-way envy, Dr. Damis. Is your middle name Burke, by any chance?"

"It is. My father was an admirer of Edmund Burke."

"Did you know that Campion's been using part of your name as an alias? He's been calling himself Burke Damis."

He flushed with displeasure. "Blast him, I wish he'd leave me and my things alone."

"Has he been at your things?"

"I mean this place. He left it like a pigsty when he moved out last fall. I had to spend most of the last week cleaning it up. Frankly, I've had enough of Bruce and his messy life and his *outré* relationships."

"Are you thinking of his relationships with women?"

"I was, yes. We won't go into them. I've long since given up trying to purge those Augean stables."

"I wish you would go into them."

"I prefer not to. They're excessively boring to me. They invariably follow the same sado-masochistic pattern. Bruce has always regarded women as his legitimate prey."

"Prey is quite a dramatic word. It reminds me of your hawk."

He nodded, as though I'd paid them both a subtle compliment. The hawk sat still as a figurine on his hand. It occurred to me that this Damis might be attached to Campion and the hawk in similar ways, watching through rimless spectacles as the two predators vaulted into space and took their pleasure.

"It brings up the fact," I went on, "that Campion's wife was strangled two months ago. Campion is wanted for the murder. Did you know that, Dr. Damis?"

"I most assuredly did not. I just flew in from Italy last week, and I came directly here." He was pale as bone now, and almost chattering. "I've been utterly out of touch with everyone and everything."

"But you've been in touch with Campion."

"How do you know that?"

"Call it intuition. You'd talk about him differently if you

hadn't seen him for a year. Now when and where did you see him?"

"This morning," he said with his eyes on the floor. "Bruce came here this morning. He'd walked halfway around the lake during the night, and he looked perfectly ghastly."

"What did he come to you for?"

"Refuge, I suppose. He admitted that he was in trouble, but he didn't say what kind, and I swear he said nothing about his wife. He wanted to stay here with me. I didn't see that it was possible, or that I owed it to him. He's always been the taker and I've been the giver, as it is. Besides, I've reached a crucial stage in training my hawk." He smoothed the long feathers of its tail.

"When did he leave here?"

"Around noon. I gave him lunch. Naturally I had no idea that I was harboring a fugitive from justice."

"How did he leave?"

"He took my car," Damis said miserably.

"By force?"

"I wouldn't say that. He is bigger than I am, and more— forceful." He had dropped his pride, and he looked very young without it. "Bruce has an ascendancy over me. I suppose you're quite right, I've secretly envied his life, his success with women—"

"You can stop doing that now. Will you please describe your car—make and model?"

"It's a 1959 Chevrolet convertible, red, with a checkered red and black top. California license number TKU 37964." As I was making a note of the number, he added: "Bruce promised I'd have it back within twenty-four hours. He knows I'm stuck out here without transportation."

"I imagine he couldn't care less. I'll see what I can do about getting it back for you. Do you want me to report it as a theft?"

"It wasn't a theft. I was a fool to do it, but I lent it to him voluntarily."

"Did he explain why he wanted the car, or where he was going with it?"

"No." He hesitated. "On second thought, he did give some indication of where he intended to go. He originally proposed that when he was finished with the convertible, he should leave it in Berkeley, in my garage. It certainly suggests that he was headed in that direction."

"And he was alone when he came here and when he left?"

"Oh yes, definitely."

"Did Campion say anything about the girl he'd been with?"

"He didn't mention a girl. As a matter of fact, he did very little talking. Who is she?"

"She is, or was, a tall blonde girl named Harriet Blackwell."

"I never heard of her, I'm afraid. Has something happened to her?"

"The indications are that she's in the lake."

He was shocked, and his feeling communicated itself to the bird on his fist. The hawk spread its wings. Damis calmed it with his hand before he spoke.

"You can't mean that Bruce drowned her?"

"Something like that. When he came here this morning, were there any signs that he'd been in a struggle? Scratch marks on his face, for instance?"

"Yes, his face *was* scratched. His clothes were in bad shape, too."

"Were they wet?"

"They looked as though they had been wet. He looked generally as though he'd had a rough night."

"He's in for rougher ones," I said. "Just in case he does come back this way, we'll want to station a man here. Is it all right with you?"

"I'd welcome it. I'm no more of a physical coward than the

next person, but—" His apprehensive look completed the sentence.

"It's unlikely that he will come back," I told him reassuringly. "Assuming he doesn't, I'd like to have your ideas on where to look for him. Also, I want your Berkeley address, in case he follows through on his original plan."

"Couldn't we skip the Berkeley address? My mother lives there with me, and I don't wish her to be alarmed unnecessarily. I'm sure that she's in no danger from him."

"Does she know Campion?"

"Very slightly. Minimally. We had him to dinner, once, a couple of years ago. Mother didn't like him at all—she said he had a dark aura. At that time, though Mother didn't know it, he was living with some black-stockinged tramp in Sausalito. He'd previously lived in Carmel, Santa Barbara, San Diego, Los Angeles, and probably a number of other places. I wouldn't know where to start looking for him. Unless," he added after some thought, "he's gone to his sister."

"Campion has a sister?"

"He has, but it's far from likely that he's with her. She's a very stuffy Peninsula type, he told me. They don't get along."

"Where does she live on the Peninsula, and what's her name?"

"I'd have to look it up. I've never met the woman. I only happen to have her address because Campion used it as a mailing address when he was moving around."

Carrying the hawk with him, Damis went to a table in the corner of the room. He opened a drawer and got out a shabby brown leather address book. I stood beside him as he flipped the pages to the C's.

Bruce Campion was the first name on the page. Scribbled under and around it were addresses in the various cities Damis had mentioned. They were all scratched out except for a Menlo Park address—c/o Mrs. Thor Jurgensen, 401 Schoolhouse Road—which I made a note of.

"I used to think we were good friends," Damis was saying. His eyes were fixed on the hawk, as though it was feeding him his lines by mental telepathy. "But over the years I caught on to the pattern of our relationship. I heard from Bruce only when he wanted something—a loan or a recommendation or the use of something I owned. I'm heartily sick of the man. I hope I never see him again."

I made no comment. He said to the hawk: "Are you hungry, Angelo? How about another sparrow wing?"

I left him communing with the silent bird and drove Fawn into State Line. We had *filets mignons,* carelessly served in one of the gambling clubs. The fat drunk in the white Stetson was balanced precariously on a stool at the bar. He seemed to have shifted gears under his load. His imperfectly focused eyes were watching the girls in the place, especially Fawn.

She had some wine with her meat, and it set her talking about Ralph again. He used to take her fishing at Luna Bay when she was in her early teens and he was in his late ones. Once he rescued her from the San Gregorio surf. Her memories had a dreamlike quality, and I began to wonder if she had dreamed them in the first place. But she ended by saying: "I can't take your twenty dollars. It's the least I can do for Ralph."

"You might as well take it—"

"No. There has to be something I won't do for money. I mean it."

"You're a good girl."

"He said as she lifted his wallet. The hustler with the heart of gold—cold and yellow."

"You're being hard on yourself, Fawn."

"And don't keep calling me Fawn. It isn't my name."

"What do you want me to call you?"

"Don't call me anything."

"Tell me your real name."

"I hate my real name." Her face was as blank as a wall.

"What is it, though?"

"Mabel," she said with disgust. "My parents had to give me the most unglamorous name in the world."

"Where are your parents, by the way?"

"I put them out for adoption."

"Before or after you changed your name to Fawn?"

"If you have to know," she said, "I changed my name the night King went AWOL on me and left me in this hole. The funny thing is, I'm getting sick of calling myself Fawn. I used to think it was glamorous, but now it just sounds like nothing. I'm getting ready to change my name again. Do you have any suggestions?"

"Not on the spur of the moment."

She leaned toward me, smiling intensely and nudging the edge of the table with her papillae. "Let's go to my place and have another drink and talk about it."

"Thanks, but I have work to do."

"It can wait, can't it? I stood up my date for you."

"Also, you're too young for me."

"I don't get it," she said with her puzzled frown. "You're not *old.*"

"I'm getting older fast." I rose and laid some money on the table. "Do you want me to drop you anywhere?"

"I'll stay here. It's as good a place as any."

Before I reached the door, the drunk was moving in on her with his white Stetson in his hand and his bald head glowing.

chapter **18**

I FOUND A telephone booth and called Arnie Walters's office in Reno. He answered the telephone himself.

"Walters here."

"This is Lew Archer. I have some information on Campion's movements. He's driving a red Chevvie convertible—"

"We know that." Arnie's voice was low and fast. "Campion's been seen in Saline City, talking to the key boy of one of the local motels. A patrol cop made him but he didn't pick him up right away. He wanted to check with our bulletin, and he had an idea that Campion was checking in. But when he got back to the motel, Campion had cleared out. This happened within the last couple of hours. Do you have later information?"

"You're 'way ahead of me. Did you get the name of the motel?"

"The Travelers, in Saline City. It's a town in the East Bay."

"What about Harriet?"

"Nothing so far. We're starting dragging operations in the morning. The police lab established that the blood in the hat is her type, B, but that doesn't mean much."

"How do you know her blood type?"

"I called her father," Arnie said. "He wanted to come up here, but I think I talked him out of it. If this case doesn't break pretty soon, he's going to blow a gasket."

"So am I."

By midnight I was in Saline City looking for the Travelers Motel. It was on the west side of town at the edge of the salt flats. Red neon outlined its stucco façade and failed to mask its shabbiness.

There was nobody in the cluttered little front office. I rang the handbell on the registration desk. A kind of grey-haired youth came out of a back room with his shirttails flapping.

"Single?"

"I don't need a room. You may be able to give me some information."

"Is it about the murderer?"

"Yes. I understand you talked to him. What was the subject of conversation?"

He groaned, and stopped buttoning up his shirt. "I already

told all this to the cops. You expect a man to stay up all night chewing the same cabbage?"

I gave him a five-dollar bill. He peered at it myopically and put it away. "Okay, if it's all that important. What you want to know?"

"Just what Campion said to you."

"Is that his name—Campion? He said his name was Damis. He said he spent the night here a couple months ago, and he wanted me to look up the records to prove it."

"Was he actually here a couple of months ago?"

"Uh-huh. I remembered his face. I got a very good memory for faces." He tapped his low forehead lovingly. "'Course I couldn't say for sure what date it was until I looked up the old registration cards."

"You did that, did you?"

"Yeah, but it didn't do him no good. He took off while I was out back checking. The patrol car stopped by, the way it always does around eight o'clock, and it must of scared him off."

"I'd like to see that registration card."

"The cops took it with them. They said it was evidence."

"What was the date on it?"

"May five, I remember that much."

It was evidence. May the fifth was the night of Dolly Campion's death.

"You're sure the man who registered then was the same man you talked to tonight?"

"That's what the cops wanted to know. I couldn't be absotively certain, my eyes aren't that good. But he looked the same to me, and he talked the same. Maybe he was lying about it, though. He said his name was Damis, and it turns out that's a lie."

"He registered under the name Damis on the night of May the fifth, is that correct?"

"They both did."

"Both?"

"I didn't get to see the lady. She came in her own car after he registered for them. He said his wife was gonna do that, so I thought nothing of it. She took off in the morning, early, I guess."

"How do you remember all that, when you're not even certain it was the same man?"

"He sort of reminded me. But I remembered all right when he reminded me."

He was a stupid man. His eyes were glazed and solemn with stupidity. I said: "Do you have any independent recollections of the night of May the fifth?"

"The date was on the registration card."

"But he could have registered another night, and said that it was May the fifth? And the man who signed in on May fifth could have been another man?"

I realized that I was talking like a prosecutor trying to confuse a witness. My witness was thoroughly confused.

"I guess so," he said dejectedly.

"Did Campion tell you why he was so interested in pinning down the date?"

"He didn't say. He just said it was important."

"Did he give you money?"

"He didn't have to. I said I'd help him out. After all, he was a customer."

"But you'd only seen him once before?"

"That's right. On the night of May five." His voice was stubborn.

"What time did he check in that night?"

"I couldn't say. It wasn't too late."

"And he stayed all night?"

"I couldn't say. We don't keep watch on the guests." He yawned, so wide I could count his cavities.

"What's your name?" I said.

"Nelson Karp."

"My name is Archer, Nelson. Lew Archer. I'm a private detective, and I have to ask you to return the five dollars I gave you. I'm sorry. You're probably going to be a witness in a murder trial, and you'll want to be able to tell the court that nobody paid you money."

He took the bill out of his pocket and dropped it on the counter. "I might of known there was a catch to it."

"I said I was sorry."

"You and who else is sorry?"

"Anyway, the State pays witnesses."

I didn't say how little, and Nelson Karp cheered up.

"When Campion left here tonight, which way did he go?"

"'Crost San Mateo Bridge. I heard them say that."

"By 'them' you mean the cops?"

"Yeah. They did a lot of telephoning from here." He gestured toward the pay phone on the wall.

I stepped outside and looked across the flats, where piles of salt rose like ephemeral pyramids. The lights of the Peninsula winked blearily in the haze across the Bay. As the crow flies, or the hawk, I wasn't more than ten miles from Menlo Park.

I went back into the office and got some change from Karp and placed a toll call under the name John Smith to Campion's sister Mrs. Jurgensen. Her phone rang thirteen times, and then a man's voice answered.

"Hello."

"I have a person call for Mrs. Thor Jurgensen," the operator intoned.

"Mrs. Jurgensen isn't here. Can I take a message?"

"Do you wish to leave a message, sir?" the operator said to me.

I didn't. Campion knew my voice, as I knew his.

Shortly after one o'clock I parked in the three-hundred block of Schoolhouse Road in Menlo Park. I crossed into the next

block on foot, examining the mailboxes for the Jurgensens'
number. It was a broad and quiet street of large ranch-
type houses shadowed by oaks that far predated them. Bay-
shore was a murmur in the distance.

At this hour most of the houses were dark, but there was
light in a back window of 401. I circled the house. My footsteps were muffled in the dew-wet grass. Crouching behind
a plumbago bush, I peered through a matchstick bamboo blind
into the lighted room.

It was a big country-style kitchen divided by a breakfast bar
into cooking and living areas. A used-brick fireplace took up
most of one wall. Campion was sleeping peacefully on a couch
in front of the fireplace. A road map unfolded on his chest
rose and fell with his breathing.

He had on the remains of his grey suit. There were dark
stains on it, oil or mud or blood. His face was scratched, and
charred with beard. His right arm dragged on the floor and he
had a gun there at his fingertips, a medium-caliber nickel-
plated revolver.

No doubt I should have called the police. But I wanted to
take him myself.

A detached garage big enough for three cars stood at the
rear of the property. I approached it through a flower garden
and let myself in through the unlocked side door. One of the
two cars inside had the outlines of a Chevrolet convertible.

It was Dr. Damis's car. I read his name on the steering post
in the light of my pencil flash. The keys were in the ignition.
I took them out and pocketed them.

I looked around for a weapon. There was a work bench
at the rear of the garage, and attached to the wall above it was
a pegboard hung with tools. I had a choice of several hammers.
I took down a light ball-peen hammer and hefted it. It would
do.

I went back to the Chevrolet and stuck a matchbook between the horn and the steering wheel. It began to blow like Gabriel's horn. I moved to the open side door and flattened myself against the wall beside it, watching the back of the house. My ears were hurting. The enclosed space was filled with yelling decibels which threatened to crowd me out.

Campion came out of the house. He ran through the garden, floundering among camellias. The nickel-plated revolver gleamed in his hand. Before he reached the garage he stopped and looked all around him, as though he suspected a trick. But the pull of the horn was too strong for him. He had to silence it.

I ducked out of sight and saw his shadowy figure enter the doorway. I struck him on the back of the head with the hammer, not too hard and not too easily. He fell on his gun. I got it out from under him and dropped it in my jacket pocket. Then I unjammed the horn.

A man was swearing loudly in the next yard. I stepped outside and said: "Good evening."

He turned a flashlight on me. "What goes on? You're not Thor Jurgensen."

"No. Where are the Jurgensens?"

"They're spending the night in the City. I was wondering who was using their house."

He came up to the fence, a heavy-bodied man in silk pajamas, and looked me over closely. I smiled into the glare. I was feeling pretty good.

"A wanted man was using it. I'm a detective, and I just knocked him out."

"Evelyn's brother?"

"I guess so."

"Does Evelyn know he was here?"

"I doubt it."

"Poor Evelyn." His voice held that special blend of grief and glee which we reserve for other people's disasters. "Poor old Thor. I suppose this will be in the papers—"

I cut him short: "Call the Sheriff's office in Redwood City, will you? Tell them to send a car out."

He moved away, walking springily in his bare feet.

chapter 19

ROYAL AND I waited outside the hospital room while Campion returned to consciousness. It took him the better part of an hour. I had time to fill the Captain in on my activities, and Campion's.

Royal was unimpressed by my findings in Saline City. "He's trying to fake an alibi for his wife's murder."

"Or establish one. I think you should talk to the key boy Nelson Karp, and see if that registration card is genuine. It's in the hands of the Saline City police."

Royal said without much interest: "Alibis like that one come a dime a dozen and you know it. He could have checked in at this motel and even spent part of the night, then driven back to Luna Bay and done her in. It's only about thirty miles between the two places."

"Which makes it all the easier to check."

"Look," he said, "I've got other things on my mind. Take it up with Deputy Mungan if you like. He's in charge of the sub-station at Luna Bay, and he's been handling the evidential details."

I didn't pursue the argument. Royal was a good cop but like other good cops he had an inflexible mind, once it was made up. We sat in uneasy silence for a few minutes. Then a young resident wearing a white coat and a high-minded expression came out of Campion's room and announced that, in view of the importance of the case, his patient could be questioned.

Royal and I went in past the uniformed guard. It was an ordinary small hospital room, with the addition of heavy steel

screening on the window. Campion's bed was slightly raised
at the head. He lay still and watched us. His heavy eyes recognized each of us in turn, but he didn't speak. His head was
bandaged, and the flesh around his eyes was turning purple.
Scratches stood out on his pale cheeks.

I said: "Hello, Campion."

Royal said: "Long time no see, Bruce."

Campion said nothing. The turbanlike bandage on his head,
the grimace of pain on his mouth, made him look a little like
an Indian fakir lying on a bed of spikes.

Royal's shadow fell across him. "What did you do with Harriet Blackwell, Bruce?"

"I didn't do anything with her."

"She was last seen in your company."

"I can't help it."

"You can't help killing people, you mean?"

"I've never killed anyone."

"What about your little wife Dolly?"

"I didn't kill Dolly."

"Come on now, Bruce. We know different. You've had your
little burst of freedom. This is the end of the trail. The end of
the trail and the beginning of the trial." Royal grinned at
his own bad joke. "Anything you say can be used against you,
true, but I'm advising you to speak out now, tell us the whole
thing freely. It'll be easier on you in the long run."

"Sure," Campion said. "They'll put a cushion on the chair in
the gas chamber and perfume the cyanide."

Royal leaned over the bed, his wide shoulders blotting out
Campion's face. "You know you're headed for the gas chamber,
eh? So why not give me the full story, Bruce? I been waiting a
long time to hear it. Just come clean about Dolly, and I'm your
friend. I'll do what I can to save you from the green room."

"Don't do me any favors, cop. And get away from me. You
have bad breath."

Royal's open hand jerked up. "Why, you dirty little bas—"

He bit the word in two and backed away, with a sideways glance at me.

Campion said: "Go ahead and hit me. Hitting people is what you people are for. I've hated you people all my life. You sell out justice to the highest bidder and let the poor people take the gaff."

"Shut up, you." Royal was shouting. "You lie there crying about justice with women's blood on your hands."

Campion flapped his hands in front of his face. "I don't see any blood."

"That's right, you didn't shed any blood when you killed Dolly. You used a stocking around her neck. Her own stocking." Royal made a spitting noise. "What goes on in a mind like yours, Bruce? I'd like to know."

"You never will. You're too ignorant."

"I'm not too ignorant to know a psycho when I see one, fooling around with paintboxes and living on women. Why don't you do a man's work?"

"Like vagging prostitutes and shaking them down?"

"Don't talk to me about prostitutes. I read a book about that whoring psycho French painter—the one that cut off his ear and committed suicide. How psycho can you get?"

Campion sat up in bed. "If you weren't so ignorant you'd speak of Van Gogh with respect. Incidentally, he wasn't a Frenchman. He was a Dutchman, and a great religious genius."

"And you're another? Is that what you're trying to say? You're a great religious genius who goes in for human sacrifice?"

"You're the one who puts people in the gas chamber."

"I'm the one, and that's where you're going."

I stepped between them, facing Royal. His face was congested with blood, and his eyes had an oily sheen. I'd never seen him out of control before. Campion had lain back and closed his eyes.

I opened them with a question: "How did the blood get on Harriet's hat?"

"What hat?"

"The hat I fished out of the lake today. What was it doing in the lake, and how did her blood and hair get on the lining?"

"You better ask *her*. It's her hat."

"You knew it was in the lake?"

"You just told me, and I know you wouldn't lie. Cops never lie."

"Change the record, boy. How did that hat get into the lake?"

"I said, why don't you ask her?"

"She isn't available. Where is she, Campion?"

"I wouldn't know. I have a suggestion, however."

"What is it?"

"Disappear. I'm a sick man. I need rest."

"The doctor says you're questionable."

"Not me. I'm incommunicado. It's my reputation that's questionable."

"Stop playing word games."

"Why? A man needs some amusement in the long night watches. Storm troopers make dull companions."

Hot blood rose in my face. I felt a growing solidarity with Royal.

"You don't show much concern for your fiancée."

"My what?"

"You were going to marry her, weren't you?"

"Was I?"

"Answer me."

"You already know all the answers. Cops always do."

"If you weren't going to marry her, why did you take her to Tahoe? Because the lake is deep?"

Campion looked up at me with a deathly boredom. Royal spoke behind me in a new quiet voice: "Mr. Archer deserves an answer, Bruce. He's gone to a lot of trouble to ask you that question."

"Mr. Archer can take a running jump in the lake."

"Is that what Harriet did," I said, "with a little help from you?"

"I don't know what she did. I never touched her."

"How did you get those marks on your face?"

One of his hands crawled up to his face. His fingers explored it like a blind man's fingers palpating a strange object.

"I was wandering around in the woods last night. I must have scratched myself on the bushes."

"This was after your trouble with Harriet?"

He nodded almost imperceptibly.

"What was the trouble about?"

He lay and looked at me. "What trouble?"

"You mentioned trouble with Harriet."

"You were the one who mentioned trouble," he said.

"But you agreed that trouble had occurred."

"You must have been hearing things."

"I saw you nod your head."

"I have a slight tremor. Please excuse it. It comes from being beaten half to death by storm troopers. Now why don't you go away?"

"We're not going away," Royal said at my shoulder. "You admitted you had trouble with the girl. You've taken the first step toward the truth. You might as well give us the rest of it and get it over with. How about it, Bruce?"

"Don't call me Bruce."

"Bruce is your name, isn't it?"

"Not to you. To my friends."

"What friends?" Royal said in bitter contempt.

"I have friends."

"Where are they? Under the ground?"

Campion turned his face away.

"Did Ralph Simpson call you Bruce?" I said.

"What?" he said to the wall.

"Did Ralph Simpson call you Bruce?"

"Yes, he did."

"You were friends?"

"Yes."

"Then why did you knock him off and steal his papers?"

His eyes rolled in my direction. "I didn't steal his papers."

"We found his birth certificate in your pocket," Royal said.

"Ralph lent it to me."

"The same night you stuck the icepick in him?"

Campion's mouth became rectangular. I could see the red tongue curled behind his teeth. He raised his voice and cried out. His eyes turned up, and their veined whites glared at us as he went on yelling inarticulately.

Royal and I exchanged shameful looks. For some reason we were feeling guilty, at least I was. When Campion stopped his noise and fell back onto the pillow, other noises could be heard in the corridor. A woman seemed to be arguing with more than one man.

Royal started for the door. It was flung open before he reached it. The woman who burst in resembled Campion, though she was older and softer and better cared for.

"What are you doing to my brother?"

"Nothing, ma'am," Royal said. "That is, we had some questions—"

"Have you been torturing him?"

"It's been more like the other way around."

She moved past him to the bed. "They've hurt you, Bruce."

Campion looked at her bleakly. "If I can stand it, you can. Go away."

"He's right, Mrs. Jurgensen," Royal said. "You shouldn't be in here, you know."

The guard spoke up from the doorway. "That's what I was trying to tell her, Captain. I didn't know if I should use physical force."

Royal shook his head curtly. A tall man came in past the guard. He had greying blond crewcut hair and a long face. His mouth was pinched as though he'd been sucking a lemon. He took the woman by the arm and tried to drag her away from the bed.

She resisted his efforts without looking at him. She was staring hungrily at her brother's face.

"Don't you want me to help you?"

"You were among the missing when I needed it. You know what you can do with it now. Get lost."

"You heard him, Evelyn," the tall man said. He had a faint Scandinavian accent, more a lack of timbre than an accent. "He wants no part of us. We want no part of him."

"But he's my brother."

"I *know* that, Evelyn. Do you want everyone in the Bay area to know it? Do you want young Thor to lose his fraternity connection? Do you want people pointing me out on Montgomery Street?"

"You hear your husband," Campion said. "Why don't you amscray, sister? Fold your tensions like the Arabs and silently steal away."

The resident doctor appeared with a nurse in tow. He cast a withering glance around the room.

"May I remind you this is a hospital, Captain. This man is your prisoner but also my patient. I gave you permission to question him on the understanding that it would be quiet and brief."

Royal started to say: "I'm not responsible—"

"I am. I want this room cleared immediately. That includes you, Captain."

"I'm not finished with my interrogation."

"It can wait till morning."

Royal dropped the issue. He had the trial to think of, and the use that Campion's defense could make of the doctor's testimony. He walked out. The rest of us went along.

Not entirely by accident, I met the Jurgensen couple in the parking lot. They pretended not to see me, but I planted myself between them and their Mercedes sedan and made a fast pitch to her.

"I'm a private detective working on this case and it's come to my attention that there are some holes in the case against your brother. I'd like very much to talk to you about it."

"Don't say a word, Evelyn," her husband said.

"If we could sit down and have an exchange of views, Mrs. Jurgensen—"

"Pay no attention, Evelyn. He's simply trying to pump you."

"Why don't you stay out of this?" I said. "He isn't your brother."

She turned to him. "I'm worried about him, Thor, and I'm ashamed. All these months we've pretended he didn't exist, that we had no connection—"

"We *have* no connection. We decided that between us and that's the way it's going to be."

"Why don't you let the lady do her own talking?" I said.

"There isn't going to be any talking. You get out of the way."

He took me by the shoulder and pushed me to one side. There was no point in hitting him. The Mercedes whisked them away to their half-acre earthly paradise.

I checked in at a Camino Real motel and went to sleep trying to think of some one thing I could do that would be absolutely right and final. I dreamed that Campion was innocent and I had to prove it by re-enacting the crimes with paper dolls that stuck to my fingers. Then I found Harriet's body in the lake. She had talon marks on her head.

I awoke in a cold sweat. The late night traffic whirred with a sound like wings along the highway.

chapter 20

I GOT UP into the sharp-edged uncertainties of morning and drove across the county to Luna Bay. Patrick Mungan, the deputy in charge there, was a man I knew and trusted. I hoped the trust was reciprocal.

When I entered the bare stucco substation, his broad face generated a smile which resembled sunlight on a cliff.

"I hear you've been doing our work for us, Lew."

"Somebody has to."

"Uh-huh. You look kind of bedraggled. I keep an electric razor here, in case you want to borrow it."

I rubbed my chin. It rasped. "Thanks, it can wait. Captain Royal tells me you handled the evidence in the Dolly Campion murder."

"What evidence there was. We didn't pick up too much. It wasn't there to be picked up."

Mungan had risen from his desk. He was a huge man who towered over me. It gave me the not unpleasant illusion of being small and fast, like a trained-down welterweight. He opened the swinging door at the end of the counter that divided the front office.

"Come on in and sit down. I'll send out for coffee."

"That can wait, too."

"Sure, but we might as well be comfortable while we talk." He summoned a young deputy from the back room and dispatched him for coffee. "What got you so involved in the Campion business?"

"Some Los Angeles people named Blackwell hired me to look into Campion's background. He'd picked up their daughter Harriet in Mexico and was romancing her, under an alias. Three days ago they ran away together to Nevada, where she disappeared. The indications are that she's his second victim, or his third."

I told Mungan about the hat in the water, and about the dusty fate of Quincy Ralph Simpson. He listened earnestly, with the corners of his mouth drawn down like a bulldog's, and said when I'd done: "The Blackwell girl I don't know about. But I don't see any reason why Campion would stab Ralph Simpson. It may be true what he said about Simpson lending him his papers to use. They were friends. When the Campions moved here last fall, it was Simpson who found them a house. Call it a house, but I guess it was all they could afford. They had a tough winter."

"In what way?"

"Every way. They ran out of money. The wife was pregnant and he wasn't working, unless you call painting pictures work. They had to draw welfare money for a while. The county cut 'em off when they found out Campion was using some of it to buy paints. Ralph Simpson helped them out as much as he could. I heard when the baby was born in March, he was the one paid the doctor."

"That's interesting."

"Yeah. It crossed my mind at the time that maybe Simpson was the baby's father. I asked him if he was, after Dolly got killed. He denied it."

"It's still a possibility. Simpson was a friend of Dolly's before she knew Campion. I found out last night that Simpson was responsible for bringing them together in the first place. If Simpson got her pregnant and let Campion hold the bag, it would give Campion a motive for both killings. I realize that's very iffy reasoning."

"It is that."

"Have you had any clear indication that Campion wasn't the father?"

Mungan shook his ponderous head. "All the indications point the other way. Remember she was well along when he married her in September. A man doesn't do that for a woman unless he's the one."

"I admit it isn't usual. But Campion isn't a usual man."

"Thank the good Lord for that. If everybody was like him, the whole country would be headed for Hades in a handbasket. A hand-painted handbasket." He laid his palm on the desk as if he was covering a hole card. "Personally I have my doubts that those two killings, Dolly and Simpson, are connected. I'm not saying they aren't connected. I'm only saying I have my doubts."

"They have to be connected, Pat. Simpson was killed within a couple of weeks of Dolly—a couple of weeks which he apparently spent investigating her death. Add to that the fact that he was found buried in her home town."

"Citrus Junction?"

I nodded.

"Maybe he went to see the baby," Mungan said thoughtfully. "The baby's in Citrus Junction, you know. Dolly's mother came and got him."

"You seem to like my idea after all."

"It's worth bearing in mind, I guess. If you're going down that way, you might drop in on Mrs. Stone and take a look at the little tyke. He's only about four months old, though, so I wouldn't count on his resembling anybody."

The young deputy came back with a hot carton in a paper bag. Mungan poured black coffee for the three of us. In response to unspoken signals, the young deputy carried his into the back room and closed the door. Mungan said over his paper cup: "What I meant a minute ago, I meant the two killings weren't connected the way you thought, by way of Campion. This isn't official thinking, so I'm asking you to keep it confidential, but there's some doubt in certain quarters that Campion killed Dolly."

"What quarters are you talking about?"

"These quarters," he said with a glance at the closed door.

"Me personally. So did Ralph Simpson have his doubts. We talked about it. He knew that he was a suspect himself, but he insisted that Campion didn't do it. Simpson was the kind of fellow who sometimes talked without knowing what he was talking about. But now that he's dead, I give his opinion more weight."

I sipped my coffee and kept still while Mungan went on in his deliberate way: "Understand me, Lew, I'm not saying Bruce Campion didn't kill his wife. When a woman gets herself murdered, nine times out of ten it's the man in her life, her boy friend or her husband or her ex. We all know that. All I'm saying, and I probably shouldn't be saying it, we don't have firm evidence that Campion did it."

"Then why was he indicted?"

"He has his own stupidity to thank for that. He panicked and ran, and naturally it looked like consciousness of guilt to the powers that be. But we didn't have the evidence to convict him, or maybe even arraign him. After we held him twenty-four hours, I recommended his release without charges. The crazy son-of-a-gun took off that same night. The Grand Jury was sitting, and the D.A. rushed the case in to them and got an indictment. They never would have indicted if Campion hadn't run." Mungan added with careful honesty: "This is just my opinion, my unofficial opinion."

"What's Royal's unofficial opinion?"

"The Captain keeps his opinion to himself. He's bucking for Sheriff, and you don't get to be Sheriff by fighting the powers that be."

"And I suppose the D.A. is bucking for Governor or something."

"Something. Watch him make a circus out of this."

"You don't like circuses?"

"I like the kind with elephants."

He finished his coffee, crumpled the cup in his fist, and

tossed it into the wastebasket. I did the same. It was a trivial
action, but it seemed to me to mark a turning point in the case.

"Exactly what evidence do you have against Campion?"

Mungan made a face, as if he had swallowed and regurgi-
tated a bitter pill. "It boils down to suspicion, and his lack of
an alibi, and his runout. In addition to which, there's the purely
negative evidence: there was no sign that the place had been
broken into, or that Dolly had tried to get away from the killer.
She was lying there on the floor in her nightgown, real peaceful
like, with one of her own silk stockings knotted around her
neck."

"In her bedroom?"

"The place has no bedroom. I'll show you a picture of the
layout."

He went to his files in the back room and returned with
several photographs in his hands. One was a close-up of a full-
breasted young blonde woman whose face had been savagely
caricatured by the internal pressure of her own blood. The
stocking around her neck was almost hidden in her flesh.

In the other pictures, her place on the floor had been taken
by a chalk outline of her figure. They showed from various
angles a roughly finished interior containing an unmade bed,
a battered-looking child's crib, a kitchen table and some chairs,
a gas plate and a heater, a palette and some paints on a bench
by the single large window. This window, actually the glazed
door opening of the converted garage, had a triangular hole in
a lower corner. Unframed canvases hung on the plasterboard
walls, like other broken windows revealing a weirdly devas-
tated outside world.

"How did the window get broken, Pat?"

"Ralph Simpson said that it had been broken for weeks.
Campion just never got around to fixing it. He was too high
and mighty, too busy throwing paint at the wall to see that the
wife and child got proper care."

"You don't like him much."

"I think he's a bum. I also think he's got a fair shake coming
to him."

Mungan tossed the pictures onto his desk. He took a button
out of the pocket of his blouse and rolled it meditatively between his thumb and forefinger. It was a large brown button
covered with woven leather, and it had a few brown threads
attached to it. I'd seen a button like it in the last few days, I
couldn't remember where.

"Apparently the baby slept in the same room."

"There's only the one room. They lived like shanty Irish," he
said in the disapproving tone of a lace-curtain Irishman.

"What happened to the child on the night of the murder?"

"I was going to bring that up. It's one of the queer things
about the case, and one reason we suspected Campion from
the start. Somebody, presumably the killer, took the baby out
of his crib and stashed him in a car that was parked by the
next house down the road. The woman who lives there, a
Negro woman name of Johnson, woke up before dawn and
heard the baby crying in her car. She knew whose baby it was
—her and Dolly were good neighbors—so naturally she took
it over to the Campions'. That's how Dolly's body was discovered."

"Where was Campion that night, do you know?"

"He said he was gone all night, drinking until the bars
closed, and then driving, all over hell and gone. It's the kind
of story you can't prove or disprove. He couldn't or wouldn't
name the bars, or the places he drove afterward. He said
along toward dawn he went to sleep in his car in a cul-de-sac
off Skyline. That wouldn't be inconsistent with him doing the
murder. Anyway, we picked him up around nine o'clock in
the morning, when he drove back to his place. There's no
doubt he had been drinking. I could smell it on him."

"What time was his wife killed?"

"Between three and four A.M. The deputy Coroner was out

there by eight, and he said she couldn't have been dead longer than four or five hours. He went by body temp. and stomach contents, and the two factors checked each other out."

"How did he know when she'd eaten last?"

"Campion said they ate together at six the previous night. He brought in a couple of hamburgers—some diet for a nursing mother—and the carhop at the drive-in confirmed the time. Apparently he and Dolly had an argument over the food, so he took what money there was in the house and went and got himself plastered."

"What was the argument about?"

"Things in general, he said. They hadn't been getting along too well for months."

"He told you this?"

"Yeah. You'd think he was trying to make himself look bad."

"Did he say anything about another woman?"

"No. What's on your mind, Lew?"

"I think we can prove he was lying about what he did on the night of May the fifth. Have you talked to Royal this morning?"

"He phoned to tell me he had Campion. He wants me to go over to Redwood City and take a hand in the questioning."

"Has Campion admitted anything yet?"

"He's not talking at all. Royal's getting kind of frustrated."

"Did he say anything to you about the Travelers Motel in Saline City?"

"Not a word." Mungan gave me a questioning look.

"According to their night clerk, Nelson Karp, Campion spent the night of May fifth there with a woman. Or part of the night. They registered as Mr. and Mrs. Burke Damis, which is one of the aliases Campion has been using. The Saline City police lifted the registration card last night after Campion was seen there. He seems to have been trying to set up an alibi."

"A good one or a phony?"

"You can find that out quicker than I can."

Mungan stood up and looked down the rocky slopes of his

face at me. "Whyn't you give me the word on it in the first place?"

"I gave the word to Royal last night. He wasn't interested. I thought I'd wait and see if you were."

"Well, I am. But if this is no phony, why did Campion hold it out until now?"

"Ask him."

"I think I will."

He dropped the leather button he had been playing with on his desk. It rolled onto the floor, and I picked it up.

"Is this part of the evidence, Pat?"

"I honestly don't know. The baby had it in his fist when Mrs. Johnson found him in her car. She didn't know where it came from. Neither did anybody else."

I was still trying to remember where I had seen a button or buttons like it. I dredged deep in my memory, but all that came up was the smell of the sea and the sound of it.

"May I have this button?"

"Nope. I read a story once about a button solving a murder, and I have a special feeling about this button."

"So have I."

"But I'm holding onto it." His smiling eyes narrowed on my face. "You sure you don't want to borrow the use of my razo before you go?"

"I guess I'd better."

He got the electric razor out of the bottom drawer of his desk. I took it into the washroom and shaved myself. All I uncovered was the same old trouble-prone face.

chapter 21

MUNGAN WAS GONE when I came out. I used his telephone to call Vicky Simpson's house. No answer. The young deputy in the back room told me that so far as he knew Vicky was still in Citrus Junction waiting for the authorities to release her husband's body. I turned in the U-drive car at the San Francisco airport, caught a jet to Los Angeles, picked up my own car at the airport there, and drove out through the wedding-smelling orange groves to Citrus Junction.

I went first to see the baby. His grandmother lived on the west side of town in the waste that the highway builders had created. It was mid-afternoon when I got there. Earth movers were working in the dust like tanks in a no man's land.

An overgrown pittasporum hedge shielded the house from the road. The universal dust had made its leaves as grey as aspen. The house was a two-story frame building which needed paint. Holes in the screen door had been repaired with string. I rattled it with my fist.

The woman who appeared behind the screen looked young to be a grandmother. The flouncy dress she wore, and her spike heels, were meant to emphasize her slender figure. She had a blue-eyed baby face to which the marks of time clung like an intricate spider web. She was blonder than the picture I'd seen of her daughter.

"Mrs. Stone?"

"I'm Mrs. Stone."

I told her my name and occupation. "May I come in and talk to you for a bit?"

"What about?"

"Your daughter Dolly and what happened to her. I know it must be a painful subject—"

"Painful subject is right. I don't see any sense in going over and over the same old ground. You people know who killed her as well as me. Instead of coming around torturing me, why don't you go and catch that man? He has to be some place."

"I took Campion last night, Mrs. Stone. He's being held in Redwood City."

A hungry eagerness deepened the lines in her face and aged her suddenly. "Has he confessed?"

"Not yet. We need more information. I'm comparatively new on the case, and I'd appreciate any help you can give me."

"Sure. Come in."

She unhooked the screen door and led me across a hallway into her living room. It was closely blinded, almost dark. Instead of raising a blind, she turned on a standing lamp.

"Excuse the dust on everything. It's hard to keep a decent house with that road work going on. Stone thought we should sell, but we found out we couldn't get our money out of it. The lucky ones were the people across the way that got condemned by the State. But they're not widening on this side."

An undersong of protest ran through everything she said, and she had reason. Grey dust rimed the furniture; even without it the furniture would have been shabby. I sat on a prolapsed chair and watched her arrange herself on the chesterfield. She had the faintly anachronistic airs of a woman who had been good-looking but had found no place to use her looks except the mirror.

At the moment I was the mirror, and she smiled into me intensively. "What do you want me to tell you?"

"We'll start with your son-in-law. Did you ever meet him?"

"Once. Once was enough. Jack and me invited the two of them down for Christmas. We had a hen turkey and all the trimmings. But that Bruce Campion acted like he was on a slumming expedition. He hauled poor Dolly out of here so fast you'd think there was a quarantine sign on the house. Little did he know that some of the best people in town are our good friends."

"Did you quarrel with him?"

"You bet I did. What did he have to act so snooty about? Dolly told me they were living in a garage, and we've owned our own house here for twenty-odd years. So I asked him what he planned to do for her. When was he going to get a job and so on? He said he married her, didn't he, and that was all he planned to do for her, said he already had a job doing his own work. So I asked him how much money he made and he said not very much, but they were getting along with the help of friends. I told him my daughter wasn't a charity case, and he said that's what *I* thought. Imagine him talking like that to her own mother, and her six months pregnant at the time. I tried to talk her into cutting her losses and staying here with us, but Dolly wouldn't. She was too loyal."

Mrs. Stone had the total recall of a woman with a grievance. I interrupted her flow of words: "Were they getting along with each other?"

"*She* was getting along with him. It took a saint to do it and that's what she was, a saint." She rummaged in a sewing basket beside her. "I want to show you a letter she wrote me after Christmas. If you ever saw a devoted young wife it was her."

She produced a crumpled letter addressed to her and post-marked "Luna Bay, Dec. 27." It was written in pencil on a sheet of sketching paper by an immature hand:

Dear Elizabeth,

I'm sorry you and Bruce had to fight. He is moody but he is really A-okay if you only know him. We appresiate the twenty—it will come in handy to buy a coat—I only hope Bruce does not get to it first —he spends so much on his painting—I realy need a coat. Its colder up here than it was in Citrus J. I realy

appresiate you asking me to stay (I'm a poet and
dont know it!) but a girl has to stick with her "hubby"
thru thick and thin—after all Bruce stuck with me.
Maybe he is hard to get along with but he is a lot
better than "no hubby at all." Dont you honestly think
hes cute? Besides some of the people we know think
his pictures are real great and he will make a "killing"
—then you will be glad I stuck with Bruce.

Love to Jack
Dolly
(*Mrs. Bruce Campion*)

"Doesn't it tear your heart out?" Mrs. Stone said, plucking
at the neighborhood of hers. "I mean the way she idolized
him and all?"

I assumed a suitably grim expression. It came naturally
enough. I was thinking of the cultural gap between Dolly and
Harriet, and the flexibility of the man who had straddled it.

"How did she happen to marry him, Mrs. Stone?"

"It's the old old story. You probably know what happened.
She was an innocent girl. She'd never even been away from
home before. He corrupted her, and he had to take the con-
sequences." She was a little alarmed by what she had said.
She dropped her eyes, and added: "It was partly my own
fault, I admit it. I never should have let her go off to Nevada
by herself, a young girl like her."

"How old?"

"Dolly was just twenty when she left home. That was a year
ago last May. She was working in the laundry and she wasn't
happy there, under her father's thumb. She wanted to have
more of a life of her own. I couldn't blame her for that. A girl
with her looks could go far."

She paused, and her eyes went into long focus. Perhaps she
was remembering that a girl with her own looks hadn't. Per-

haps she was remembering how far Dolly had gone, all the way out of life.

"Anyway," she said, "I let her go up to Tahoe and get herself a job. It was just to be for the summer. She was supposed to save her money, so she could prepare herself for something permanent. I wanted her to go to beauty school. She was very good at grooming herself—it was the one real talent she had. She took after me in that. But then she ran into *him*, and that was the end of beauty school and everything else."

"Did she make any other friends up at the lake?"

"Yeah, there was one little girl who helped her out, name of Fawn. She was a beauty operator, and Dolly thought very highly of her. She even wrote me about her. I was glad she had a girl friend like that. I thought it would give her some ambition. Beauty operators command good money, and you can get a job practically anywhere. I always regretted I didn't take it up myself. Jack makes a fair salary at the laundry, but it's been hard these last years, with inflation and all. Now we have the baby to contend with."

She raised her eyes to the ceiling.

"I'd like to see the baby."

"He's upstairs sleeping. What do you want to see him for?"

"I like babies."

"You don't look the type. I'm not the type myself, not any more. You get out of the habit of attending to their needs. Still," she added in a softer voice, "the little man's a comfort to me. He's all I have left of Dolores. You can come and take a look—long as you don't wake him."

I followed her up the rubber-treaded staircase. The baby's room was dim and hot. She turned on a shaded wall light. He was lying uncovered in the battered crib which I had seen in Mungan's glaring photographs. As Mungan had predicted, he didn't resemble anyone in particular. Small and vulnerable and profoundly sleeping, he was simply a baby. His breath was sweet.

His grandmother pulled a sheet up over the round Buddha eye of his umbilicus. I stood above him, trying to guess what he would look like when he grew up. It was hard to imagine him as a man, with a man's passions.

"This was Dolly's own crib," Mrs. Stone was saying. "We sent it up with them at Christmas. Now we have it back here." I heard her breath being drawn in. "Thank God his crazy father spared him, anyway."

"What's his name?"

"Dolly called him Jack, after her father. Dolly and her father were always close. What do you think of him?"

"He's a fine healthy baby."

"Oh, I do for him the best I can. It isn't easy to go back to it, though, after twenty years. My only hope is that I can bring him up properly. I guess I didn't do such a good job of bringing Dolly up."

I murmured something encouraging as we started downstairs. Like other women I had known, she had the strength to accept the worst that could happen and go on from there. Moving like a dreamer into the living room, she went to the mantel and took down a framed photograph.

"Did you ever see a picture of my daughter?"

"Not a good one."

The picture she showed me was an improvement on Mungan's, but it wasn't a good one, either. It looked like what it was, a small-town high-school graduation picture, crudely retouched in color. Dolly smiled and smiled like a painted angel.

"She's—she was pretty, wasn't she?"

"Very," I said.

"You wouldn't think she'd have to settle for a Bruce Campion. As a matter of fact, she didn't have to. There were any number of boys around town interested. There used to be a regular caravan out here. Only Dolly wasn't interested in the boys. She wanted to get out of Citrus for life. Besides, she always went for the older ones. I think sometimes," she said quite innocently, "that came from being so fond of her father and all. She never felt at home with boys her own age. The truth is, in a town this size, the *decent* older ones are already married off."

"Was Dolly friends with some of the other kind?"

"She most certainly was not. Dolly was always a good girl, and leery of bad company. Until that Campion got ahold of her."

"What about her friends at Tahoe? Were there other men besides Campion in her life?"

"I don't know what you mean by in her *life*." Almost roughly, she took the picture of Dolly out of my hands and replaced it on the mantel. With her back still turned, she said across the width of the room: "What are you getting at, mister?"

"I'm trying to find out how Dolly lived before she married Campion. I understand she lost her job and got some help from friends, including Fawn King. You said she wrote you about Fawn. Do you have the letter?"

"No. I didn't keep it."

"Did she mention any other friends besides Fawn?"

She came back toward me shaking her head. Her heels made dents in the carpet. "I think I know what you're getting at. It's just another one of his dirty lies."

"Whose lies?"

"Bruce Campion's lies. He's full of them. When they were here Christmas, he tried to let on to Jack that he wasn't the father, that he married her out of the goodness of his heart."

"Did he say who the father was?"

"Of course he didn't, because there wasn't anybody else. I asked Dolly myself, and she said *he* was the father. Then he turned around and admitted it then and there."

"What did he say?"

"He said he wouldn't argue, said he made his bargain and he would stick to it. He had his gall, talking about her like she was a piece of merchandise. I told him so, and that was when he marched her out of the house. He didn't want her talking any more. He had too much to hide."

"What are you referring to?"

"His lies, and all his other shenanigans. He was a drinker, and heaven knows what else. Dolly didn't say much—she never complained—but I could read between the lines. He went through money like it was water—"

I interrupted her. "Did Dolly ever mention a man named Quincy Ralph Simpson?"

"Simpson? No, she never did. What was that name again?"

"Quincy Ralph Simpson."

"Isn't that the man they found across the street—the one that was buried in Jim Rowland's yard?"

"Yes. He was a friend of your daughter's."

"I don't believe it."

"He was, though. Simpson was the one who introduced her to Campion. After they got married, Simpson gave them a good deal of help, including financial help."

"That doesn't prove anything."

"I'm not trying to make it prove anything. But I'm surprised that Dolly never mentioned Simpson to you."

"We didn't keep in close touch. She wasn't much of a letter writer."

"When did you see Dolly and Campion last?"

"Christmas. I told you about that."

"You didn't see Campion in May?"

"I did not. Jack drove me up there the day they found her, but I shunned *him* like a rattlesnake."

"And he wasn't here in Citrus Junction, after the police released him?"

"How would I know? He wouldn't come to us."

"He may have, in a sense. He may have been across the road burying Ralph Simpson. Whoever buried Simpson must have had a reason for picking the house across from yours."

She squinted at me, as if the light had brightened painfully. "I see what you mean."

"Are you sure Ralph Simpson never came here to your house?"

"There's no reason he should. We didn't even know him." Mrs. Stone was getting restless, twining her hands in her lap.

"But he knew Dolly," I reminded her. "After she was killed, and you brought the baby here, he may have been watching your house."

"Why would he do that?"

"It's been suggested that he was the baby's father."

"I don't believe it." But after a pause, she said: "What kind of a man *was* Ralph Simpson? All I know about him is what I read in the papers, that he was stabbed and buried in the Rowlands' yard."

"I never knew him in life, but I gather he wasn't a bad man. He was loyal, and generous, and I think he had some courage. He spent his own last days trying to track down Dolly's murderer."

"Bruce Campion, you mean?"

"He wasn't convinced that it was Campion."

"And you aren't, either," she said with her mouth tight.

"No. I'm not."

Her posture became angular and hostile. I was trying to rob her of her dearest enemy.

"All I can say is, you're mistaken. I *know* he did it. I can feel it, here." She laid her hand over her heart.

"We all make mistakes," I said.

"Yes, and you made more than one. I *know* that Bruce Campion was the baby's father. Dolly wouldn't lie to me."

"Daughters have been known to lie to their mothers."

"Maybe so. But if this Simpson was the father, why didn't he marry her? Answer me that."

"He was already married."

"Now I *know* you're wrong. Dolly would never mess with a married man. The one time she did—" Her eyes widened as though she had frightened herself again. She clamped her mouth shut.

"Tell me about the one time Dolly messed with a married man."

"There was no such time."

"You said there was."

"I'm saying there wasn't. I was thinking about something entirely different. I wouldn't sully her memory with it, so there."

I tried to persuade her to tell me more, with no success. Finally I changed the subject.

"This house across the way where Simpson was found buried—I understand it wasn't occupied at the time."

"You understand right. The Rowlands moved out the first of the year, and the house was standing empty there for months. It was a crying shame what happened to it and the other condemned houses. Some of the wild kids around were using them to carry on in. Jack used to find the bottles and the beer cans all around. They smashed the windows and everything. I hated to see it, even if it didn't matter in the long run. The State just tore the houses down anyway." She seemed to be mourning obscurely over the changes and losses in her own life. "I hated to see them do it to the Jaimet house."

"The Jaimet house?"

She made a gesture in the direction of the road. "I'm talking about that same house. Jim Rowland bought it from Mrs. Jaimet after her husband died. It was the original Jaimet ranch house. This whole west side of town used to be the Jaimet ranch. But that's all past history."

"Tell me about Jim Rowland."

"There's nothing much to tell. He's a good steady man, runs the Union station up the road, and he's opening another station in town. Jack always swears by Rowland. He says he's an honest mechanic, and that's high praise from Jack."

"Did Dolly know him?"

"Naturally she knew him. The Rowlands lived across the street for the last three-four years. If you think it went further than that, you're really off. Jim's a good family man. Anyway, he sold to the State and moved out the first of the year. He wouldn't come back and bury a body in his own yard, if that's what you're thinking."

I was thinking that you never could tell what murderers would do. Most of them were acting out a fantasy which they couldn't explain themselves: destroying an unlamented past which seemed to bar them from the brave new world, erasing the fear of death by inflicting death, or burying an old malignant grief where it would sprout and multiply and end by destroying the destroyer.

I thanked Mrs. Stone for her trouble and walked across the road. The earth movers had stopped for the day, but their dust still hung in the air. Through it I could see uprooted trees, houses smashed to rubble and piled in disorderly heaps. I couldn't tell where Rowland's house had stood.

chapter 22

THE DEPUTY on duty at the Citrus Junction courthouse was a tired-looking man with his blouse open at the neck and a toothpick in his mouth. A deep nirvanic calm lay over his office. Even the motes at the window moved languidly. The ultimate slowdown of the universe would probably begin in Citrus Junction. Perhaps it already had.

I asked the tired man where Sergeant Leonard was. He regarded me morosely, as if I'd interrupted an important meditation.

"Gone to town on business."

"Which town?"

"L.A."

"What business?"

He looked me over some more. Perhaps he was estimating my Bertillon measurements. He belonged to the Bertillon era.

"Anything to do with the Simpson case?" I said.

He removed his toothpick from between his teeth and examined it for clues, such as toothmarks. "We don't discuss official business with the public. You a newspaper fellow?"

"I'm a private detective working with Leonard on the Simpson case."

He was unimpressed. "I'll tell the Sergeant when he comes in. What's your name?"

"S. Holmes."

He reinserted his toothpick in his mouth and wrote haltingly on a scratch pad. I said: "The 'S.' stands for Sherlock."

He looked up from his laborious pencil work. The old crystal set he was using for a brain received a faint and far-off signal: he was being ribbed.

"What did you say the first name was?"

"Sherlock."

"That supposed to be funny? Ha ha," he said.

I started over: "My name is Archer, and Leonard will want to see me. When are you expecting him back?"

"When he gets here."

"Oh, thanks."

"You're welcome." He tore up the paper he had been writing on and let the pieces flutter down onto the counter between us.

"Can you give me Leonard's home address?"

"Sure I can. But you're the great detective. Find it for yourself."

Archer the wit. Archer the public relations wizard. I took my keen sense of humor and social expertise for a walk down the corridor. There was nobody at the information desk inside the front door, but a thin telephone directory was chained to the side of the desk. Wesley Leonard lived on Walnut Street. An old man watering the courthouse chrysanthemums told me where Walnut Street was, a few blocks from here. Archer the bloodhound.

It was a middle-middle-class street of stucco cottages dating from the twenties. The lawn in front of Leonard's cottage was as well kept as a putting green. A stout woman who was not so well kept answered the door.

Pink plastic curlers on her head gave her a grim and defiant expression. She said before I asked: "Wesley's not here. And I'm busy cooking supper."

"Do you know when he'll be back?"

"He's generally home for supper. Wesley likes a good hot supper."

"What time would that be?"

"Six. We eat an early supper." Supper was a key word in her vocabulary. "Who shall I tell him?"

"Lew Archer. I'm the detective who brought Vicky Simpson here last Monday night. Is Mrs. Simpson still with you?"

"No. She only stayed the one night." The woman said in a sudden gush of confidence: "Wesley's such a good Samaritan, he doesn't realize. Are you a real good friend of Mrs. Simpson's?"

"No."

"Well, I wouldn't want to insult her. She has her troubles. But it's hard on an older woman having a younger woman in the house. A younger woman with all those troubles, it puts a strain on the marriage." She ran her fingers over her curlers, as if they were holding the marriage precariously together. "You know how men are."

"Not Wesley."

"Yes, Wesley. He's not immune. No man is." She looked ready to be disappointed in me at any moment. "Wesley was up half the night letting her cry on his shoulder. Heating milk. Making a grilled cheese sandwich at four A.M. He hasn't made

me a sandwich in ten years. So after she woke up at noon and
I gave her her lunch I tactfully suggested that she should try
the hotel. Wesley says I acted hardhearted. I say I was only
heading off trouble in the marriage."

"What's she using for money?"

"Her boss wired her an advance on her wages, and I guess
the boys in the courthouse chipped in some. Mrs. Vicky Simpson is comfortably ensconced."

"Where?"

"The Valencia Hotel, on Main Street."

It had stood there for forty or fifty years, a three-story cube
of bricks that had once been white. Old men in old hats were
watching the street through the front window. Their heads
turned in unison to follow my progress across the dim lobby.
It was so quiet I could hear their necks, or their chairs, creak.

There was nobody on duty at the desk. I punched the handbell. It didn't work. One of the old men rose from his chair near
the window and shuffled past me through a door at the back.
He reappeared behind the desk, adjusting a glossy brown
toupee which he had substituted for his hat. It settled low on
his forehead.

"Yessir?"

"Is Mrs. Simpson in?"

He turned to inspect the bank of pigeonholes behind him.
The back of his neck was naked as a plucked chicken's.

"Yessir. She's in."

"Tell her there's someone who wants to speak to her."

"No telephone in her room. I guess I could go up and tell
her," he said doubtfully.

"I'll go. What's her number?"

"Three-oh-eight on the third floor. But we don't like gentle-
men visitors in a lady's room." Somehow his toupee made this
remark sound lowbrow and obscene.

"I'm no gentleman. I'm a detective."

"I see."

He and his friends by the window watched me go up the stairs. I was the event of the day. A red bulb lit the third-floor corridor. I tapped on the door of 308.

"Who is it?" Vicky said in a dull voice.

"Lew Archer. Remember me?"

Bedsprings made a protesting noise. She opened the door and peered out. Her face had thinned.

"What do you want?"

"Some talk."

"I'm all run out of talk."

Her eyes were enormous and vulnerable. I could see myself mirrored in their pupils, a tiny red-lit man caught in amber, twice.

"Let me in, Vicky. I need your help."

She shrugged and walked away from the open door, sprawling on the bed in a posture that seemed deliberately ugly. Her breasts and hips stood out under her black dress like protuberances carved from something hard and durable, wood or bone. A Gideon Bible lay open on the bed. I saw when I sat down in the chair beside it that Vicky had been reading the Book of Job.

"I didn't know you were a Bible reader."

"There's lots of things you don't know about me."

"That's true. Why didn't you tell me Ralph was a friend of the Campions?"

"That should be easy to figure out. I didn't want you to know."

"But why?"

"It's none of your business."

"We have business in common, Vicky. We both want to get this mess straightened out."

"It'll never get straightened out. Ralph's dead. You can't change that."

"Was he involved in Dolly's murder? Is that why you covered for him?"

"I didn't cover for him."

"Of course you did. You must have recognized Campion from the description I gave you. You must have known that Dolly had been murdered. You knew that Ralph was close to her."

"He wasn't—not in the way you mean."

"In what way was he close to her?"

"He was more like her financial adviser," she said in a halting voice.

"Dolly had no use for a financial adviser. She was stony broke."

"That's what you think. I happen to know she was loaded at the time she was killed. Ralph told me she had at least a thousand dollars in cash. She didn't know what to do with it, so she asked Ralph."

"You must be mistaken, Vicky. The Campions had no money. I was told that Ralph had to pay the doctor when their child was born."

"He didn't *have* to. He had a good day at the race track and gave them the money. When Ralph won a little money he thought he was Santa Claus. Don't think I didn't put up a squawk. But she paid him back after all."

"When?"

"Just before she was killed. Out of the money she had. That's how he financed his trip to Tahoe."

It was a peculiar story, peculiar enough to be true.

"Did Ralph actually see all the money Dolly claimed she had?"

"He saw it. He didn't count it or anything, but he saw it. She asked him to take it and hold it for her, so she could make a down payment on a tract house. Ralph didn't want the responsibility. He advised her to put it in the bank, but she was afraid Bruce would find out, and it would be gone with the wind. Like the other money—the money she had when he married her."

"I didn't know she had any."

"What do you think he married her for? She had plenty, according to Ralph, another thousand anyway. Bruce took it and blew it. She was afraid he'd do the same with the new money."

"Where did all the money come from?"

"Ralph said she got it out of a man. She wasn't saying who."

"Was the man the father of her child?"

She lowered her eyes demurely. "I always thought Bruce was the father."

"Bruce denied it."

"I never heard that."

"I did, Vicky. Do you have any idea who the father was if it wasn't Bruce?"

"No."

"Could it have been Ralph?"

"No. There was nothing between him and Dolly. For one thing, he had too much respect for Bruce."

"But the child was conceived long before she married Campion. Also you tell me she confided in Ralph about her money problems. Didn't you say she wanted him to look after her thousand dollars?"

"Yes, and maybe he should have." She glanced around the little room as if someone might be spying at the keyhole or the window. She lowered her voice to a whisper: "I think she was killed for that money."

"By Bruce, you mean?"

"By him, or somebody else."

"Did Ralph tell the police about it?"

"No."

"And you didn't either?"

"Why should I ask for trouble? You get enough trouble in this life without coming out and asking for it."

I rose and stood over her. Late afternoon sunlight slanted in through the window. She sat rigid with her legs under her, as if the shafts of light had transfixed her neck and shoulders.

"You were afraid Ralph killed her."

Her eyes shifted away from mine and stayed far over in the corners of her head. "Deputy Mungan made Ralph come down to the station and answer a lot of questions. Then Ralph went off to Nevada right after. Naturally I was scared."

"Where was Ralph the night Dolly was killed?"

"I don't know. He was out late, and I didn't wake up when he came in."

"You still think Ralph murdered her?"

"I didn't say I *thought* it. I was scared."

"Did you ask him?"

"Of course I didn't ask him. But he kept talking about the murder. He was so upset and shaky he couldn't handle a cup of coffee. This was the night after it happened. They had Bruce Campion in the clink, and Ralph kept saying that Bruce didn't do it, he knew Bruce didn't do it."

"Did Ralph see Bruce before he left for Tahoe?"

"Yeah, Bruce came to the house in the morning when they let him out. I wouldn't of let him *in* if I'd been there."

"What happened between Bruce and Ralph that morning?"

"I wouldn't know. I was at work. Ralph phoned me around noon and said he was going up to Tahoe. Maybe Bruce went with him. He dropped out of sight that same day, and I never saw him again. A couple of days after that, the papers were full of him running away, and the Grand Jury brought in a murder conviction."

"The Grand Jury indicted him," I said. "There's a big difference between an indictment and a conviction."

"That's what Ralph said, the day he came back from the lake. I thought a week or so away from it all would get it off his mind. But he was worse than ever when he came back. He was obsessed with Bruce Campion."

"Just how close were they?"

"They were like brothers," she said, "ever since they were in Korea together. Bruce had more on the ball than Ralph had, I guess, but somehow it was Ralph who did the looking after. He thought it was wonderful to have Bruce for a friend. He'd give him the shirt off his back, and he practically did more than once."

"Would Ralph give Bruce his birth certificate to get out of the country?"

She glanced up sharply. "Did he?"

"Bruce says he did. Either Ralph gave it to him voluntarily, or Bruce took it by force."

"And killed him?"

"I have my doubts that Bruce killed either one of them. He had no apparent motive to kill Ralph, and the money Dolly had puts a new complexion on her case. It provides a motive for anyone who knew she had it."

"But why would anybody want to kill Ralph?"

"There's one obvious possibility. He may have known who murdered Dolly."

"Why didn't he say so, then?"

"Perhaps he wasn't sure. I believe he was trying to investigate Dolly's murder, up at the lake and probably here in Citrus Junction. When he came back from Tahoe, did he say anything to you about the Blackwells?"

"The Blackwells?" There was no recognition in her voice.

"Colonel Mark Blackwell and his wife. They brought me into this case, because their daughter Harriet had taken up with Campion. The Blackwells have a lodge at Tahoe, and Harriet was there with Campion the night before last. Then she disappeared. We found her hat in the lake with blood on it. Campion has no explanation."

Vicky rose on her knees. Moving awkwardly, she backed away to the far side of the bed. "I don't know nothing about it."

"That's why I'm telling you. The interesting thing is that

Ralph spent some time in the Blackwells' lodge last May. He worked as their houseboy for a week or so. They fired him, allegedly for stealing."

"Ralph might of had his faults," she said from her corner, "but I never knew him to steal anything in his life. Anyway, there's no sense trying to pin something on a dead man."

"I'm not, Vicky. I'm trying to pin murder on whoever killed him. You loved him, didn't you?"

She looked as though she would have liked to deny it and the pain that went with it. "I couldn't help it. I tried to help it, but I couldn't stop myself. He was such a crazy guy," she murmured, so softly that it sounded like an endearment. "Sometimes when he was asleep, when he was asleep and out of trouble, I used to think he was beautiful."

"He's asleep and out of trouble now," I said. "What about the bundle of clothes he brought back from Tahoe?"

"There was no bundle of clothes, there was just the coat. He had this brown topcoat with him. But I know he didn't steal it. He never stole in his life."

"I don't care whether he stole it or not. The question is where did he get it?"

"He *said* somebody gave it to him. But people don't give away that kind of a coat for free. It was real good tweed, imported like. Harris tweed, I think they call it. It must of cost a hundred dollars new, and it was still in new condition. The only thing the matter with it, one of the buttons was missing."

"Can you describe the buttons?"

"They were brown leather. I wanted to try and match the missing one so he could wear it. But he said leave it as it was, he wasn't going to wear it." Tears glistened in her eyes. "He said he wasn't going to wear it and he was right."

"Did he bring it with him when he came down south?"

"Yeah. He was carrying it over his arm when he got on the bus. I don't know why he bothered dragging it along with him. It was warm weather, and anyway it had that button missing."

"Which button on the coat was missing, Vicky?"

"The top one." She pointed with her thumb between her breasts.

I wished I had Mungan's button with me. I remembered now where I had seen other buttons like it, attached to a coat that answered Vicky's description. One of the girls in the zebra-striped hearse had been wearing it

chapter 23

I DROVE BACK to the coast and hit the surfing beaches southward from the fork of 101 and 101 Alternate. Some of the surfers recalled the black-and-white hearse, but they didn't know the names of any of the occupants. Anyway they claimed they didn't—they're a closemouthed tribe.

I had better luck with the Highway Patrol in Malibu. The owner of the hearse had been cited the previous week end for driving with only one headlight. His name was Ray Buzzell, and he lived in one of the canyons above the town.

"Mrs. Sloan Buzzell" was stenciled on the side of the rustic mailbox. An asphalt driveway zigzagged down the canyon side to her house. It was a redwood and glass structure with a white gravel roof, cantilevered over a steep drop. A small Fiat stood in the double carport, but there was no hearse beside it.

A violently redheaded woman opened the front door before I got to it, and stepped outside. Her hard, handsome face was carefully made up, as though she'd been expecting a visitor. I wondered what kind of visitor. Her black Capri pants adhered like oil to her thighs and hips. The plunging neckline of her shirt exhibited large areas of chest and stomach. She was carrying a half-full martini glass in her hand and, to judge by her speech, a number of previous martinis inside of her.

"Hello-hello," she said. "Don't I know you from somewhere?"

"I'm just a type. How are you, Mrs. Buzzell?"

"Fine. Feen. Fane." She flexed her free arm to prove it, and inflated her chest, which almost broke from its moorings. "*You* look sort of beat. Come in and I'll pour you a drink. I hope you drink."

"Quantities, but not at the moment, thanks. I'm looking for Ray."

She frowned muzzily. "People are always looking for Ray. Has he done something?"

"I hope not. Where can I find him?"

She flung out her arm in a gesture which included the whole coast. From the height we stood on, we could see a good many miles of it. The sun was low in the west, and it glared like a searchlight through barred clouds.

"I can't keep track of my son any more," she said in a soberer voice. "I haven't seen him since breakfast. He's off with his crowd somewhere. All they care about is surfing. Some weeks I don't set eyes on him for days at a time." She consoled herself with the rest of her martini. "Sure you won't come in for a drink? I just made a fresh shaker, and if I have to drink it all by myself I'll be smasherooed."

"Pour it out."

"The man is mad." She studied my face with exaggerated interest. "You must be a wandering evangelist or something."

"I'm a wandering detective investigating a murder. Your son may be able to help me."

She moved closer to me and whispered through her teeth: "Is Ray involved in a murder?"

"That I doubt. He may have some information that will help me. Are you expecting him home for dinner?"

"I never know. Sometimes he's out all night with his crowd. They have bedrolls in the hearse." She burst out angrily: "I could *kill* myself for letting him buy that thing. He practically *lives* in it." Her mind veered back to the point. "What do you mean, he has information?"

"I said he may have."

"Who was murdered?"

"A man named Simpson, Quincy Ralph Simpson."

"I never heard of any such man. Neither did Ray, I'm sure."

I said: "When Simpson was last seen alive by his wife, he was carrying a brown Harris tweed topcoat with brown leather buttons; the top button was missing. That was two months ago. The other day I saw one of the girls in Ray's crowd wearing that topcoat, or one exactly like it."

"Mona?"

"She was a big chesty blonde."

"That's Ray's girl, Mona Sutherland. And the coat is his, too. I know it well. His father gave it to him the last time Ray visited him, so you see you've made a mistake. It's a different coat entirely."

"Now tell me where Ray really got it, Mrs. Buzzell."

The manifestations of mother love are unpredictable. She threw her empty glass at my head. It missed me and smashed on the flagstones. Then she retreated into the house, slamming the door behind her.

I got into my car and sat. The sun was almost down, a narrowing red lozenge on the cloud-streaked horizon. It slipped out of sight. The whole western sky became smoky red, as if the sun had touched off fires on the far side of the world.

After a while the front door opened. The lady appeared with a fresh glass in her hand.

"I've just been talking to my ex on the long-distance telephone. He'll back me up about the coat."

"Bully for him."

She looked at the glass in her hand as if she was considering throwing it, too. But it had liquor in it.

"What right have you got sitting on my property? Get off my property!"

I turned the car and drove up past her mailbox and parked at the roadside and watched the horizontal fires die out and the dark come on. The sky was crowded with stars when the woman came out again. She plodded up the slope and balanced her teetering weight against the mailbox.

"I'm smasherooed."

I got out and approached her. "I told you to pour it out."

"I couldn't do that to good gin. It's been my dearest friend and beloved companion for lo these many yea-hears." She reached for me like a blind woman. "I'm frightened."

"I didn't mean to frighten you, and I don't believe your son is involved in this murder. But I have to know where he got the tweed topcoat. His father had nothing to do with it, did he?"

"No. Ray told me he found it."

"Where?"

"On the beach, he said."

"How long ago was this?"

"About two months. He brought it home and brushed the sand out of it. That's why I got so frightened, on account of the timing. You said two months. That's why I lied to you."

She was leaning on me heavily, one hand on my shoulder, the other clutching my upper arm. I let her lean.

"Ray couldn't murder anyone," she said. "He's a little hard to regiment but he's not a bad boy really. And he's so *young*."

"He's not a murder suspect, Mrs. Buzzell. He's a witness, and the coat is evidence. How he got it may be significant. But I can't establish that without talking to him. You must have some idea where I can find him."

"He did say something this morning—something about spending the night at Zuma. I know he took along some things to cook. But what he says and what he actually does are often two different things. I can't keep track of him any more. He needs a father."

She was talking into the front of my coat, and her grip had tightened on me. I held her for a bit, because she needed holding, until a car came up the road and flashed its head-lights on her wet startled face.

The striped hearse was standing empty among other cars off the highway above Zuma. I parked behind it and went down to the beach to search for its owner. Bonfires were scattered along the shore, like the bivouacs of nomad tribes or nuclear war survivors. The tide was high and the breakers loomed up marbled black and fell white out of oceanic darkness.

Six young people were huddled under blankets around one of the fires. I recognized them: one of the girls was wearing the brown tweed coat. They paid no attention when I ap-proached. I was an apparition from the adult world. If they pretended I wasn't there, I would probably go away like all the other adults.

"I'm looking for Ray Buzzell."

One of the boys cupped his hand behind his ear and said: "Hey?"

He was an overgrown seventeen- or eighteen-year-old with heavy masculine features unfocused by any meaning in his eyes. In spite of his peroxided hair, he looked like an Indian in the red firelight.

"Ray Buzzell," I repeated.

"Never heard of him." He glanced around at the others. "Anybody ever hear of a Ray Buzzell?"

"I never heard of a Ray Buzzell," the girl in the coat said. "I knew a man named Heliogabalus Rexford Buzzell. He had a long grey beard and he died some years ago of bubonic plague."

Everybody laughed except me and the girl. I said to the boy: "You're Ray, aren't you?"

"Depends who you are." He rose in a sudden single move-ment, shedding his blanket. The three other boys rose, too. "You fuzz?"

"You're getting warm, kid."

"Don't call me kid."

"What do you want me to call you?"

"Anything but kid."

"All right, Mr. Buzzell. I have some questions to ask you, about the coat Miss Sutherland is wearing."

"Who you been talking to? How come you know our names?"

He took a step toward me, his bare feet noiseless in the sand. His little comitatus grouped themselves behind him. They crossed their arms on their chests to emphasize their muscles, and the red firelight flickered on their biceps.

With a little judo I thought I could handle all eight of their biceps, but I didn't want to hurt them. I was an emissary from the adult camp. I flashed the special-deputy's badge which I carried as a souvenir of an old trouble on the San Pedro docks.

"I've been talking to your mother, among other people. She said you found the coat on the beach."

"Never believe her," he said with one eye on the girls. "Never believe a mother."

"Where did you get it then?"

"I wove it underwater out of sea lettuce. I'm very clever with my hands." He wiggled his fingers at me.

"I wouldn't go on playing this for laughs, Buzzell. It's a serious matter. Have you ever been in Citrus Junction?"

"I guess I passed through."

"Did you stop over long enough to kill and bury a man?"

"Bury a man?" He was appalled.

"His name was Quincy Ralph Simpson. He was found buried in Citrus Junction last week, with an icepick wound in his heart. Did you know him?"

"I never heard of him, honest. Besides, we've had the coat for a couple of months." His voice had regressed five years, and sounded as though it was changing all over again. He turned to the girl. "Isn't that right, Mona?"

She nodded. Her sea-lion eyes were wide and scared. With scrabbling fingers she unbuttoned the coat and flung it off. I held out my hands for it. Ray Buzzell picked it up and gave it to me. His movements had lost their certainty.

The coat was heavy, with matted fibers that smelled of the sea. I folded it over my arm.

"Where did you get it, Ray?"

"On the beach, like Moth—like the old lady said. It was salvage, like I'm always living off the beach, picking up salvage and jetsam. Isn't that right, Mona?"

She nodded, still without breaking silence.

His voice rushed on in an adolescent spate: "It was soaked through, and there were stones in the pockets, like somebody chunked it in the drink to get rid of it. But there was a strong tide running, and the waves washed it up on the beach. It was still in pretty good condition, this Harris tweed is indestructible, so I decided to dry it out and keep it. It was like salvage. Mona wears it mostly—she's the one that gets cold."

She was shivering in her bathing suit now, close by the fire. The other girl draped a plaid shirt over her shoulders. The boys were standing around desultorily, like figures relaxing out of a battle frieze.

"Can you name the beach?"

"I don't remember. We go to a lot of beaches."

"I know which one it was," Mona said. "It was the day we had the six-point-five and I was scared to go out in them and you all said I was chicken. *You* know," she said to the others, "that little private beach above Malibu where they have the shrimp joint across the highway."

"Yeah," Ray said. "We ate there the other day. Crummy joint."

"I saw you there the other day," I said. "Now let's see if we can pin down the date you found the coat."

"I don't see how. That was a long time ago, a couple months."

The girl rose and touched his arm. "What about the tide tables, Raybuzz?"

"What about them?"

"We had a six-point-five tide that day. We haven't had many this year. You've got the tide tables in the car, haven't you?"

"I guess so."

The three of us went up the beach to the zebra-striped hearse. Ray found the dog-eared booklet, and Mona scanned it under the dashboard lights.

"It was May the nineteenth," she said positively. "It couldn't have been any other day."

I thanked her. I thanked them both, but she was the one with the brains. As I drove back toward Los Angeles, I wondered what Mona was doing on the beach. Perhaps if I met her father or her mother I could stop wondering.

chapter 24

THE BLACKWELL HOUSE was dark. I pressed the bell push, and the chimes inside gave out a lonely tinkling. I waited and rang again and waited and rang and waited.

Eventually I heard footsteps inside. The veranda light went on over my head, and the little maid looked out at me sleepily. She was out of uniform and out of sorts.

"What do *you* want?"

"Are the Blackwells in?"

"She is. He isn't."

"Tell her Mr. Archer would like to speak to her."

"I can't do that. She's in bed asleep. I was asleep myself." She yawned in my face, and hugged her rayon bathrobe more closely around her.

"You go to bed early, Letty."

"I had to get *up* early this morning, so I thought I might as well catch up on my rest. Mrs. Blackwell took some sleeping pills and left strict orders not to be disturbed. She went to bed right after dinner."

"Is Mrs. Blackwell all right?"

"She said she had a blinding headache but she gets those from time to time."

"How many sleeping pills did she take?"

"A couple."

"What kind?"

"The red kind. Why?"

"Nothing. Where's the lord and master?"

"He left early this morning. He had a phone call, about Miss Harriet, and he made me get up and make breakfast for him. It isn't a regular part of my duties but the cook sleeps out—"

I cut in on her explanations: "Do you know where he is now?"

"He went up to Tahoe to help them search for her body. That's where the phone call was from."

"They haven't found her, then?"

"No. What do you think happened to her?"

"I think she's in the lake."

"That's what he said." She stepped outside, partly closing the door behind her. "He was in bad shape at breakfast. He couldn't eat he was so broken up. I didn't think he should go off there by himself. But he wouldn't let me wake up Mrs. Blackwell, and what could I do?"

She crossed the veranda and looked up at the stars. She sighed, and laid a hand on her round pink rayon bosom.

"How long have you been working for the Blackwells?"

"Two months. It seems like longer. I mean with all the trouble in the house."

"Trouble between Mr. and Mrs. Blackwell?"

"They've had their share. But it don't behoove me to talk about it."

"Don't they get along?"

"They get along as well as most, I guess. A-course they've

only been married eight or nine months. It's the long pull that counts, my daddy says, and the Colonel must be twenty years older than her."

"Is that an issue between the Blackwells?"

"No, I don't mean that. Only it makes you wonder why she married him. Mrs. Blackwell may have her faults, but she's not the gold-digging type."

"I'm interested in what you think of her and her faults."

"I don't talk behind people's backs," she said with some spirit. "Mrs. Blackwell treats me good, and I try to treat her good back. She's a nice lady to work for. He isn't so bad either."

"Did they take you up to Tahoe in May?"

"That was before I started with them. Just my luck. They were talking about going up again in September, but it's probably all off now. They wouldn't want to stay in the lodge so soon after what happened there. I wouldn't want to myself."

"Were you fond of Harriet?"

"I wouldn't say that. I never saw much of her. But I felt kind of sorry for her, even before this happened. She was a real sad cookie, even with all that money. It's too bad she had to die before she had any happiness in life. She put on a pretty good front, but you ought to seen the crying tantrums she threw in the privacy of her own room. My mother is a practical nurse, and I tried to calm her down a couple of times."

"What was she crying about?"

"Nobody loved her, she said. She said she was ugly. I told her she had a real nice figure and other attractive features, but she couldn't see it. This was in June, before she went to Mexico. It's easy to understand why she was such a pushover for that artist guy—the one with all the names that murdered her." She looked at the stars again, and coughed at their chilliness. "I think I'm catching cold. I better get back to bed. You never can tell when they'll get you up around here."

She went back into the dark house. I went down the hill

and turned left on Sunset toward my office. I drove automatically in the light evening traffic. My mind was sifting the facts I'd scraped together, the facts and the semi-facts and the semi-demi-semi-facts. One of the semi-facts had become a certainty since I'd learned that the tweed coat had been found near the Blackwells' beach house: the Blackwell case and the Dolly Campion case and the Ralph Simpson case were parts of one another. Dolly and Ralph and probably Harriet had died by the same hand, and the coat could be used to identify the hand.

I spread it out on the desk in my office and looked at it under the light. The leather buttons were identical with the one Mungan had shown me. Where the top one had been pulled off there were some strands of broken thread corresponding with the threads attached to Mungan's button. I had no doubt that an identification man with a microscope could tie that button and this coat together.

I turned the coat over, scattering sand across the desk and the floor. It had a Harris label on the right inside breast pocket, and under it the label of the retailers: Cruttworth, Ltd., Toronto. My impulse was to phone the Cruttworth firm right away. But it was the middle of the night in Toronto, and the best I could hope for was a chat with the night watchman.

I searched in vain for cleaners' marks. Perhaps the coat had never been cleaned. In spite of its rough usage on the beach, the cuffs and the collar showed no sign of wear.

I tried the thing on. It was small for me, tight across the chest. I wondered how it would fit Campion. It was a heavy coat, and a heavy thought, and I began to sweat. I struggled out of the coat. It hugged me like guilt.

I knew a man named Sam Garlick who specialized in identifying clothes and connecting them with their rightful owners in court. He was a Detective Sergeant in the L.A.P.D. His father and his grandfather had been tailors.

I called Sam's house in West Los Angeles. His mother-in-law informed me that the Garlicks were out celebrating their twenty-second wedding anniversary. She was looking after the three smaller children, and they were a handful, but she'd finally got them off to bed. Yes, Sam would be on duty in the morning.

While the receiver was in my hand, I dialed my answering service. Both Arnie Walters and Isobel Blackwell had called me earlier in the day. The most recent calls were from Sergeant Wesley Leonard and a woman named Mrs. Hatchen, who was staying at the Santa Monica Inn. Mrs. Hatchen. Harriet's mother. The long loops were intersecting, and I was at the point of intersection.

I put in a call to the Santa Monica Inn. The switchboard operator told me after repeated attempts that Mrs. Hatchen's room didn't answer. The desk clerk thought she'd gone out for a late drive. She had checked into a single late that afternoon.

I returned Leonard's call. He answered on the first ring.

"Sergeant Leonard here."

"Archer. You wanted to talk to me?"

"I thought you wanted to talk to me. The wife mentioned you were here this afternoon."

"I had some evidence that should interest you. I have more now than I had then."

"What is it?"

"The coat Ralph Simpson had with him when he left home. I'm hoping it will lead us to the killer."

"How?" he said, rather competitively.

"It's a little complicated for the phone. We should get together, Sergeant."

"I concur. I've got something hotter than the coat." He was a simple man, and simple pride swelled in his voice. "So hot I can't even tell you over the phone."

"Do you come here or do I go there?"

"You come to me. I have my reasons. You know where I live."

He was waiting for me on the lighted porch, looking younger and taller than I remembered him. There was a flush on his cheeks and a glitter in his eyes, as if the hotness of his evidence had raised his temperature.

I suspected that he was letting me in on it because he secretly doubted his competence to handle it. He had anxiety in him, too. He pumped my hand, and seemed to have a hard time letting go.

Mrs. Leonard had made lemonade and egg-salad sandwiches, and laid them out on a coffee table in the small over-furnished living room. She poured two glasses of lemonade from a pitcher clinking with ice. Then she retreated into the kitchen, shutting the door with crisp tact. I had forgotten to eat, and I wolfed several sandwiches while Leonard talked.

"I've found the murder weapon," he announced. "I didn't find it personally, but it was my own personal idea that led to its disclosure. Ever since we uncovered Simpson's body, I've had a crew of county prisoners out there mornings picking over the scene of the crime. This morning one of them came across the icepick and turned it in."

"Let me see it."

"It's down at the courthouse, locked up. I'll show it to you later."

"What makes you certain it's the weapon?"

"I took it into the L.A. crime lab today. They gave it a test for blood traces, and got a positive reaction. Also, it fits the puncture in Simpson's body."

"Any icepick would."

"But this is it. This is the one." He leaned toward me urgently across the plate of sandwiches. "I had to be sure, and I made sure."

"Fingerprints?"

"No. The only prints were the ones from the prisoner that found it. It was probably wiped clean before the murderer stuck it in the dirt. I've got something better than fingerprints. And worse, in a way."

"You're talking in riddles, Sergeant."

"It's a riddle for sure." He glanced at the closed door to the kitchen, and lowered his voice. "The icepick was part of a little silver bar set which was sold right here in town last October. I had no trouble tracking down the store because there's only the one good hardware store here in town. That's Drake Hardware, and Mr. Drake identified the icepick personally tonight. He just had the one set like it in stock, and he remembered who he sold it to. She's a local citizen—a woman my wife has known for years."

"Who is she?"

Leonard raised his hand as if he was back on traffic point duty. "Not so fast. I don't know that I'm justified telling you her name. It wouldn't mean anything to you, anyway. She's a Citrus Junction woman, lived here all her life. Always had a clean record, till now. But it looks dark for her, or maybe her husband. There's more than the icepick tying them into the murder. They live directly across the road from the site where we found the icepick *and* the body."

"Are we talking about Mr. and Mrs. Stone?"

He looked at me in surprise. "You know Jack and Liz Stone?"

"I interviewed her this afternoon. He wasn't there."

"What were you doing—questioning her about the Simpson killing?"

"We discussed it, but I didn't consider her a suspect. We talked mostly about her daughter Dolly—and what happened to her."

Leonard made a lugubrious face. "That was a bad blow to the Stone couple. The way I figure it, psychologically speaking, the murder of their girl could of drove them over the edge.

Maybe Simpson had something to do with that murder, and they killed him in revenge."

"It's a possible motive, all right. Simpson was definitely involved with Dolly and her husband. Have you questioned the Stones?"

"Not yet. I just got Mr. Drake's identification of the icepick tonight. I talked it over with the Sheriff and he says I should wait until the D.A. gets back from Sacramento. He's due back tomorrow. We wouldn't want to make a serious mistake, the Sheriff says." Clear sweat, like distilled anxiety, burst out on his forehead. "The Stones aren't moneyed folks but they've always had a good reputation and plenty of friends in town. Liz Stone is active in the Eastern Star." He took a long gulp of lemonade.

"Somebody ought to ask her about the icepick."

"That's my opinion, too. Unfortunately my hands are tied until the D.A. gets back."

"Mine aren't."

He regarded me appraisingly. Clearly he was asking himself how far he could trust me. He tossed down the rest of his lemonade and got up.

"Okay. You want to take a look at it first?"

We rode in my car to the courthouse. The icepick was in Leonard's second-floor office, where a map of Citrus County took up one whole wall. He got the thing out of a locker and set it on the table under a magnifying glass on a flexible arm.

A tag bearing Leonard's initials was wired to the handle, and the wire sealed with lead. The square-cut silver handle felt cold to my fingers. The point of the icepick was sharp and dirty, like a bad death.

"There's a corkscrew that goes with it, part of the set," he said. "If Liz and Jack Stone have the corkscrew, it ties it up."

"Maybe. Are they the sort of people that would use a silver bar set, or any kind of a bar set?"

"I never heard that they drank, but you never can tell. One of them could be a secret drinker."

"Secret drinkers don't fool around with fancy accessories. Do I have your permission to show them this thing, and ask for an explanation?"

"I guess so." He wiped his forehead. "Long as you don't go to them in my name, I guess it's all right. But don't make any accusations. We don't want them to panic and go on the run."

I let him out on the sidewalk in front of his house and drove to the west side. The Stones had an upstairs light on. The man who came to the front door was in his pajamas. He was a thin man with bushy sandy hair and defeated eyes.

"Mr. Stone?"

"Yessir."

"I had some conversation with your wife today."

"You're the detective, are you?" he said in a flat voice.

"Yes. I'd appreciate a few minutes more with your wife, and with you, too."

"I dunno, it's getting pretty late. Mrs. Stone is on her way to bed." He glanced up the stairs which rose from the hallway. "Is it about Dolly?"

"It's connected with Dolly."

"Maybe I can handle it, eh?" He squared his narrow shoulders. "It was a terrible sorrow to my wife what happened to Dolly. I hate to see her dragged back to it all the time."

"I'm afraid it's necessary, Mr. Stone."

He took my word for it and went upstairs to fetch her, · climbing like a man on a treadmill. They came down together wearing bathrobes. He was holding her arm. Her face and neck were shiny with some kind of cream or oil.

"Come in," she said. "You shouldn't keep a man waiting on the doorstep, Jack. It isn't polite."

We went into the living room, where the three of us stood and looked at each other. The awkwardness developed into tension. The woman pulled at the oily skin of her throat.

"What brings you here so late? Have you found something out?"

"I keep trying, Mrs. Stone." I got the icepick out of my pocket and held it out by the tip. "Have you seen this before?"

"Let me look at it."

She reached out and took it from me by the handle. Her husband leaned at her shoulder, one arm around her waist. He seemed to depend on physical contact with her.

"It looks like the one you bought for Mrs. Jaimet," he said.

"I believe it is. What's this little wire tag doing on it?"

"It's just to identify it. Where did you buy it, Mrs. Stone?"

"At Drake Hardware. It's part of a set I got for Mrs. Jaimet as a wedding gift. Jack thought I spent too much money on it, but I wanted to get her something nice for once. She was always good to us and Dolly. Twelve dollars wasn't too much for all she's done." Her eye was on her husband, and she was speaking more to him than to me.

"It cost sixteen," he corrected her. "I work all day for sixteen dollars take-home. But I'm not kicking. She *was* a good friend to Dolly."

His wife took up the sentiment and breathed more life into it. "She was *wonderful* to Dolly, a second mother. Remember when Dolly used to call her Aunt Izzie? Not every woman in Izzie Jaimet's position would permit that, but she's no snob. She gave our Dolly some of her happiest hours."

They clung to each other and to this warm fragment of the past. The icepick in her hand brought her back to the sharp present.

"How did you get ahold of this? I sent it to Mrs. Jaimet for a wedding gift. She doesn't even live in town any more."

"She used to live in town?"

"Right across the road," Stone said. "We were neighbors with the Jaimets for close to twenty years. She sold out to the Rowlands after Jaimet died, and moved to Santa Barbara.

But Liz and her kept in touch. She even invited Liz to attend her wedding. Liz didn't go though. I convinced her she'd be out of place—"

His wife interrupted him: "Mr. Archer didn't come here to listen to a lot of ancient history." She said to me: "You haven't answered my question. Where did you get ahold of this?"

She shook the icepick at me. I held out my hand, and she relinquished it. I put it away in my pocket.

"I can't answer that question, Mrs. Stone."

"I've been answering *your* questions, all day and half the night."

"It hasn't been quite that bad. Still I'm sorry that I can't make things even with you. You'll find out soon enough what this is about."

"Is it the man they found across the road?"

I didn't affirm it or deny it. "This may be important to you personally. It may lead to a solution of Dolly's murder."

"I don't understand how."

"Neither do I. If I did, I wouldn't be here asking you questions. How well and how long did Mrs. Jaimet know Dolly?"

"All her life." She sat down suddenly on the chesterfield. The net of time had drawn tight on her face, cutting deep marks. "That is, until about three and a half years ago, when she moved to Santa Barbara. But it didn't stop then. She invited Dolly to come and visit her in Santa Barbara. I tried to talk Dolly into it—Mrs. Jaimet could do a lot for her—but Dolly never made the trip."

"How could Mrs. Jaimet do a lot for her?"

"The way she did do a lot for her. Mrs. Jaimet is an educated woman; her husband was the principal of the high school. She used to give Dolly books to read, and take her on picnics and all. I was working in those days, and she was a real good neighbor. She just loved Dolly. So if you're thinking she had anything to do with Dolly's death, you're 'way off the beam."

"'Way off the beam," her husband echoed. "She was like a second mother to Dolly, being she had no children of her own."

"Which was her secret sorrow. She never will have children now—she's too old."

Elizabeth Stone looked down at her own body. Jack Stone put his arm around her shoulders. She crossed her legs.

"Where can I get in touch with Mrs. Jaimet?"

"She's living in L.A. with her new husband. I ought to have her address some place. She remembered me with a card at Christmastime. I think I still have that card in the bureau." She started to get up, and froze in a leaning posture. "If I give you the address, you have to promise you won't tell her who gave it to you."

"I could promise, but it's bound to come out. Nearly everything does in the long run."

"Yeah, you have something there." She turned to her husband. "Jack, will you get it for me? It's in the top drawer of the bureau with the other special cards I saved—the one with the silver bells."

He rose quickly and left the room, and she subsided onto the chesterfield. Her baby-blue eyes were strained and speculative.

"The man across the road was stabbed with an icepick. It said so in the paper. The icepick you have there, the one I bought for Mrs. Jaimet's wedding—it couldn't be the one, could it?"

"Yes. It could be."

"I don't get it. How would a lady like her get mixed up in a killing?"

"Some of the darndest people do."

"But she's a real lady."

"What makes you so sure?"

"I may not be a lady myself, but I know one when I see one. Isobel Jaimet has class, the kind that doesn't have to flaunt itself. I happen to know she has very good connections. Matter of fact, she married one of them the second time around. Her second husband was her first husband's second cousin, if you can follow that. I met him years ago when he was staying with the Jaimets. He was very important in the military. The Jaimet family itself used to own the whole west side, before they lost it."

"What is her second husband's name?"

"Let's see, it's on the tip of my tongue. Anyway, it's on the card she sent me."

"Would it be Blackwell?"

"That's it! Blackwell. You know him?"

I didn't have to answer her. Her husband's slippered feet were clop-clopping down the stairs. He came into the room carrying a square envelope, which he handed to his wife. She opened it.

"Merry Christmas and Happy New Year," the bright card said. "Colonel and Mrs. Mark Blackwell."

chapter 25

SERGEANT LEONARD was waiting for me at the front of his house. He was wearing an eager expression, which sharpened when our eyes met under the light.

"Did they break down and confess?"

"They had nothing to confess. Elizabeth Stone bought the bar set as a wedding present for an old neighbor."

"It sounds like malarkey to me. They don't have the money to buy that kind of presents for the neighbors."

"They did, though."

"Who was the neighbor?"

"Mrs. Jaimet."

"Mrs. Ronald Jaimet? That's malarkey. She couldn't have had anything to do with this."

I would have liked to be able to agree with him. Since I couldn't, I said nothing.

"Why, her and her husband were two of our leading citizens," he said. "They had a front-page editorial in the paper when he died. He was a member of a pioneer county family and the best principal we ever had at the union high school."

"What did he die of?"

"He was a diabetic. He broke his leg in the Sierra and ran out of insulin before they could get him back to civilization. It was a great loss to the town, and just about as big a loss when Mrs. Jaimet moved away. She was the head of the Volunteer Family Service and half a dozen other organizations." He paused reflectively. "Did the Stones say where she is now?"

I lit a cigarette and considered my answer. Between my duty to the law and a man who trusted me, and my duty to a client I no longer trusted, my ethics were stretched thin. Leonard repeated his question.

"I think they said she was married in Santa Barbara last year. You'd better talk to them yourself."

"Yeah. I better. In the morning." He scratched at his hairline. "It just came to my mind, the Jaimets lived right across the road from the Stones. We found Simpson buried right spang in their back yard, their use-to-was back yard. What do you make of that?"

"I don't like it," I said honestly, and changed the subject before he could ask me further questions. "I have that coat in the car if you want to look it over."

"Yeah. Bring it in."

I spread it out on the carpet in his living room. While I told him what I knew of its history, he was down on his knees, examining it inside and out.

"Too bad there's no cleaners' marks," he said. "But we may be able to trace the ownership through these Cruttworth people in Toronto. Another long trip for somebody."

"I'm getting used to long trips."

Leonard rose with his hands in the small of his back, then got down on his knees beside the coat again.

"Sometimes," he said, "the older-established cleaners put their marks inside the sleeves."

He turned back the right cuff. Several code letters and figures were written in indelible ink in the lining: BX1207. He stood up smiling.

"It's a lucky thing I looked."

"Do you recognize the mark, Sergeant?"

"No, it isn't local. But we can trace it. I know an officer in L.A. who has a pretty complete collection of these marks."

"Sam Garlick."

"You know Sam too, do you? We'll get to work on it first thing in the morning. You may not have to go to Toronto after all."

I left the coat with Leonard and went back to Bel Air. The Blackwell house had lights in it, and there was a taxi standing in the drive. The sound of my feet in the gravel woke the driver. He looked at me as if I might be about to hold him up.

"It's a nice night," I said.

"Uh-huh."

"Who are you waiting for?"

"A fare. Any objections?" His broken sleep had made him a little surly. He had a seamed dark face, and the eyes of a loner.

"I have no objections."

He said with aggressive politeness: "If I'm in your way I can move. Just say the word."

"You're not in my way. What happened, brother—did a bear bite you?"

"I don't like these long waits. These dames have no consideration. She must of been in there nearly an hour." He looked at his watch. "Over an hour."

"Who is she?"

"I dunno. Some big blonde dame in a leopard coat. I picked her up in Santa Monica."

"Is she old or young?"

"She isn't young. You ask a lot of questions."

"I'll bet you two dollars you didn't pick her up at the Santa Monica Inn."

"You lose. Are you her husband?"

"A friend." I gave him two dollars and went back to my car. We sat and had a waiting competition which lasted another fifteen or twenty minutes. Then the front door opened.

Pauline Hatchen backed out saying good night to Isobel Blackwell. I had a good look at Isobel before she closed the door. She was fully and formally dressed in a dark suit. Her heavy make-up didn't entirely hide her pallor or the patches of funeral crepe under her eyes. She didn't notice me.

I was waiting beside the cab when Pauline Hatchen reached it. "How are you, Mrs. Hatchen? I'm not as surprised to see you here as you might think. I got your call, and tried to return it."

"It's Mr. Archer. How nice." But she didn't sound too happy. "I've been wanting to talk to you again. It was one of my main reasons for coming back. The other night, in Ajijic, I didn't truly *realize* the situation. I suppose I'm what they call slow on the uptake."

"Did you fly in?"

"Yes. Today." She looked around at the large and quiet night. The lights in the Blackwell house were going out progressively. "Is there somewhere we can go and talk?"

"Will my car do? I prefer not to leave here right now. I want to see Isobel before she goes back to bed."

"I suppose it will have to do." She turned to the driver. "Do you mind waiting a few more minutes?"

"It's your time, ma'am. You're paying for it."

We walked back to my car. She seemed very tired, so tired that she had forgotten her self-consciousness. She leaned on my arm, and let me help her into the lighted front seat. Her leopard coat was genuine but shabby. She pulled it around her not inelegant legs, and I shut the door.

I sat behind the wheel. "You want to talk about Harriet."

"Yes. Is there any word from her? Anything at all?"

"Nothing that will give you any comfort."

"So Isobel said. I thought perhaps she was holding back on me. She's always been a great one for deciding what other people ought to know. And I had the very devil of a time getting in touch with her. She'd gone to bed and refused to answer the phone. How any woman can *sleep* through a thing like this! But of course she's not Harriet's mother. That makes the difference. Blood is thicker than water."

She sounded like an algebra student quoting a formula which she was just learning how to apply.

"Do you know Isobel well?"

"I've known her for a long time. That isn't quite the same thing, is it? Her first husband, Ronald Jaimet, was Mark's cousin, and incidentally one of his best friends. Mark is a very family-minded man, and naturally we saw a good deal of the Jaimets. But Isobel and I were never close. I always felt she envied me my position as Mark's wife. Ronald was a decent-enough fellow, but he was nothing but a high-school teacher. He was one of those dedicated souls. Perhaps his diabetes had something to do with it."

"Do you know anything about his death?"

"Not much. He had an accident in the mountains. Mark was with him at the time. Why don't you ask Mark?"

"Mark isn't available. Or is he?"

"No, he's not here. According to Isobel, he's gone up to Tahoe." She leaned toward me, and her clothes emitted a gust of perfume. "Just what is the situation up there, Mr. Archer?"

"I haven't been in touch with it today. They're searching for Harriet, of course. She was last seen there, and a blood-stained hat belonging to her was found in the water. I found it myself."

"Does that mean she's been killed?"

"I keep hoping it doesn't. All we can do is hope."

"You think Harriet's dead." Her voice was low and dull. "Did Burke Damis kill her?"

"He says he didn't."

"But what would he have to gain?"

"Not all murders are for profit."

We sat in close silence, listening to each other breathe. I was keenly aware of her, not so much as a woman, but as a fellow creature who had begun to feel pain. She had lost her way to the happy ending and begun to realize the conse-quences of the sealed-off past.

"You came a long way to ask me a few questions, Mrs. Hatchen. I'm sorry I can't give you better answers."

"It isn't your fault. And it wasn't just to ask questions that I came back. I heard from Harriet, you see. It brought home to me—"

"You heard from Harriet? When?"

"Yesterday, but please don't get your hopes up. She wrote the letter last Sunday, before this thing erupted. It was a very touching little letter. It made me see myself, and Harriet, in quite a new light."

"What did she have to say?"

"I can't repeat it verbatim, though I must have read it a dozen times on the plane. You can read it yourself if you like."

I turned on the overhead light. She rummaged in her leopard bag and produced a crumpled airmail envelope. It was addressed to Mrs. Keith Hatchen, Apartado Postal 89, Ajijic, Jalisco, Mexico, and had been postmarked in Pacific Palisades the previous Monday morning at 9:42. The en-

velope contained a single sheet crowded with writing. The
first few lines slanted up to the right; the rest slanted down
increasingly, so that the concluding lines were at a thirty-
degree angle from the bottom of the page.

Dear Mother,

This is a difficult letter to write because we've
never talked to one another as woman to woman
(all my fault) and it was stupid and childish of me
to leave without saying good-by. I was afraid (it
seems I'm always afraid of something, doesn't it?)
you would disapprove of me and Burke, and that I
couldn't bear. He's my moon and stars, my great brilliant moon and my cruel bright stars. You didn't know
I had such feelings, did you? Well, I do. I love him
and I'm going to marry him, I don't care what Mark
says. When I'm with Him I feel quite different from
my ordinary sad shy self (alliteration's artful aid!)
—he's a Prince, a dark Prince, who fits crystal slip-
pers on my Cinderella feet and teaches me to dance
to music I never heard before—the music of the
spheres. When he touches me the dead cold world
comes alive, dead cold Harriet comes alive.

That sounds like gibberish, doesn't it, but believe
me I mean every word of it, but I will try to write
more calmly. I need your help, Mother. I know I
can count on you, in spite of all the wasted years between us. You have known passion and suffered for
it—but here I am going on again like a nineteenth-
century romance. The point is, we need money and
we need it right away if we are to get married. Burke
is in some sort of trouble (nothing serious) and I
should never have brought him back to this country.
We plan to fly to South America—keep this under
your hat!—if we can get the money, and you are

the only one we can turn to. Mark is no help at all.
He hates Burke, I even think he hates me, too. He
says he'll hire detectives to stop the wedding! Since
he is one of the controllers of Aunt Ada's trust, I
can't do anything in that direction until I'm twenty-
five. So I am asking you to lend me five thousand
dollars till January. If you will do this please have it
ready for me and I will get in touch with you when
we reach Mexico. We have enough money to reach
Mexico.

Dear Mother, please do this. It's the only thing
I've ever asked of you. It's the only thing I ask of
life, that Burke and I have a chance to be happy together. If I can't have him, I'll die.

Your loving daughter,
Harriet.

I folded the letter along its creases and tucked it into the
envelope. Mrs. Hatchen watched me as if it was a live thing
which I might injure.

"It's a strangely beautiful letter, isn't it?"

"It didn't strike me in quite that way. I'm not too crazy
about some of the implications. Harriet wasn't thinking too
well when she wrote it."

"What do you expect?" she said defensively. "The poor
girl was under great strain. She'd just had a fearful battle with
her father—Isobel told me something about it. Harriet was
fighting for everything she holds dear."

"So was Campion. Everything that he holds dear seems to
be five thousand dollars."

"Campion?"

"Campion is Burke Damis's real name. He's in jail in Redwood City at the moment. What about the five thousand
dollars, Mrs. Hatchen? Would you have been willing to lend
it to her?"

"Yes. I still am, if she is alive to use it. I brought it with me. Keith and I went into Guadalajara yesterday afternoon and took it out of the bank. It's part of my settlement from Mark, and Keith had no real objection."

"I hope you're not carrying it around."

"It's in the safe at the hotel."

"Leave it there. Harriet certainly won't be needing it. I don't believe it was her idea, anyway." I turned to look at her under the light. "You're a generous woman, Mrs. Hatchen. I took you for something different."

"I am something different." She narrowed her eyes and drew down the corners of her mouth. "Please turn off the light and don't look at me. I'm an ugly old woman, trying to buy back the past. But I came back here about fifteen years too late. I had no right to leave Harriet. Her life would have turned out better if I'd stayed."

"You can't be sure of that." I switched off the light, and noticed that all the lights in the Blackwell house had gone out. "Do you mind telling me just why you left Mark Blackwell? Did it have anything to do with Isobel?"

"No, he wasn't interested in her. He wasn't interested in any woman, and that includes me." Her voice had become harsher and deeper. "Mark was a mother's boy. I know that sounds like a peculiar statement to make about a professional military man. Unfortunately it's true. His mother was the widow of the late Colonel, who was killed in the First War, and Mark was her only son, and she really lavished herself on him, if 'lavish' is the word. 'Ravish' may be closer.

"She spent the first years of our marriage with us, and I had to sit in the background and watch him dance to her tune, playing skip-rope with the silver cord. It's a common story— I've heard it from other women, in and out of the service. You marry them because they're idealistic and make no passes. The trouble is, they stay that way. Mark was like a little boy in bed. You'll never know the contortions I had to go through to get a child. But we won't go into that.

"When his mother died, I thought he'd turn to me. I was a dreamer. He transferred his fixation—yes, I've talked to the doctors—he transferred his fixation to poor little Harriet. It's a terrible thing to see a person converting another person into a puppet, a kind of zombie. He supervised her reading, her games, her friends, even her thoughts. He made her keep a diary, which he read, and when he was away on duty she had to send it to him. He got her so confused that she didn't know whether she was a girl or a boy, or if he was her father or her lover.

"He was worse than ever after the war, when he got back from Germany. The war was a disappointment to Mark; it didn't do what he'd hoped for his career. Actually he only chose that career because it was a family tradition and his mother insisted on it. I think he would have been happier doing almost anything else. But by the time they retired him, he thought it was too late to start something new. And he had money, so he didn't have to. There's always been scads of money in the family, and he could afford to spend all his time on Harriet. He conceived the grand idea of turning her into a sort of boy-girl who would make everything come right in the end for him. He taught her to shoot and climb mountains and play polo. He even took to calling her Harry.

"It sickened me. I'm not the aggressive type, and I'd always been afraid of him—you get that way living with a man you don't love. But I finally forced a showdown. I told him I would divorce him if he didn't get some help, psychiatric help. Naturally he thought I was the one who was crazy—he couldn't afford to think otherwise. Maybe I was, to stay with him for twelve years. He told me to go ahead and divorce him, that he and Harriet were enough for each other. She was only eleven years old at the time. I wanted to take her with me, but Mark said he would fight me to the limit. I couldn't afford a court battle. Don't ask why. Everything catches up with you in the end. So I lost my daughter, and now she's really lost."

We sat and let the darkness soak into our bones. I tried to relieve it.

"There's a small chance that Harriet's all right," I said. "She and Campion may have decided to travel separately. It would account for his refusal to say what happened to her. She may turn up in Mexico after all."

"But you don't really think she will?"

"No. It's just one of several possibilities. The others aren't so pleasant to contemplate."

There was a stir of life in the cab ahead. The driver got out and slouched toward us.

"You said a few minutes, ma'am. I don't mind waiting if I know how long I got to wait. It's this uncertainty that makes me nervous."

"Things are rough all over," I said.

"I was speaking to the lady." But he went back to his cab.

Mrs. Hatchen opened the door on her side. "I've kept you longer than I meant to. You said you wanted to talk to Isobel."

"Yes."

"Do you think she knows something she hasn't told?"

"People nearly always do," I said. "It's why I have a hard life, and an interesting one."

She reached for the letter, which was still in my hand. "I'd like that back if you don't mind. It's very important to me."

"I'm sorry. The police will have to see it. I'll try to get it back to you eventually. Will you be staying at the Santa Monica Inn?"

"I don't know. Isobel asked me to stay with her, but that's impossible."

"Why?"

"We don't get along. We never have. She thinks I'm a silly flibbertigibbet. Maybe I am. *I* think *she* is a hypocrite."

"I'd be interested in your reasons."

"They're simple enough. Isobel has always pretended to despise money and the things it can buy. Plain living and high thinking was her motto. But I notice she grabbed Mark and his money the first good chance she got. Please don't quote me to Isobel. In fact, you better not tell her that you saw me."

I said I wouldn't. "One more question, Mrs. Hatchen. What happens to Ada's trust fund if Harriet doesn't live to enjoy it?"

"I suppose it reverts to Mark. Nearly everything does."

chapter 26

THE MAID reluctantly let me in. I waited in the hallway, counting the pieces in the parquetry and wishing that I had never seen Isobel Blackwell, or taken her money, or liked her. She finally appeared, wearing the same dark suit and the same dark patches under her eyes. Her movements were carefully controlled, as if she was walking a line.

She said with unsmiling formality: "I hope the importance of your news justifies this late-night visit."

"It does. Can we sit down?"

She took me into the drawing room, under the eyes of the ancestors. I said to them as well as to her: "I'm doing you a favor coming here. If you weren't my client, there'd be policemen instead, and reporters trampling the roses."

"Am I supposed to understand that?" Her speech was slurred; and her eyes had a drugged look. "If I am, you'll have to explain it to me. And please bear in mind that I may not be thinking too clearly—I'm full of chloral hydrate. Now what were you saying about policemen and newspapermen?"

"They'll be here tomorrow. They'll be wanting to know, among other things, if you have an icepick with a square-cut silver handle."

"We do have, yes. I haven't seen it lately, but I assume it's somewhere in the kitchen, or one of the portable bars."

"I can tell you now it isn't. It's in the hands of Sergeant Wesley Leonard of the Citrus County Sheriff's Department."

I was watching her closely, and she seemed genuinely perplexed. "Are you trying to threaten me in some way? You sound as though you were."

"The word is warn, Mrs. Blackwell."

Her voice sharpened. "Has something happened to Mark?"

"Something has happened to Ralph Simpson and Dolly Stone. I think both those people were known to you."

"Dolly Stone? I haven't even seen the girl in years."

"I hope you can prove that, because Dolly was murdered last May."

She lowered her head and moved it from side to side, as if she was trying to dodge the fact. "You must be joking." She stole a look at my face and saw that I was not. "How? How was she murdered?"

"She was strangled, by unknown hands."

Isobel Blackwell looked at her hands. They were slender and well kept, but the knuckles suggested a history of work. She massaged the knuckles, as if she might be trying to erase the history.

"You surely can't imagine that I had anything to do with it. I had no idea that Dolly was dead. I *was* quite close to her at one time—she was virtually my foster daughter—but that was years ago."

"She was your foster daughter?"

"That may be putting it too strongly. Dolly was one of my projects. The Stones lived across the road from us, and I couldn't help noticing the beginnings of antisocial tendencies in the child. I did my best to provide her with an example and steer her clear of delinquency." Her voice was cool and careful. "Did I fail?"

"Somebody failed. You sound a little like a social worker, Mrs. Blackwell."

"I was one before I married my first husband."

"Ronald Jaimet."

She raised her brows. Under them, her eyes appeared strangely naked. "Suddenly you know a great deal about my affairs."

"Suddenly your affairs are at the center of this case. When I found out tonight that you knew Dolly Stone and her parents, it knocked most of my ideas sideways. I'm trying to work up a new set of ideas, and I can't do it without your co-operation."

"I'm still very much in the dark. I'm not even sure what case we're talking about."

"It's all one case," I said, "Harriet's disappearance and Dolly's death and the murder of Ralph Simpson, who was stabbed with an icepick—"

"*My* icepick?"

"That's the police hypothesis. I share it. I'm not accusing you of doing the actual stabbing."

"How good of you."

"The fact remains that you knew Ralph Simpson, you were almost certainly aware of his death, and you said nothing about it."

"Is this the same Ralph Simpson who worked for us at Tahoe in the spring?"

"The same. A day or two after he left you he was stabbed to death and buried in the back yard of the house you used to own in Citrus Junction."

"But that's insane, utterly insane."

"You knew about it, didn't you?"

"I did not. You're quite mistaken."

"There's an account of the Simpson killing on the front page of the Citrus Junction paper in your sitting room."

"I haven't read it. I take the paper, to keep track of old

friends, but I'm afraid I seldom look at it. I haven't even glanced at it this week."

I couldn't tell if she was lying. Her face had become a stiff mask which refused to tell what went on in the mind behind it. Her eyes had veiled themselves. Guilt can effect those changes. So can innocent fear.

"You have sharp eyes, don't you, Mr. Archer? Unfriendly eyes."

"Objective eyes, I hope."

"I'm not fond of your objectivity. I thought there was a— degree of confidence between us."

"There was."

"You put that emphatically in the past tense. Since you've been operating with my money, operating on *me* in fact, I would have expected a little more tolerance, and sympathy. You realize my connection with Dolly proves nothing whatever against me."

"I'd be glad to see that proved."

"How can I prove it?"

"Tell me more about Dolly. For instance, what were the antisocial tendencies you noticed in her?"

"Must I? I've only just learned of her death. It's distressing to rake over the past under the circumstances."

"The past is the key to the present."

"You're quite a philosopher," she said with some irony.

"I'm simply a detective with quite a few murder cases under my belt. People start out young on the road to becoming murderers. They start out equally young on the road to becoming victims. When the two roads intersect, you have a violent crime."

"Are you suggesting that Dolly was a predestined victim?"

"Not predestined, but prepared. What prepared her, Mrs. Blackwell?"

"*I* didn't, if that's what you're thinking." She paused, and took a deep breath. "Very well, I'll try to give you a serious answer. I *was* concerned about Dolly, from the time she was four or five. She wasn't relating too well to other children. Her relationship with adults wasn't right, either, and it got worse. It showed up particularly in her contacts with my husband. Dolly was a pretty little thing, and her father had treated her seductively and then rejected her. It's a common pattern. The Stones aren't bad people, but they're ignorant people, lacking in insight. They were our good neighbors, however, and Ronald and I believed in helping our neighbors as best we could. We tried to provide Dolly with a more normal family constellation—"

"And yourselves with a daughter?"

"That's an unkind remark." Her anger showed through her mask. She forced it back. "It's true, we couldn't have children; Ronald had a diabetic condition. I'm also aware of the ease with which good white magic turns into bad black magic. But we made no attempt to take Dolly from her parents, emotionally or otherwise. We merely tried to give her some things they couldn't—books and music and recreation and the company of understanding people."

"Then your husband died, and you moved away."

"I'd already lost her by that time," she said defensively. "It wasn't I who failed Dolly. She'd begun to steal money from my purse and lie about it, and she did other things I prefer not to go into. She's dead: *nil nisi bonum.*"

"I wish you would go into the other things."

"I'll put it this way. I wasn't able to protect her against degrading influences—I only had a part of her life after all. She ran with the wrong crowd in high school and picked up gutter ideas of sex. Dolly was already mature at the age of fifteen."

She didn't go on. Her mouth was grave, her eyes watchful. It was possible, I thought, that Dolly had made a play for Ronald Jaimet before he died. It was possible that Jaimet had fallen for it. A daughterless man in middle age can take a sudden fall, all the way down to the bottom of the hole. It would be a suicidal hole, but suicide came easily to a diabetic. He simply had to forget his dose and his diet.

Being a murder victim came easily to a diabetic, too.

"You have that look again," Isobel Blackwell said. "That objective look, as you call it. I hope I'm not the object of your thoughts."

"In a way you are. I was thinking about Ronald Jaimet's death."

"Apparently you've come here tonight determined to spare me nothing. If you must know, Ronald died by accident. And incidentally, since I think I know what's on your mind, Ronald's relations with Dolly were pure—wonderfully pure. I knew Ronald."

"I didn't. What were the circumstances of his death? I understand Mark was with him."

"They were on a pack trip in the Sierra. Ronald fell and broke his ankle. What was worse, he broke his insulin needle. By the time Mark got him down the hill to Bishop, he was in a coma. He died in the Bishop hospital, before I could get to him."

"So you have the story from Mark."

"It's the truth. Ronald and Mark were good friends as well as cousins. Ronald was the younger of the two, and he'd always admired Mark. I could never have married Mark if that hadn't been the case."

Under the increasing pressure of my questions, she seemed to feel the need to justify the main actions of her life. I brought her back to Ronald Jaimet's death.

"Diabetics don't usually go on pack trips in the mountains. Aren't they supposed to lead a fairly sheltered life?"

"Some of them do. Ronald couldn't. I realize, I realized then, that it was risky for him to expose himself to accidents. But I couldn't bring myself to try and stop him. His annual hike was important to him, as a man. And Mark was there to look after him."

I sat for a minute and listened to the echoes of her last sentence. Perhaps she was hearing them, too.

"How did Ronald happen to take a spill?"

"He slipped and fell on a steep trail." She jerked her head sideways as if to deflect the image of his fall. "Please don't try to tell me that it was accident-proneness or unconscious suicide. I've been over all that in my mind many times. Ronald had a great sense of life, in spite of his illness. He was happy in his life. I made him happy."

"I'm sure you did."

She went on stubbornly, justifying her life and its meanings: "And please don't try to tell me that Mark had anything to do with Ronald's death. The two men were deeply fond of each other. Mark was like an older brother to Ronald. He carried him on his back for miles over rugged trails, back to the jeep. It took him most of a day and a night to bring him down the hill. When Harriet and I finally reached the hospital—she drove me up to Bishop that day—Mark was completely broken up. He blamed himself for not taking better care of Ronald. So you see, you're wandering far afield when you suggest that Mark—"

"The suggestion came from you, Mrs. Blackwell."

"No, it was you."

"I'm sorry, but you brought it up."

"I did?" She dragged her fingers diagonally across her face, pressing her eyes closed, drawing down one corner of her mouth. Her lipstick was smeared like blood there. "You're probably right. I'm very tired, and confused. I only have about half a lobe working."

"It's the chloral hydrate," I said, thinking that the drug had some of the properties of a truth serum.

"It's partly that and partly other things. Before you arrived, I had a very wearing hour with Harriet's mother. Pauline flew all the way from Guadalajara to find out what had happened. I didn't know she had so much maternal feeling."

"What went on in that hour?"

"Nothing, really. She seems to blame me for the family trouble, and I suppose I blame her. Someday, in the brave new world, we'll all stop blaming each other."

She tried to smile, and the faltering movement of her mouth charmed me. I would have preferred not to be charmed by her.

"Someday," I said, "I can stop asking questions. As it stands, I have to go on asking them. What kind of a houseboy was Ralph Simpson?"

"Adequate, I suppose. He worked for us such a short time, it's hard to say. I don't like using servants, anyway, which is why we have only the one living in. I'm accustomed to doing things for myself."

"Is that why Simpson was fired?"

"Mark thought he was too familiar. Mark likes to be treated as a superior being; Ralph Simpson was very democratic. I rather liked it. I'm not really used to the stuffy life." She glanced up at the ancestors.

"I heard a rumor at Tahoe that Ralph was fired for stealing."

"Stealing what, for heaven's sake?"

"It may have been a topcoat," I said carefully. "When Ralph got home from the lake, he had a man's topcoat which he told his wife was given him. It was brown Harris tweed with woven brown leather buttons. One of the buttons was missing. Do you know anything about the coat?"

"No. Obviously you do."

"Did your husband ever buy clothes in Toronto?"

"Not to my knowledge."

"Has he ever been in Toronto?"

"Of course, many times. We passed through there on our honeymoon last fall."

"This coat was bought from a Toronto firm named Cruttworth. Did your husband have dealings there?"

"I couldn't say. Why is this topcoat so important to you?"

"I'll tell you if you'll let me look at your husband's clothes."

She shook her head. "I couldn't possibly, without his permission."

"When do you expect him back?"

"I don't believe he'll leave Tahoe until Harriet is found."

"Then he may be there for a long time. The chances are better than even that she's dead and buried like Ralph Simpson, or sunk in the lake."

Her face was ugly with dismay. "You think Burke Damis did this to her?"

"He's the leading suspect."

"But it isn't possible. He couldn't have."

"That's his contention, too."

"You've talked to him?"

"I ran him down last night. He's in custody in Redwood City. I thought that was going to close the case, but it didn't. The case keeps opening up, and taking in more people and more territory. The connections between the people keep multiplying. Damis's real name is Campion, as you may know, and he married Dolly Stone last September. She had a child in March, and two months later she was strangled. Campion was the main suspect in her death."

"That's incredible."

"What I find hard to believe, Mrs. Blackwell, is that you were totally unaware of all this."

"But I was. I hadn't been in touch with Dolly."

"There has to be a further connection, though. You see that. Bruce Campion alias Burke Damis married your one-time foster daughter last year. This year he planned to marry your stepdaughter, with your support, and got as far as eloping with her. Coincidences come large sometimes, but I'm not buying that one."

She said in a small voice: "You're really suspicious of me."

"I have to be. You tried to keep me off Campion's back. You promoted his marriage to Harriet."

"Only because she had no one else. I was afraid of what would happen to her, to her emotions, if she went on being so bitterly lonely."

"Perhaps you were playing God with her, the way you did with Dolly? Perhaps you met Campion through Dolly, and put him up to marrying Harriet?"

"I swear I never saw him before he came to this house last Saturday night. I admit I rather liked him. People make mistakes. I seem to have made a mistake about you as well."

Her look was complexly female, asking me for renewed assurances of loyalty and fealty. Under the threat of the situation she was using all her brains now, and the full range of her temperament. I guessed that she was defending herself, or something just as dear to her as herself.

"Anyway," she said, "what possible advantage could I derive from serving as a marriage broker to Mr. Damis-Campion?"

The question was rhetorical, but I had answers for it. "If your husband disinherited Harriet, or if she was killed, you could inherit everything he has. If Harriet and your husband were killed, in that order, you could inherit everything they both have."

"My husband is very much alive."

"At last report he is."

"I love my husband. I won't say I loved Harriet, but I cared for her."

"You loved your first husband, too, and you survived him."

Tears started in her eyes. She made an effort of will which contorted her face, and cut the tears off at the source. "You can't believe these things about me. You're just saying them."

"I'm not saying them for fun. We've had two murders, or three, or four. Ralph Simpson and Dolly, Harriet, Ronald Jaimet. All of the victims were known to you; three were close."

"But we don't know that Harriet has been murdered. Ronald definitely was not. I told you the circumstances of Ronald's death."

"I heard what you told me."

"My husband will confirm my account, in detail. Don't you believe it?"

"At this point I'd be silly to commit myself."

"What kind of a woman do you think I am?" Her eyes were intent on mine, with a kind of scornful ardor.

"I'm trying to develop an answer to that question."

"I don't admire your methods. They're a combination of bullying and blackmail and insulting speculation. You're trying to make me out a liar and a cheat, perhaps even a murderer. I'm none of those things."

"I hope you're not. The facts are what they are. I don't know all of them yet. I don't know you."

"I thought you liked me, that we liked each other."

"I do. But that's my problem."

"Yet you treat me without sympathy, without feeling."

"It's cleaner that way. I have a job to do."

"But you're supposed to be working for me."

"True. I've been expecting you to fire me any minute."

"Is that what you want?"

"It would free my hand. You can't pull me off the case—I guess you know that. It's my case and I'll finish it on my own time if I have to."

"You seem to be using a great deal of my time, too. And as for freeing your hand, I have the impression that your hand is already excessively free. I can feel the lacerations, Mr. Archer."

Her voice was brittle, but she had recovered her style. That bothered me, too. Chloral hydrate or no, an innocent woman holding nothing back wouldn't have sat still for some of the things I had said. She'd have slapped my face or screamed or burst into tears or fainted or left the room or ordered me out. I almost wished that one or several of these things had happened.

"At least you're feeling pain," I said. "It's better than being anaesthetized and not knowing where the knife is cutting you."

"You conceive of yourself as a surgeon? Perhaps I should call you doctor."

"I'm not the one holding the knife. I'm not the one, either, who took your silver icepick and stabbed Ralph Simpson with it."

"I trust you've relinquished the idea that it was I."

"You're the most likely suspect. It's time you got that through your head. You knew Simpson, it was your icepick, it was your old stamping ground where he was buried."

"You don't have to get rough," she said in a rough voice. Her voice was as mutable as any I'd ever heard.

"This is a picnic compared with what you're going to have for breakfast. I kept the police out of your hair tonight by suppressing your present name and whereabouts—"

"You did that for me?"

"You are my client, after all. I wanted to give you a chance to clear yourself. You haven't used the chance."

"I see." A grim look settled like age on her mouth. "What was my motive for stabbing Ralph Simpson and burying him in the yard of our old house?"

"Self-protection of one kind or another. Most murderers think they're protecting themselves against some kind of threat."

"But why did I bury him in the yard of our house? That doesn't make any sense, does it?"

"You could have arranged to meet him there, knowing the house was empty, and killed him on the spot."

"That's a pretty picture. Why would I rendezvous with a man like Ralph Simpson?"

"Because he knew something about you."

"And what would that delightful something be?"

"It could have to do with the death of Dolly Stone Campion."

"Are you accusing me of murdering her?"

"I'm asking you."

"What was my motive?"

"I'm asking you."

"Ask away. You'll get no further answers from me."

Her eyes were bright and hard, but the grinding interchange had hurt her will. Her mouth was tremulous.

"I think I will, Mrs. Blackwell. A queer thing occurred the night Dolly was murdered—queer when you look at it in relation to murder. When the strangler had done his strangling, he, or she, noticed that Dolly's baby was in the room. Perhaps the child woke up crying. The average criminal would take to his heels when that happened. This one didn't. He, or she, went to some trouble and ran considerable risk to put the child where he'd be found and looked after. He, or she, picked up the baby and carried him down the road to a neighbor's house and left him in a car."

"This is all new to me. I don't even know where the murder took place."

"Near Luna Bay in San Mateo County."

"I've never even been there."

I threw a question at her from left field: "The Travelers Motel in Saline City—have you been there?"

"Never." Her eyes didn't change.

"Getting back to the night of Dolly's murder, a woman might think of the child's safety at such a time. So might the child's father. I'm reasonably sure it wasn't Campion. Are you willing to discuss the possible identity of the child's father?"

"I have nothing to contribute."

"I have, Mrs. Blackwell. We have evidence suggesting that the strangler was wearing the Harris tweed topcoat I mentioned. Apparently one of the buttons was loose, about to fall off. The baby got hold of it when the murderer was carrying him down the road. The neighbor woman found the brown leather button in the baby's fist." I paused, and went on: "You see why the identification of that topcoat is crucial."

"Where is the topcoat now?"

"The police have it, as I said. They'll be showing it to you tomorrow. Are you certain you've never seen one like it? Are you certain that your husband didn't buy a coat from Cruttworth's in Toronto?"

Her eyes had changed now. They were large and unfocused, looking a long way past me. Under her smudged makeup the skin around her mouth had a bluish tinge, as if my hammering questions had literally bruised her. She got to her feet, swaying slightly, and ran out of the room on awkward high heels.

I followed her. The threat of violence, of homicide or suicide, had been gathering in the house for days. She flung herself along the hallway and through the master bedroom into a bathroom. I heard her being sick there in the dark.

A light was on in the great bedroom. I opened one of the wardrobe closets and found Mark Blackwell's clothes. He had a couple of dozen suits, hanging in a row like thin and docile felons.

I turned back the right cuff of one of the jackets. Written in the lining in indelible ink was the same cleaner's code that Leonard had found in the sleeve of the topcoat: BX1207.

chapter 27

THE MAID APPEARED in the doorway. She was back in uniform but still using her unzipped personality. "Now what?"

"Mrs. Blackwell is ill. You'd better see to her."

She crossed the bedroom to the dark bathroom, dragging her feet a little. I waited until I heard the two women's voices. Then I made my way back through the house to the telephone I had used before. The Citrus Junction paper with the Simpson story on the front page lay untouched on Isobel Blackwell's desk. If she had guilty knowledge of it, I thought wishfully, she would have hidden or destroyed the newspaper.

Arnie Walters answered his phone with a grudging "Hello."

"This is Archer. Have you seen Blackwell?"

He ignored the question. "It's about time you checked in, Lew. I heard you took Campion last night—"

"I want to know if you've seen Mark Blackwell, Harriet's father."

"No. Was I supposed to?"

"He set out early Thursday morning for Tahoe, at least that was his story. Check with the people there, will you, and call me back. I'm at Blackwell's house in L.A. You know the number."

"Is he on the missing list, too?"

"Voluntary missing, maybe."

"Too bad you can't keep track of your clients. Have they all flipped?"

"Everybody's doing it. It's the new freedom."

"Stop trying to be funny. You wake me up in the middle of the night, and you don't even tell me what Campion had to say."

"He denies everything. I'm inclined to believe him."

"He can't deny the blood on the hat. It's Harriet's blood type, and she was last seen with him. He can't deny the murder of his wife."

"That was a bum beef, Arnie."

"You know that for a fact?"

"A semi-fact, anyway. Campion's no Eagle Scout, but it looks as though somebody made a patsy out of him."

"Who?"

"I'm working on it."

"Then what's your theory about Harriet? She's vanished without a trace."

"She may have met with foul play after Campion left her. She was carrying money and driving a new car. We ought to bear down on finding that car. One place to look would be the airport parking lots at Reno and San Francisco."

"You think she flew some place?"

"It's a possibility. Look into it, will you, but call me back right away on Blackwell. I have to know if the Tahoe authorities have seen him."

Isobel Blackwell spoke behind me as I hung up: "Do you doubt everything and everyone?"

She had washed her face and left it naked of make-up. Her hair was wet at the temples.

"Practically everything," I said. "Almost everyone. It's a little habit I picked up from my clients by osmosis."

"Not from me. I've never learned the habit of distrust."

"Then it's time you did. You've been deliberately cutting yourself off from the facts of life, and death, while all hell has been breaking loose around you."

"At least you believe I'm innocent."

She came all the way into the room and sat in the chair I'd vacated, turning it sideways and resting her head on her hand. She had drenched herself with cologne. I stood over her with the distinct feeling that she had come to place herself in my power or under my protection.

"Innocence is a positive thing, Mrs. Blackwell. It doesn't consist in holding back information out of a misplaced sense of loyalty. Or shutting your eyes while people die—"

"Don't lecture me." She moved her head sideways as though I'd pushed her. "What kind of woman do you think I am? I've asked you that before."

"I think we're both in the process of finding out."

"I already know, and I'll tell you. I'm an unlucky woman. I've known it for many years, since the man I loved told me he was diabetic and couldn't or shouldn't have children. When he died it confirmed my unluck. I made up my mind never to marry anyone or love anyone again. I refused to expose myself to suffering. I'd had it.

"I moved to Santa Barbara and went on schedule. My schedule was chock full of all the activities a widowed woman is supposed to fill up her time with—garden tours and bridge and adult education classes in mosaic work. I got myself to the point where I was reasonably content and hideously bored. I forgot about my basic unluck, and that was my mistake.

"Mark came to me late last summer and told me that he needed me. He was in trouble. My heart, or whatever, went out to him. I allowed myself to feel needed once again. I'd always been fond of Mark and his blundering boyish ways. That may sound like a queer description of him, but it's the Mark I know, the only one I've known. At any rate I married him and here I am."

She turned her head up to meet my eyes. The tendons in her neck were like wires in a taut cable. An obscure feeling for her moved me. If it was pity, it changed to something better. I wanted to touch her face. But there were still too many things unsaid.

"If you've been unlucky," she said, "you become unwilling to move for fear the whole house will come tumbling down."

"It's lying in pieces around you now, Mrs. Blackwell."

"I hardly need you to tell me that."

"Was Mark in trouble with a girl last summer?"

"Yes. He picked her up at Tahoe and got her pregnant. She was plaguing him for money, naturally. He didn't care about the money, but he was afraid she'd press for something more drastic. Marriage, perhaps, or a lawsuit that would ruin him in the public eye. What people think is very important to

Mark. I suppose he thought that marriage to me would protect him and tend to silence the girl." Stubbornly, she refrained from naming her.

"Did he have the gall to spell this out to you?"

"Not in so many words. His motives are usually quite transparent. He gives himself away, especially when he's afraid. He was terribly afraid when he came to my house in Santa Barbara. The girl, or one of her friends, had threatened him with criminal charges. Apparently he'd driven her across the state line."

"Did you know the girl was Dolly Stone?"

"No." The word came out with retching force. "I'd never have married Mark—"

"Why did you marry him?"

"I was willing to feel needed, as I said. He certainly needed me, and so did Harriet. I thought a marriage that started badly couldn't fail to improve. And Mark was so desperately afraid, and guilty. He believed he was on the moral skids, that he might end by molesting little children on the streets. He said I was the only one who could save him, and I believed him."

"You didn't save him from murdering Dolly. I think you know that by now."

"I've been afraid of it."

"How long have you suspected?"

"Just tonight, when we were talking about his topcoat, and I got sick. I'm not feeling very well now."

A greenish pallor had invaded her face, as though the light had changed. Without thinking about it, I touched her temple where the hair was wet. She leaned her head against my hand.

"I'm sorry you're not feeling well," I said. "You realize we have to go on to the end."

"I suppose we do. I lied to you about the topcoat, of course. He bought it when we were on our honeymoon—we ran into some cold weather in Toronto. Mark said it would come in

handy when we went up to Tahoe in the spring. I suppose
Ralph Simpson found it there, and brought it to Mark for an
accounting. Mark took the icepick the Stones had given us—"
Her voice broke. "These things are all mixed up with our mar-
riage," she said. "You'd think he was trying to make a Black
Mass of our wedding ceremony."

She shuddered. I found myself crouching with my arms
around her, her tears wetting my collar. After a while the
tears stopped coming. Later still she drew away from me.

"I'm sorry. I didn't mean to let my emotions go at your expense."

I touched the tragic hollow in her cheek. She turned away
from my hand.

"Please. Thank you, but also please. I have to think of just
one thing, and that's my duty to Mark."

"Isn't that pretty well washed out?"

She raised her eyes. "You've never been married, have you?"

"I have been."

"Well, you've never been a woman. I have to follow through
on this marriage, no matter what Mark has done to it. For my
sake as well as his." She hesitated. "Surely I won't have to
stand up in court and testify about these things—the icepick,
and the coat, and Dolly?"

"A wife can't be forced to testify against her husband. You
probably know that from your social-working days."

"Yes. I'm not thinking too well. I'm still in shock, I guess. I
feel as though I'd been stripped naked and was about to be
driven through the streets."

"There will be bad publicity. It's one reason I had to get the
facts from you tonight. I'd like to protect you as much as possible."

"You're a thoughtful man, Mr. Archer. But what can you
do?"

"I can do your talking to the police for you, up to a point."

Her mind caught on the word police. "Did I understand

from your telephone conversation just now that you're asking the Tahoe police to arrest Mark?"

"I asked a friend in Reno, a detective I've been using, to find out if your husband is up there. He's going to call me back."

"Then what?"

"Your husband will be arrested, if he's there. He may not be within five thousand miles of Tahoe."

"I'm sure he is. He was so concerned about Harriet."

"Or about his own skin."

She looked at me with sharp dislike.

"You might as well face this, too," I said. "There's a very good chance that your husband left here this morning with no intention of ever coming back. What time did he leave, by the way?"

"Early, very early. I wasn't up. He left me a note."

"Do you still have the note?"

She opened the top drawer of her desk and handed me a folded piece of stationery. The writing was a hasty scratching which I could hardly decipher:

> *Isobel,*
>
>   I'm off to Tahoe. It is too grinding to sit and wait for news of Harriet. I must do something, anything. It's best you stay here at home. I'll see you when this is over. Please think of me with affection, as I do you.
>
>   *Mark*

"It could be a farewell note," I said.

"No. I'm sure he's gone to Tahoe. You'll see."

I dropped the subject, pending Arnie's call. Some time went by. I sat in a straight-backed chair by the French doors. The dark sky was turning pale. House lights pierced the emerging hills, like random substitutes for the fading stars.

Isobel Blackwell sat with her head on her arms. She was as quiet as a sleeper, but I knew by the rhythm of her breathing that she was awake.

"There's one thing I'd like to have clear," I said to her back. "Is it possible that Mark killed Ronald Jaimet?"

She pretended not to hear me. I repeated the question in the same words and the same tone. She said without raising her head: "It isn't possible. They were dear friends. Mark went to enormous trouble to bring Ronald down from the high country. He was almost dead from exhaustion when he got to Bishop. He needed medical attention himself."

"That doesn't prove anything about the accident. Was there any indication that it was a planned accident?"

She turned on me fiercely. "There was not. What are you trying to do to me?"

I wasn't sure myself. There were obscure areas in the case, like blank spaces on a map. I wanted to fill them in. I also wanted to wean Isobel Blackwell away from her marriage before she went down the drain with it. I'd seen that happen to sensitive women who would rather die in a vaguely hopeful dream than live in the agonizing light of wakefulness.

I tried to tell her some of these things, but she cut me short.

"It's quite impossible. I know how Ronald died, and I know how Mark felt about it. He was completely broken up, as I told you."

"A murder can do that to a man. A first murder. Was Mark in love with you four years ago when Ronald died?"

"He most assuredly was not."

"Can you be certain?"

"I can be very certain. He was infatuated with—a girl."

"Dolly Stone?"

She nodded, slowly and dismally. "It wasn't what you think, not at that time. It was more of a father-daughter thing, the kind of relationship he had with Harriet when she was younger. He brought Dolly gifts when he came to visit us, he took her for little outings. She called him uncle."

"What happened on the little outings?"

"Nothing. Mark wouldn't sink that low—not with a young girl."

"You used the word 'infatuated.'"

"I shouldn't have. It was Ronald's word really. He took a much stronger view of it than I did."

"Ronald knew all about it then?"

"Oh yes. He was the one who put a stop to it."

"How?"

"He talked to Mark. I wasn't in on the proceedings, but I know they weren't pleasant. However, their friendship survived."

"But Ronald didn't."

She got to her feet blazing with anger. "You have a vile imagination and a vicious tongue."

"That may be. We're not talking about imaginary things. Did the Dolly issue come up shortly before Ronald's death?"

"I refuse to discuss this any further."

The telephone punctuated her refusal. It buzzed like a rattlesnake beside her; she started as though it was one. I walked around her and answered it.

"Arnie here, Lew. Blackwell didn't turn up at the dragging operations. Sholto was there all day, and he says that Blackwell hasn't been at the lodge since the middle of May. Got that?"

"Yes."

"Get this. Harriet's car has been spotted. It was found abandoned off the highway north of Malibu. We just got word from the CHP. What does that mean to you?"

"More driving. I'll go out there and take a look at the car."

"About Blackwell, what do we do if he shows up?"

"He won't. But if he does, stay close to him."

Arnie said with a strain of grievance in his voice: "It would help if I knew what the problem was."

"Blackwell is a suspect in two known murders, two other possibles. The ones I know about for sure are Dolly Stone and Ralph Simpson. He's probably armed and dangerous."

Isobel Blackwell struck me on the shoulder with her fist and said: "No!"

"Are you all right, Lew?" Arnie's voice had altered, become soothing, almost caressing. "You haven't been sitting up all night with a bottle?"

"I'm sober as a judge, soberer than some. You ought to be getting official confirmation in the course of the day."

I hung up before he could ask me questions I wasn't ready to answer. Isobel Blackwell was looking at me strangely, as if I had created the situation and somehow made it real by telling Arnie about it. The light from the windows was cruel on her face.

"Has my husband's car been found?"

"Harriet's. I'm going out to Malibu to look at it."

"Does it mean she's alive?"

"I don't know what it means."

"You suspect Mark of killing Harriet, too."

"We'd better not discuss what I suspect. I'll be back. If your husband should come home, don't tell him what's been said here tonight."

"He has a right to know—"

"Not from you, Mrs. Blackwell. We can't predict how he'd react."

"Mark would never injure me."

But there was a questioning note in her voice, and her hand went to her throat. Her head moved from side to side in the collar of her fingers.

chapter **28**

I DROVE OUT TO Malibu through the chilly dawn. The zebra-striped hearse was still parked by the road-side at Zuma. The sight of it did nothing for me at all.

The HP dispatcher working the graveyard shift had an open paperback on the desk in front of him, and seemed to begrudge his answers to my questions. Harriet's Buick Special was impounded in a local garage; it wouldn't be available for inspection until the garage opened at eight.

"When was it picked up?"

"Last night, before I came on duty."

"You came on at midnight?"

"That's correct."

His eyes kept straying downward to his book. He was a fat man with a frowzy unwed aura.

"Can you tell me where it was found?"

He consulted his records. "Side road off the highway about six miles north of here. According to the officer, the woman in the lunchroom said it was there all day. She got around to reporting it when she closed up for the night."

"What lunchroom is that?"

"It's one of those jumbo shrimp traps. You'll see the sign on the right as you go north."

He picked up his book. It had a picture on the cover of a man riding a horse into a kind of nuclear sunset.

I drove out of the straggling beachfront town and north on the highway to the jumbo shrimp place. It was the same establishment in which I had sat and drunk coffee long ago at the beginning of the case. Harriet's car had been abandoned within a few hundred yards of her father's beach house.

I turned left down the hill, nosed my car into the parking area, and parked at the railing beside a black Cadillac. The tide was high, and the sea brimmed up like blue mercury. Some pelicans were sailing far out over it, tiny within the amplitude of the sky.

The Cadillac had Blackwell's name on the steering post. I walked along the gangway to his beach house. I was keenly aware of every sound and movement, my own, the thumping and shushing of the waves, the distant cry of a scavenger gull following the pelicans. Then my knocking on Blackwell's door was the only sound.

Finally I let myself in with his key. Nothing had been changed in the high raftered room, except for what had been done to Campion's painting. Someone had slashed it so that the morning sun came jaggedly through it like lightning in a cloud.

I went to the head of the stairs and called down: "Blackwell! Are you there?"

No answer.

I called Harriet. My voice rang through the house. I felt like a self-deluded medium trying to summon up the spirits of the dead. I moved reluctantly down the steps and more reluctantly through the big front bedroom into the bathroom. I think I smelled the spillage before I saw it.

I turned on the bathroom light. A towel in the sink was soaked and heavy with coagulating blood. I lifted it by one corner, dropped it back into the sink. Splatters of blood were congealed on the linoleum floor. I stepped across them and opened the door into the back bedroom. It had a broken lock.

Blackwell was there, sitting in his shirtsleeves on the edge of a bare mattress. His face was white, except where it was shadowed by black beard. He looked at me like a thief.

"Good morning," he said. "It would have to be you."

"Bad morning. Who have you been killing this morning?"

He screwed up his face, as if a glare had fallen across it. "No one."

"The bathroom is a shambles. Whose blood is it?"

"Mine. I cut myself shaving."

"You haven't shaved for at least twenty-four hours."

He touched his chin absently. I sensed that he was out of contact, trying to fill the gap between himself and reality with any words he could think of from moment to moment.

"I cut myself shaving yesterday. That's old blood. Nobody died today."

"Who died yesterday?"

"I did." He grimaced in the invisible glare.

"You're not that lucky. Stand up."

He rose obediently. I shook him down, though I hated to touch his body. He had no weapon on him. I told him to sit again, and he sat.

The angry will had gone out of him. A sort of fretfulness had taken its place. I had seen that fretfulness before, in far-gone men. It was like a rat gnawing their hearts and it made them dangerous, to others and themselves.

A slow leakage of water glazed his eyes. "I've had a lonely night."

"What have you been doing?"

"Nothing in particular. Waiting. I hoped that daylight would give me the strength to get up and move. But the daylight is worse than the darkness." He sniffed a little. "I don't know why I'm talking to you. You don't like me."

I didn't try to pretend anything. "It's good you're able and willing to talk. We have the business of the confession to get over."

"Confession? I have nothing to confess. The blood in the bathroom is old blood. I didn't spill it."

"Who did?"

"Vandals, possibly. Vandals must have broken in. We've had a lot of vandalism over the years."

"We've had a lot of murders over the years. Let's start with the first one. Why did you kill Ronald Jaimet?"

He looked up like a white-haired child horribly ravaged by age. "I didn't kill him. His death was the result of an accident. He fell and broke his ankle, and his needle. It took me a day and a night to get him out of the mountains. Without his insulin he became very sick. He died of his illness. It was all completely accidental."

"Just how did the accident happen?"

"Ronald and I had a scuffle, a friendly scuffle. His foot

slipped on a stone and went over the edge of the trail. His weight came down on his ankle. I actually heard it snap."

"What was the friendly scuffle about?"

"Nothing, really. He was joshing me a bit, about my affection for a young protégée of his. It's true I was fond of the girl, but that was as far as it went. I never—I never did her any physical harm. My feelings were pure, and I told Ronald this. I think I pushed him, in a playful way, to emphasize what I was saying. I had no idea of making him fall."

"And no intention of killing him?"

He puzzled over the question. "I don't see how I could have wanted to kill him. Wouldn't I have left him there if I had?" He added, as if this would clinch it: "Ronald was my favorite cousin. He greatly resembled my mother."

He gave me a peculiar wet look. I was afraid he was going to talk about his mother. They often did.

I said: "When did you start having sexual relations with Dolly Stone?"

His eyes shifted away. They were almost lost in the puffiness around them, as if he had been beaten by intangible fists. "Oh. That."

"That."

He lay back on the bed, curling his body sideways so that his head rested on the uncovered striped pillow. He said in a hushed voice: "I swear to heaven I didn't touch her when she was a child. I merely adored her from a distance. She was like a fairy princess. And I didn't go near her after Ronald died. I didn't see her again till we met last spring at Tahoe. She was grown up, but I felt as though I'd found my fairy princess once again.

"I invited her to the lodge, simply with the idea of showing it to her. But I was too happy. And she was willing. She came back more than once on her own initiative. I lived in pure delight and pure misery—delight when I was with her, and misery the rest of my waking hours. Then she turned against me, and I was in utter misery all the time." He sighed like an adolescent lover.

"What turned her against you?"

"We ran into difficulties."

I was weary of his euphemisms. "You mean you got her pregnant."

"That, and other things, other difficulties. She turned against me finally and completely." He drew up his legs. "I went through hell last summer. She put me through hell."

"How did she do that?"

"I was fearful of losing her, and just as fearful of what would happen if I tried to hold her. I was utterly at her mercy. It was a very tense period. I couldn't stomach some of the things she said. She called me a dirty old man. Then my daughter Harriet joined me at the lodge, and the whole thing became impossible. Dolly wouldn't come to me any more, but she kept threatening to tell Harriet about us."

He squirmed and tossed like a restless sleeper. The bed creaked under him in harsh mimicry of the noises of passion.

"Was Dolly blackmailing you?"

"I wouldn't put it that way. I gave her money, altogether a good deal of money. Then I stopped hearing from her entirely. But I was still on tenterhooks. The thing could erupt publicly at any time. I didn't know she'd married until this spring."

"In the meantime you married Isobel Jaimet as a buffer."

"It was more than that," he insisted. "Isobel was an old and trusted friend. I was—I am genuinely fond of Isobel."

"Lucky Isobel."

He looked up at me with hatred in his eyes. But he was too broken to sustain it. He turned his face into the pillow. I had the queer impression that under the tangled white hair at the back of his head was another face made of blind bone.

"Tell me the rest of it," I said.

He lay so still that he didn't appear to be breathing. It occurred to me that he was holding his breath as angry children did when the world turned unpermissive.

"Tell me the rest of it, Blackwell."

He began to breathe visibly. His shoulders rose and fell. His body jerked in occasional little spasms. It was the only response I could get from him.

"Then I'll tell you, and I'll make it short, because the police will be eager to talk to you. Dolly renewed her demands for money this spring—she'd had a hard winter. You decided to put a final stop to the demands and the uncertainty. You went to her house in the middle of the night of May the fifth. Her husband wasn't there—he was out with another woman. I suppose Dolly let you in because she thought you were bringing her money. You strangled her with one of her stockings."

Blackwell groaned as though he felt the nylon around his withering neck.

"Then you noticed the baby, your own bastard son. For some reason you couldn't bear to leave him in the room with the dead woman. Perhaps you had the child's safety and welfare in mind. I'd like to think so. At any rate you picked him up and carried him down the road to a neighbor's car. The child got hold of a button on your coat which may have been loosened during your struggle with Dolly. It was still in his fist when the neighbor woman found him. The button has brought this whole thing home to you.

"When Dolly's husband was indicted for her murder, his friend Ralph Simpson set out to track down its source. He probably knew of your affair with Dolly, and had a pretty good idea where the button came from. He went up to Tahoe and got you to employ him and eventually found the coat where you had hidden it. Perhaps he confronted you with it. You fired him and came back here. Instead of taking the coat to the police, as he ought to have, he followed you south with it. He may have had a dream of solving the crime by himself— Simpson was a failure who needed a success—or maybe the dream went sour in him and turned into money-hunger. Did he attempt to blackmail you?"

He spoke inarticulately into the pillow.

"It doesn't greatly matter now," I said. "It will come out at the trial. It will come out that you took a silver icepick from your house when you went to meet Simpson. I think it was no accident that the icepick was a wedding present from Dolly's parents. It was certainly no accident that you buried his body in what had been Ronald Jaimet's back yard. I don't know what was going on in your head. I don't believe you could tell me if you tried. A psychiatrist would be interested in what went on in that back yard when Dolly was a child."

Blackwell cried out. His voice was thin and muffled. It sounded like a ghost trapped in the haunted house of his mind. I remembered his saying that he was dead and I pitied him as you pity the dead, from a long way off.

He turned his head sideways. His visible eye was open, but featureless as a mollusk in the harsh shell of his brow.

"Is that how it was?" he said. There seemed to be no irony in his question.

"I don't claim to know all the details. If you're willing to talk now, correct me."

"Why should I correct your errors for you?"

"You're talking for the record, not for me. Is that Harriet's blood in the bathroom?"

"Yes."

"Did you kill her?"

"Yes. I cut her throat." His voice was flat and unemotional.

"Why? Because she caught on to you and had to be silenced?"

"Yes."

"What did you do with her body?"

"You'll never find it." A kind of giggle rattled out of his throat and made his lips flutter. "I'm a dirty old man, as Dolly

said. Why don't you put me out of my misery? You have a
gun, don't you?"

"No. I wouldn't use it on you if I had. You're not that important to me. Where is your daughter's body?"

The giggle erupted again, and amplified itself into a laugh.
Whoops of laughter surged up into his throat and choked him.
He sat up coughing.

"Get me some water, for pity's sake."

For pity's sake I started into the bathroom. Then I heard
the furtive rustle of his movement. One of his hands was groping under the pillow. It came out holding a revolver which
wavered in my direction and then held steady.

"Get out of here or I'll shoot you. You don't want to be the
fifth one."

I backed through the doorway.

"Close the door. Stay in there."

I obeyed his orders. The bathroom seemed hideously familiar. The towel lay like a maimed thing in the sink.

Blackwell's gun went off on the other side of the door. It was
still in his mouth when I reached him, like a pipe of queer
design which he had fallen asleep smoking.

chapter 29

I GOT BACK TO Isobel Blackwell around
noon. All morning county cars had bumped down the old blacktop road, and county men had tramped back and forth along the
gangway to the beach house. I told my story, and Blackwell's,
till it grated on my tongue. If I had any doubts of Blackwell's
credibility, I suppressed them. I was bone-tired, and eager to
see the case ended.

They trundled his body away. We searched for Harriet's

body in the house and under it, and up and down the beach. We went back to Malibu and examined her car. It told us nothing.

"The consensus is that Harriet's in the sea," I told Isobel Blackwell, "that he disposed of her body in the same way he disposed of the topcoat. And like the topcoat it will probably come in with the next big tide."

We were in her sitting room. The drapes were closed, and she had left the lights off. Perhaps she didn't want me to see her face; perhaps she didn't want to see mine. She sat in a long chair and peered at me through the artificial gloom as if I was as monstrous as the things I had had to tell her. The side-to-side movement of her head, the gesture of incomprehension and denial, was threatening to become habitual.

"I'm sorry, Mrs. Blackwell. I thought you'd rather hear it from me than get it from the police or read it in the newspapers."

"Does it have to be in the newspapers?"

"It will be. You don't have to read them. After you've gathered yourself together, you ought to take a long trip, put all this behind you." My suggestion sounded feeble in my own ears.

"I couldn't face a journey now." After a pause, she said in a softer voice: "I thought horrors like this only occurred in Greek plays."

"The horrors will pass. Tragedy is like a sickness, and it passes. Even the horrors in the Greek plays are long since past."

"That's not much comfort to me here and now."

"It's something to think about."

"I don't want to think." But she sat locked in thought, as still as ancient marble, her mind transfixed by the Medusa fact: "How could he bring himself to kill Harriet? He loved her."

"In a sick way. Where girls were concerned, even his own,

he was a mother's boy playing with dolls in the attic. Love like that can change to hatred if it's threatened. You cut off the doll's head—"

"He cut off her head?"

"I was speaking figuratively. Apparently he cut her throat with an old razor blade. He used the same blade to slash Campion's painting."

Her head had begun its sidewise movement again. "I can understand why Mark had to kill Dolly, or thought he had to. Once he'd used her, she threatened him by her very existence. Ralph Simpson was a threat, and even Ronald must have seemed to be. But Harriet was his own daughter."

"I suspect she was another threat to him, the most intimate one of all. Did Harriet know about his affair with Dolly?"

"I'm afraid so. Mark had a horrible habit of confession. I don't suppose he poured it all out, but he did say something to Harriet last spring. He may have felt it was bound to come out, and it was his duty to prepare her. It didn't have the desired effect."

"How do you know?"

"Because Harriet came to me with it. She said she had to talk to someone. She was greatly upset, much more deeply upset than I'd ever seen her. She regressed to a very low age level; she was literally bawling with her head in my lap. I didn't think she should be encouraged to throw childish fits at her age. I told her she ought to be able to take it if I could."

"How did she handle that?"

"She got up and left the room. We didn't discuss the subject again. I felt that Mark had made a mistake in telling her. It didn't improve the situation among the three of us."

"When did this happen?"

"Some time in March or April. I imagine Mark was concerned about the birth of the child, and that's why he spoke to Harriet, though he never said a word about it to me. Looking back, it does throw some light on what Harriet was feeling.

Dolly had displaced her in Mark's affections, as she thought. A couple of months later she attached herself to Dolly's widower. Do you suppose she was aware of what she was doing?"

"Yes," I said, "and Campion knew what he was doing, but neither of them told the other. I believe that Campion took up with her in Mexico precisely because she was Mark's daughter. He suspected Mark of killing his wife, and cooked up an affair with Harriet in order to get close to him. He surely wouldn't have come back from Mexico, with an indictment hanging over him, unless he hoped to clear himself."

"Why didn't he ever say anything?"

"He did, last Monday afternoon, when your husband turned a shotgun on him. I failed to get the message. He hasn't talked since then because he knew he wouldn't be believed. Campion's a maverick, an authority-hater, with a certain pride of his own. But he'll be talking now, and I want to be there when he spills over. You can pay my time and expenses if you like."

"I'll be glad to."

"You're a generous woman. After some of the things I said to you last night—"

She cut me short with a movement of her head. "They helped me, Mr. Archer. You were cruel at the time, but actually you were preparing me—for this."

"I was doing more than that. I considered you a possible murder suspect."

"I know. The point is that you don't any more. It's over."

"Almost over. Campion's testimony should wind up the case."

"What do you suppose he will have to say?"

"He probably made the mistake of speaking out to Harriet at the lodge, accusing Mark of Dolly's murder. She couldn't take it; it completely destroyed her image of her father. It must have been a shock, too, to learn that Campion had been using her, that his interest in her was mainly on his dead wife's account. They quarreled, violently. Campion got his face scratched, she was hit on the head, somehow her hat got knocked into the water. She couldn't have been badly hurt—she was well enough to drive to Malibu—but Campion didn't know that. Judging by his attitude the other night, he may have thought he killed her, or injured her seriously."

"But she drove herself from Tahoe to Malibu?"

"Apparently. It took her more than twenty-four hours. She may have had her head wound attended to on the way. She reached the beach house early yesterday morning and telephoned her father. Perhaps she accused him of murder over the phone, or asked him to deny it. He left you a note to put you off the track, went to the beach house, and killed her. He carried her body down to the beach and let it go out with the tide.

"But he had killed once too often. This doll bled. It was his daughter's blood, and it was real. He was so paralyzed he couldn't clean up after his final murder. He sat in the back bedroom all day and all night trying to gather the strength to kill himself. Perhaps he had to talk to someone before he did. I happened to be the one."

"I'm glad it was you, Mr. Archer. And I'm glad he didn't kill you. Truly glad."

She rose up in the ruins of her life and gave me her hand. I said I would be seeing her again. She didn't deny it, even with a movement of her head.

chapter 30

CAMPION HAD BEEN MOVED to the San Mateo County jail. He still wasn't talking. After some palaver with Captain Royal and his chief, and telephone calls to their opposite numbers in Los Angeles, I got permission to interview him alone. Royal brought him into the interrogation room and left us together, locking the steel-sheathed door behind him.

Campion stood with his back to the door. He didn't say hello or nod his head. Bad nights had left their nightmare tracks on his face, but he still had a kind of frayed intensity. He looked at me as though I might lunge at him with a rubber hose.

"How are you, Bruce? Sit down."

"Is that an order?"

"It's an invitation," I said in a mollifying tone. "Mark Blackwell has confessed your wife's murder. Did Royal tell you?"

"He told me. It came a little late. I'm going to sue you all for false arrest."

"That doesn't sound like such a wise idea. You're pretty vulnerable."

"Then when are they going to let me out? I've got work to go on with."

"You've got some talking to do first. If you'd leveled with the cops, you wouldn't be here—"

"Don't snow me. I know cops. They make patsies out of the little ones and let the big ones go."

"You made a patsy out of yourself. Think about it."

I left him standing and moved around the bright barred room. Campion's eyes followed me warily. After a while he sat down at a metal table, resting his bandaged head on one hand.

I approached him and touched his shoulder. "Listen, Bruce—"

He raised both arms to protect his head.

"Relax. I'm not your enemy."

He twisted under my hand. "Then don't stand over me. I've always hated people standing over me."

I sat down across the table from him. "I assume you're a serious man in spite of the cop-hater nonsense. You've been through some rough experiences, and I respect that. You could have spared yourself some of the roughness by trusting other people."

"Who was there to trust?"

"Me, for one. Royal can be trusted, too. He's not a bad cop. Why didn't you tell us the truth the night before last? You let us believe that Harriet was dead and you had drowned her."

"You would have gone on believing it no matter what I said."

"But you didn't give us a chance. You didn't give her a chance, either. You might have saved her life."

His right fist clenched on the table. "I tried. I tried to stop her. But I can't swim too well. She got away from me in the dark."

"We seem to be talking past each other. When did she get away from you?"

"That night at the lake, Tuesday night I think it was. She went berserk when I told her I suspected her father of killing Dolly. She came at me clawing—I had to hit her to get her off me. It was a bad scene, and it got worse. Before I knew what she was doing, she ran out of the lodge and down to the lake. I plunged in after her, but she was already gone. I'm afraid I panicked then."

"Is this the truth?"

His eyes came up to mine. "I swear it is. I didn't tell you and Royal because you would have taken any such admission as a confession of guilt." He looked at his fist; slowly it came unclenched. "I still can't prove I didn't knock her out and drown her."

"You don't have to. She didn't drown in Tahoe. If suicide was in her mind that night, she changed her mind. Evidently she came out of the water after you'd gone."

"Then she's still alive!"

"She's dead, but you didn't kill her. Her father did. He confessed it along with his other murders before he shot himself."

"Why in the name of God did he do that?"

"God only knows. She probably accused him to his face of murdering Dolly."

Emotions warred across Campion's face: incredulity and relief and self-reproach. He tried to wipe them away with his hand.

"I should never have told Harriet about her father," he said. "I see now why I should have been honest with you. But I thought you were working for Blackwell, covering up for him."

"We were both mistaken about each other. Do you want to straighten me out about a few other matters?"

"I suppose so. I seem to be on the truth kick."

"You were in serious trouble during the Korean War," I said by way of testing him. "What was it?"

"It was after the war. We were sitting around in Japan waiting for transport." He made an impatient outward gesture with his arm. "To make a long story short, I hit the officer in charge of the staging point. I broke his nose. He was a Colonel."

"Did you have a reason, apart from the fact that you don't like Colonels?"

"My reason may sound foolish to you. He caught me sketching one day and thought it would be dandy if I painted his portrait. I told him I didn't take orders about my work. We got into a battle of wills. He threatened to keep me over there till I painted him. I hit him. If he'd had a little less rank, or a little more, or if he'd belonged to our unit, it wouldn't have been so bad. But face had to be saved and I got a year in a detention camp and a D.D. I didn't paint him, though," he added with bitter satisfaction.

"You're a pretty good hater. What do you like?"

"The life of the imagination," he said. "It's all I'm good for. Every time I try to do something in the actual world I make a mess of it. I never should have married Dolly, for instance."

"Why did you?"

"It's a hard question. I've been thinking about the answers

to it ever since I got into this jam. The main thing was the money, of course—I'd be a hypocrite if I denied that. She had a little money, call it a dowry. I was trying to prepare a series of pictures for a show, and I needed money to do it. You always need money, at least I do, and so we struck a bargain."

"You knew about her pregnancy?"

"It was one of the attractions, in a way."

"Most men would feel the opposite way."

"I'm not most men. I liked the idea of having a child but I didn't want to be anybody's father. I didn't care who the father was, so long as it wasn't me. Does that sound foolish? It may have something to do with the fact that my old man did the disappearing-father act when I was four years old." There was a growl of resentment in his voice.

"Did your father have trouble with the law?"

He said with a sour mocking grin: "My father was the law. He was a lousy Chicago cop, with both front feet in the trough. A bad act. I remember the last time I saw him. I was eighteen at the time, hacking my way through art school. He was helping a blonde into a Cadillac in front of an apartment hotel on the Gold Coast." He cleared his throat. "Next question."

"Getting back to Dolly—I'm not quite clear how you felt about her."

"Neither am I. I started out feeling sorry for her. I thought it might develop into something real—that's an old boyish dream of mine." His mouth curled in self-irony. "It didn't. You know the pity that chills the heart? Oddly enough I never went to bed with her. I loved to paint her, though. That's my way of loving people. I'm not much good at the other ways."

"I thought you were a devil with the ladies."

He flushed. "I've done my share of rutting. A lot of them think it's artistic to bed with an artist. But there was only one in my life I cared about—and that one didn't last. I was too fouled up."

"What was her name?"

"Does it matter? Her first name was Anne."

"Anne Castle."

He gave me a bright astonished look. "Who told you about her?"

"She did. I was in Ajijic two or three nights ago. She spoke of you with great affection."

"Well," he said. "That's a fresh note for a change. Is Anne all right?"

"She probably would be if she didn't have you to worry about. It broke her heart when you decamped with Harriet. The least you can do is write her a letter."

He sat quiet for a time. I think he was composing the letter in his head. To judge by his frowning concentration, he was having a hard time with it.

"If Anne was important to you," I said, "why did you take up with Harriet?"

"I'd already made a commitment." His eyes were still turned inward on himself.

"I don't follow you, Campion."

"I didn't meet Harriet in Mexico, as you seem to think. I met her in my own house in Luna Bay several weeks before I went to Mexico. She came to see Dolly and the baby. She and Dolly were old friends. But Dolly wasn't there that afternoon —she'd taken the baby in for his monthly checkup. Harriet stood around watching me paint. She was an amateur painter herself, and she got very excited over what I was doing. She was quite an excitable girl."

"So?"

Campion looked at me uneasily. "I couldn't help thinking what she could do for me, with a little encouragement. I was broke, as usual, and she obviously wasn't. I thought it would be pleasant to have a patroness. I could stop worrying about the light bill and simply do my work. I made a date with her before Dolly got back with the baby. I saw her that night, and before long we were spending nights together.

"I didn't know what I was letting myself in for. Harriet acted as though she'd never been with a man. She fell so hard it scared me. She drove over from Tahoe a couple of times a week, and we were in and out of the motels. I should have had the sense to pull out of the situation. I had a feeling that it would lead to trouble." He drew in a deep breath.

"What kind of trouble?"

"I didn't know. But she was a serious girl, too serious, and terribly passionate. I shouldn't have led her on."

"Did you suspect that Blackwell was the baby's father?"

He hesitated. "I may have, more or less subconsciously. Harriet said something once, when she was holding the baby in her arms. She called him little brother. It stuck in my mind, though I didn't realize she was speaking literally."

"And Dolly never told you?"

"No. I didn't press the point, while she was alive. I didn't really want to know who the father was. I thought I could love the baby better if he was anonymous. But it turned out I couldn't love him too well. Him or anybody. Then I messed the whole thing up when I tried to go into orbit with Harriet. I should have stayed home and looked after Dolly and the baby."

His voice was low, and I thought I heard the growl of manhood in it. He rose and struck his open left palm with his closed right fist. Shaking hands with himself in an embarrassed way, he went to the window.

"I was with Harriet the night Dolly was killed," he said with his back turned.

"Harriet was the woman you slept with in the Travelers Motel?"

"That's right. Slept isn't quite accurate. We had an argument, and she started back to Tahoe in the middle of the night. I stayed in the room and got drunk. She'd brought me a bottle of her father's Scotch." He seemed to take a painful pride in spelling out the details of his humiliation.

"What was the argument about?"

"Marriage. She wanted to buy me a Reno divorce. I won't deny I was tempted, but when it came to a showdown I found I couldn't do it. I didn't love Harriet. I didn't love Dolly, either, but I had made a bargain with her to give the boy my name. I kept hoping if I stuck with it I'd learn to love the boy. But it was already too late. When I sobered up enough to drive myself home, Dolly was dead and the boy was gone and the cops were there."

"Why didn't you tell them where you'd spent the night? You had an alibi of sorts."

"It didn't look as if I'd have to use it. They questioned me and let me go. As soon as I was free, I got in touch with Harriet at Tahoe. She said I mustn't on any account drag her or her family into it. She was protecting her father, obviously, though she didn't say so. She sold me the idea of hiding out after they indicted me, and I spent a bad couple of weeks shut up in their beach house. I wanted to go on to Mexico—Ralph lent me his birth certificate with that in mind—but I had no money.

"Harriet finally gave me the money for the flight. She said that she would join me in Mexico later, and we could pretend to be strangers, and pick up where we'd left off. We could stay in Mexico or go further down into South America." He turned from the window—his face had been opened by the light. "I suppose she saw her chance to sew me up for life. And I was tempted, again. I'm a very ambivalent guy."

"I'm wondering about Harriet's motive. You suggested she was protecting her father. Did she know, at that time, that he had murdered Dolly?"

"I don't see how she could have." He fingered the scratches on his face. "Look how she reacted when I told her about my suspicions the other night."

"Just when did you develop those suspicions?"

"It happened over a period of time. Ralph Simpson brought

up the name before I left Luna Bay. He'd seen Dolly with Blackwell last summer. Ralph fancied himself as a detective, and he was very interested in a leather button that was found at the scene of the crime. The police mentioned it, too. Do you know anything about that button?"

"Too much." I summarized the history of the wandering top-coat.

"So Blackwell killed Ralph."

"He confessed the murder this morning, along with the others."

"Poor old Ralph." Campion lowered himself into a chair and sat for a while in blank-eyed silence. "Ralph should never have got mixed up with me. I'm a moral typhoid carrier."

"It's a thought," I said. "But you were telling me about your suspicions of Blackwell and how they grew."

After another silence he went on: "Ralph started me thinking about Blackwell. Bits and pieces, associations, began to gather, and eventually I had a sort of Gestalt. Some of the things that went into it were Harriet's interest in the baby, and the slip she made, if it was a slip, about her little brother. Then Dolly started getting money from somewhere, about the time that Harriet turned up at our house. I didn't understand the relationship between Dolly and Harriet. It was pleasant enough on the surface, but there was a good deal of hostility under it."

"That would be natural enough, if Dolly knew you were making love to Harriet."

"She didn't. Anyway, the relationship didn't change from the first afternoon Harriet came to the house. They greeted each other like two sisters who hated each other but refused to admit it. I can see now why that would be: Harriet knew about Dolly's fling with her father, and Dolly knew she knew."

"You still haven't told me when you found out."

"I got my Gestalt one night in Mexico, after Harriet came. We were talking in my studio, and the subject of her father's lodge at Tahoe came up, I don't know how." He turned his head to one side, as though he had overheard a distant voice. "Yes, I do know. She was hot on the marriage trail again, in spite of the fact that I was wanted for murder. She was fantasying about going back to the States where we could settle down in the lodge and live happily ever after. She got quite lyrical in her descriptions of the place. Oddly enough, I'd heard it all before."

"From Harriet?"

"From Dolly. Dolly used to tell me stories about the sweet old lady who befriended her when she was on her uppers in State Line last summer. She gave me detailed descriptions of the sweet old lady's house—the beamed ceilings, the lake view, the layout of the rooms. It suddenly hit me that it was Blackwell's house and that Blackwell was the sweet old lady and probably the father of my"—he swallowed the word—"the father of Dolly's child. I didn't say a word to Harriet at the time, but I decided to go back to the States with her. I wanted to find out more about the sweet old lady. Well, I have."

A complex grief controlled the lines of his face like a magnetic field.

chapter 31

GETTING OUT OF my cab at the San Francisco airport, I saw a woman I vaguely recognized standing with a suitcase in front of the main terminal building. She was wearing a tailored suit whose skirt was a little too long for the current fashion. It was Anne Castle, minus her earrings and with the addition of a rakish hat.

I took the suitcase out of her hand. "May I carry this, Miss Castle?"

She looked up at my face. Her own was so deeply shadowed

by trouble that her vision seemed clouded. Slowly her brow cleared.

"Mr. Archer! I intended to look you up, and here you are. Surely you didn't follow me from Los Angeles?"

"You seem to have followed me. I imagine we both came here for the same reason. Bruce Campion, alias Burke Damis."

She nodded gravely. "I heard a report yesterday on the Guadalajara radio. I decided to drop everything and come here. I want to help him even if he did kill his wife. There must be mitigating circumstances."

Her upward look was steady and pure. I caught myself on the point of envying Campion, wondering how the careless ones got women like her to care for them so deeply. I said: "Your friend is innocent. His wife was murdered by another man."

"No!"

"Yes."

Tears started in her eyes. She stood blind and smiling.

"We need to talk, Anne. Let's go some place we can sit down."

"But I'm on my way to see him."

"It can wait. He'll be busy with the police for some time. They have a lot of questions to ask him, and this is the first day he's been willing to answer."

"Why do they have to question him if he's innocent?"

"He's a material witness. He also has a good deal of explaining to do."

"Because he used a false name to cross the border?"

"That doesn't concern the local police. It's the business of the Justice Department. I'm hoping they won't press charges. A man who's been wrongly indicted for murder has certain arguments on his side—what you called mitigating circumstances."

"Yes," she said. "We'll fight it. Has he done anything else?"

"I can't think of anything that's actionable. But there are

some things you should know before you see him. Let me buy
you a drink."

"I don't think I'd better. I haven't been sleeping too well,
and I have to keep my wits about me. Could we have coffee?"

We went upstairs to the restaurant, and over several cups
of coffee I told her the whole story of the case. It made more
sense in the telling than it had in the acting out. Reflected in
her deep eyes, her subtle face, it seemed to be transformed
from a raffish melodrama into a tragedy of errors in which
Campion and the others had been caught. But I didn't whitewash him. I thought she deserved to know the worst about
him, including his sporadic designs on Harriet's money and his
partial responsibility for her death.

She reached across the table and stopped me with her hand
on my sleeve. "I saw Harriet last night."

I looked at her closely. Her eyes were definite, alive with
candor.

"Harriet isn't dead. Her father must have been lying, or
hallucinating. I know I wasn't."

"Where did you see her?"

"In the Guadalajara airport, when I went in to make my
reservation. It was about nine-thirty last night. She was waiting for her bag at the end of the ticket counter. I heard her
call out that it was *azul*—blue—and I knew her voice. She'd
evidently just come in on the Los Angeles plane."

"Did you speak to her?"

"I tried to. She didn't recognize me, or pretended not to.
She turned away very brusquely and ran out to the taxi stands.
I didn't follow her."

"Why not?"

She answered carefully: "I felt I had no right to interfere
with her. I was a little frightened of her, too. She had that
terribly bright-faced look. I don't know if I'm making myself
clear, but I've seen that look on other people who were far
out."

chapter 32

I FOUND HER late Monday afternoon in a village in Michoacán. The village had an Aztec name which I forget, and a church with Aztec figures carved in some of its ancient stones. A roughly cobbled road like the bed of a dry creek ran past the church.

A beggar woman in widow's black met me at the door and followed me into the nave reciting griefs I couldn't understand, though I could see the scars they had left on her. Her face broke up in wrinkled smiles and blessings when I gave her money. She went out and left me alone in the church with Harriet.

She was kneeling on the stone floor close to the chancel. She had a black *rebozo* over her head, and she was as still as the images of the saints along the walls.

She scrambled to her feet when I said her name. Her mouth worked stiffly, but no words came out. The shawl covering her hair accentuated the stubborn boniness of her face.

"Do you remember me?"

"Yes." Her small voice was made smaller by the cavernous space around us. "How did you know—?"

"The *posadero* told me you've been here all day."

She moved her arm in an abrupt downward gesture. "I don't mean that. How did you know I was in Mexico?"

"You were seen—by other Americans."

"I don't believe you. Father sent you to bring me back, didn't he? He promised that he wouldn't. But he never kept his promises to me, not once in my life."

"He kept this one."

"Then why have you followed me here?"

"I didn't make any promises, to you or anyone."

"But you're supposed to be working for Father. He said when he put me on the plane that he would call off the dogs once and for all."

"He tried to. There isn't anything more he can do for you now. Your father is dead, Harriet. He shot himself Friday morning."

"You're lying! He can't be dead!"

The force of the words shook her body. She raised her hands to cover her face. I could see in her sleeves the flesh-colored tape securing the bandages at her wrists. I had seen such bandages before on would-be suicides.

"I was there when he shot himself. Before he did, he confessed the murders of Ralph Simpson and Dolly. He also said that he had murdered you. Why would your father do that?"

Her eyes glittered like wet stone between her fingers. "I have no idea."

"I have. He knew that you had committed those two murders. He tried to take the blame for them and arrange it so we wouldn't press the search for you. Then he silenced himself. I don't think he wanted to live in any case; he had too much guilt of his own. Ronald Jaimet's death may have been something less than a murder, but it was something more than an accident. And he must have known that his affair with Dolly led indirectly to your murdering her and Ralph Simpson. He had nothing to look forward to but your trial and the end of the Blackwell name—the same prospect you're facing now."

She removed her hands from her face. It had a queer glazed look, as if it had been fired like pottery. "I hate the Blackwell name. I wish my name was Smith or Jones or Gomez."

"It wouldn't change you or the facts. You can't lose what you've done."

"No." She shook her head despondently. "There's no hope for me. No deposit, no return, no nothing. I've been in here since early morning, trying to make contact. There is no contact."

"Are you a member of this Church?"

"I'm not a member of anything. But I thought I could find peace here. The people seemed so happy yesterday coming out of Mass—so happy and peaceful."

"They're not running away from another life."

"You call it life, what I had?" She screwed up her face as though she was trying to cry, but no tears came. "I did my best to end my so-called life. The first time the water was too cold. The second time Father wouldn't let me. He broke in the bathroom door and stopped me. He bandaged my wrists and sent me here; he said that Mother would look after me. But when I went to her house in Ajijic she wouldn't even come out and talk to me. She sent Keith out to the gate to fob me off with a lie. He tried to tell me that she had gone away and taken the money with her."

"Keith Hatchen told you the truth. I've talked to him, and your mother as well. She went to California to try and help you. She's waiting in Los Angeles."

"You're a liar." Her sense of grievance rose like a storm in her throat. "You're all liars, liars and betrayers. Keith betrayed me to you, didn't he?"

"He said that you had been to his house."

"See!" She pointed a finger at my eyes. "Everybody betrayed me, including Father."

"I told you he didn't. He did his best to cover up for you. Your father loved you, Harriet."

"Then why did he betray me with Dolly Stone?" She stabbed the air with her finger like a prosecutor.

"Men get carried away sometimes. It wasn't done against you."

"Wasn't it? I know better. She turned him against me when we were just little kids. I wasn't so little, but she was. She was

so pretty, like a little doll. Once he bought her a doll that was
almost as big as she was. He bought me a doll just like it to
make it up to me. I didn't want it. I was too old for dolls. I
wanted my daddy."

Her voice had thinned to a childish treble. It sounded
through the spaces of the old building like an archaic voice
piping out of the crypts of the past.

"Tell me about the murders, Harriet."

"I don't have to."

"You want to, though. You wouldn't be here if you didn't."

"I tried to tell the priest. My Spanish wasn't good enough.
But you're no priest."

"No, I'm just a man. You can tell me, anyway. Why did you
have to kill Dolly?"

"At least you understand that I did *have* to. First she stole
my father and then she stole my husband."

"I thought Bruce was her husband."

She shook her head. "It wasn't a marriage. I could sense
that it wasn't a marriage as soon as I saw them with each other.
They were just two people living together, facing in opposite
directions. Bruce wanted out of it. He told me so himself, the
very first day."

"Why did you go there that first day?"

"Father asked me to. He was afraid to go near her himself,
but he said that no one could criticize me if I paid her a visit
and gave her a gift of money. I had to see the baby, anyway.
My little brother. I believed that seeing him would make me
feel—differently. I was so terribly torn asunder when Father
told me about him." She raised both fists beside her head and
shook them, not at me. She said between her fists: "And there
Bruce was. I fell in love with him as soon as I saw him. He
loved me, too. He didn't change till afterward."

"What changed him?"

"*She* did, with her wiles and stratagems. He turned against
me suddenly one night. We were in a motel on the other side

of the Bay, and he sat there drinking my father's whisky and said he wouldn't leave her. He said he'd made a bargain he couldn't break. So I broke it for him. I took it into my hands and broke it."

She brought her fists together and broke an invisible thing. Then her arms fell limp at her sides. Her eyes went sleepy. I thought for a minute she was going to fall, but she caught herself and faced me in a kind of shaky somnambulistic defiance.

"After I killed her, I took the money back. I'd seen where she hid it, in the baby's mattress. I had to move him to get at it, and he started crying. I took him in my arms to quiet him. Then I had an overmastering urge to take him out of that place and run away with him. I started down the road with him, but suddenly I was overcome by fear. The darkness was so dense I could hardly move. Yet I could see myself, a dreadful woman walking in darkness with a little baby. I was afraid he'd be hurt."

"That you would hurt him?"

Her chin pressed down onto her chest. "Yes. I put him in somebody else's car for safekeeping. I gave him up, and I'm glad I did. At least my little brother is all right." It was a question.

"He's all right. His grandmother is looking after him. I saw him in Citrus Junction the other day."

"I almost did," she said, "the night I killed Ralph Simpson. It's funny how these things keep following you. I thought I was past the sound barrier but I heard him crying that night, in Elizabeth Stone's house. I wanted to knock on the door and visit him. I had my hand lifted to knock when I saw myself again, a dreadful woman in outer darkness, in outer space, driving a man's dead body around in my car."

"You mean Ralph Simpson."

"Yes. He came to the house that night to talk to Father. I recognized the coat he was carrying and intercepted him. He agreed to go for a drive and discuss the situation. I told him

Bruce was hiding in the beach house—he said any friend of Bruce was a friend of his, poor little man—and I drove him out to the place above the beach. I stabbed him with the ice-pick that Mrs. Stone gave my father." Her clenched fist struck weakly at her breast. "I intended to throw his body in the sea, but I changed my mind. I was afraid that Bruce would find it before I got him out of there. I threw the coat in the sea instead and drove to Citrus Junction."

"Why did you pick Isobel's yard to bury him in?"

"It was a safe place. I knew there was nobody there." Her eyes, her entire face, seemed to be groping blindly for a meaning. "It kept it in the family."

"Were you trying to throw the blame on Isobel?"

"Maybe I was. I don't always know why I do things, especially at night. I get the urge to do them and I do them."

"Is that why you wore your father's coat the night you killed Dolly?"

"It happened to be in the car. I was cold." She shivered with the memory. "It isn't true that I wanted him to be blamed. I loved my father. But he didn't love me."

"He loved you to the point of death, Harriet."

She shook her head, and began to shiver more violently. I put my arm around her shoulders and walked her toward the door. It opened, filling with the red sunset. The beggar woman appeared in it, black as a cinder in the blaze.

"What will happen now?" Harriet said with her head down.

"It depends on whether you're willing to waive extradition. We can go back together, if you are."

"I might as well."

The beggar held out her hands to us as we passed. I gave her money again. I had nothing to give Harriet. We went out into the changing light and started to walk up the dry river-bed of the road.